the lighter side of LIFE and DEATH

c. k. kelly martin

WITHDRAWN

random house new york

Visit us on the Web! www.randomhouse.com/teens

Educators and librarians, for a variety of teaching tools, visit us at
www.randomhouse.com/teachers

Library of Congress Cataloging-in-Publication Data
Martin, C. K. Kelly.
The lighter side of life and death / by C. K. Kelly Martin. — 1st ed.
p. cm.
Summary: After the last, triumphant night of the school play,
fifteen-year-old Mason loses his virginity to his good friend and secret crush,
Kat Medina, which leads to enormous complications at school just as his home life
is thrown into turmoil by his father's marriage to a woman with two children.
ISBN 978-0-375-84588-8 (trade) — ISBN 978-0-375-95588-4 (lib. bdg.) —
ISBN 978-0-375-84589-5 (trade pbk.) — ISBN 978-0-375-84590-1 (pbk.) —
ISBN 978-0-375-89327-8 (e-book)
[1. Interpersonal relations—Fiction. 2. Sex—Fiction. 3. High schools—Fiction.
4. Schools—Fiction. 5. Remarriage—Fiction. 6. Theater—Fiction.] I. Title.
PZ7.M3644Lig 2010
[Fic]—dc22 2009015608

Printed in the United States of America

10 9 8 7 6 5 4 3 2 1

First Edition

For Paddy, who was my friend first

I'm stuck on your heart,
I hang on every word you say.
—"Simply the Best," Tina Turner

———

rage on

the lighter side of
LIFE and DEATH

one

THere are certain things you know you'll always re-member. Like the way Miracle stares at me when we hear the gun-shot. Our eyes lock fast. Hers shine with resignation, pain and the kind of love I can only begin to understand. Suddenly I can't catch my breath. I'm beyond anything I ever wanted to feel. It's low and high, intertwined like a double helix, and I mumble to Monica G as I rush offstage, my body racked with dread.

But this isn't the end. Not yet. I stumble back under the lights, bury my head in Miracle's chest and try to speak. *Don't,* she says. She has the last lines. There's nothing else for me to remember, nothing to do but watch her and let the final moments roll over me. My eyes burn as I look and listen but I don't fight it. I want to be fearless like Miracle. I want it to hurt so everyone can see.

Then there's just silence stretched out in front of us in the dark-ness. I wipe my face as we scramble offstage, and Miracle grabs my sleeve and whispers something I can't quite hear. I nod anyway, feeling wounded and amazed. It's like we're all incredible—me, Miracle, Monica G, Charlie Kady, Y and Z, Jamie and everyone else who made this happen. We're even better than last night and the night before that. It makes me wonder just how good we could be if there was a next time.

Everyone claps for us. Not just polite applause but like they really got it. On stage we hold hands and bow, and the feeling just keeps growing. We did good; we did awesome. I love these people next to me, Miracle channeling Meryl Streep and Monica G squeezing my hand and Jamie pulling strings in the background and Y and Z looking deep in love with each other, beaming with pride. I tell you, if you could bottle what I'm feeling right now, you'd be a billionaire. My cells are singing an anthem.

They're still singing when I stride out to the lobby afterwards. I'm swarmed by people clapping me on the shoulder and hurling praise in my direction. Then it's Dad's turn and he grins at Nina like he's showing me off for the first time. "Mason, you were fabulous," she says with a smile. "You should be so proud."

Nina's the only one of Dad's girlfriends that I've ever spent more than thirty minutes with, and I thank her and shift my focus to Brianna, next to her. Brianna happens to be the only one of us who isn't smiling. She's a thirteen-year-old tragedy-in-waiting, that kid. The face of gloom. As far as I can see, it doesn't have much to do with Dad and Nina's engagement either. She's been like that ever since we met.

"Your dad tells me you're off to celebrate now," Nina says with a cheerful nod. "Don't let us keep you."

I smile wider because Nina's got my number. Yolanda Solomon's extremely cool parents have handed over their house until one-thirty. There's not a second to lose. "Say hi to Burke for me, okay?" I tell her. Burke is Brianna's six-and-a-half-year-old brother. He's so normal that you'd never guess they share DNA.

"Will do," Nina replies. "I'll see you at the engagement shower."

The engagement shower's doubling as a housewarming party. Everything but the wedding has been pushed forward on account of Nina's landlord selling their condo—they weren't supposed to move in with us until the end of September. Not that I mind. I only have a year and a half before I go away to university, and Nina's okay.

"Do you need any cash?" Dad asks. He was here on opening night too but he wanted to come back with Nina.

"Well, I won't turn it down." My jaw aches from smiling so hard. It's impossible to stop.

Dad pulls out his wallet and hands me forty bucks, and then I'm edging my way through the crowd towards Jamie. "You guys got a ride?" Yolanda asks, tapping me on the shoulder. "Miracle still has a couple spots in the van."

"We're cool," Jamie says, charging towards us. "We're going with Charlie and Chris." I never have a clue what's going on. Jamie always handles the logistics.

"Perfect," Y says, scanning the lobby for Zoe. "See you at my place."

"Have you seen Kat?" I ask, turning towards Jamie. Kat Medina was Jamie's discovery when her family moved to Glenashton from Kitchener three years ago. She's about five feet tall with this cute little Filipino accent and curves like Jennifer Lopez. I think Jamie meant to keep her for himself, but that didn't work out; Jamie can never hide anything from me. Besides, Jamie isn't Kat's type. Lucky for him, I'm not either, which means we all evolved into close friends instead.

I can't count the number of nights the three of us have hung out in Kat's backyard along with her girls, Michelle Suazo and Sondra, barbecuing ribs and eating her mom's pancit noodles. Used to be that nearly every time a bunch of us would watch slasher movies together, I'd get a late-night call from Kat, scared to shut her eyes. I'd camp out on the phone with her talking about the funniest, most nonthreatening things I could imagine until she was too dog-tired to be freaked out anymore. Those movies don't spook her as much now but we still do the late-night conversations when one of us can't sleep.

"I think she already left with Hugo," Jamie says. Hugo's this half-Asian, half-black senior from the track team—the flawless-specimen-of-the-human-race type that Kat always falls for. They've been together two months.

"Okay," I tell him. "Let's roll."

And we're off. Charlie cranks M.I.A. on the stereo and in no time we're pulling into Yolanda's drive, helping her and Zoe set up the coolers and munchies. "Can someone call for pizza?" Z asks, looking right at Jamie. If you want something done right, he's your man. He's always one of the most responsible people in a room, even when he's partying. Two months ago I saw him steal this guy Anthony's jacket (with his car keys inside) at the end of a party to stop him from driving drunk. He was scared Anthony would pound him into the carpet, so wouldn't admit to taking it at the time, but what counts is that he stopped Anthony from climbing behind the wheel. In the end someone else might've too, but Jamie's usually the first one to think of these things.

"I'll start the pizza fund," I volunteer, fumbling around for one of Dad's twenties. People are already sauntering through the front door, grabbing beer, and I point them in the direction of the pizza fund and talk to Charlie Kady and Dustin over the sound of the music. None of us have come down from our performance high yet and we don't intend to. The music gets louder and the beer chills and before you know it everybody's there and it's happening just like Y and Z planned—the perfect party.

The cast and crew buzz around each other, dancing and laughing and knocking back beer, and no one cares that there's no drugs because this party isn't about that; this party's about us. Kat and her girls, Michelle and Sondra, slide in and out of the scene too, shaking their asses like they're in an old Destiny's Child video, and they look really sexy doing it and they know it too but they're only having fun. And all of a sudden someone gets smart and throws on "Lose My Breath" and then we're all dancing like Destiny's Child and it's funnier than ever but it's good too. Dustin, the terminally shy techie guy that never says two words to anyone outside the play, sings along and swivels his hips, his hair flying in a hundred directions. He's Dustin the Diva and I edge closer to him, just to catch some of the fallout vibes. It's the most fantastic party I've ever been to and it hasn't reached its zenith yet.

I grab another slice of double-cheese pizza from the kitchen because suddenly I'm ravenous and if I wait much longer there won't be any left. Charlie comes in after me and palms a pepperoni for himself. Jamie's next and the three of us get to talking so deep that no one can bear to leave the room. Charlie says he doesn't know what he wants to do now that the play's finished. Like all of a sudden he won't know where to focus his energy and he'll have to join Greenpeace or something and save the polar bears.

Jamie says that's a good idea and that we should all go save polar bears and that'd be better than any play, and of course he's right but we have to debate it anyway because I know the play was as important to him as it was to me. Charlie tries to debate too but he hasn't decided which side he's on, and somewhere in the middle of it Miracle appears and announces that she's leaving and does anyone need a ride?

"But the party's just getting started," I say.

"Yeah, well, I'm tired," Miracle complains, conjuring a yawn. "I guess all those weeks of rehearsals have caught up with me."

It's not that at all. Miracle doesn't know how to cut loose unless she's in front of an audience. In real life she's as serious as they come.

"You stopped dancing. That's the problem." I grab her hand and guide her back out to where the music's playing. When I spin to look at her, she's frowning but she humors me and starts dancing just the same. "You were amazing tonight," I tell her. "That *look*." I shake my head in admiration. "I don't know how you do it."

Y and Z are dancing next to us and soon Charlie, Christopher Cipolla and Dustin are there too and everyone's smiling and having such a good time that I think I just might have convinced Miracle to stay. It's one of those moments that you wish you could slow down and savor, but even now Jamie's pulling me out of it from across the room, giving me this anxious look, like the sky's falling. Kat's standing next to him in her poncho and suede hat, agitated as hell.

I don't want to stop dancing but of course I do. Jamie's eyes are pulling me towards them like a tractor beam and I stride across the room and say, "Hey, what's going on?"

Kat turns her head, leaving the answer to Jamie. "She wants to go," he replies awkwardly. "Have you seen her purse around?"

First off, why does she want to go? Secondly, all purses look the same to me. I wouldn't recognize Kat's if Jamie was balancing it on his head. "Sorry," I say, shaking my head at them both. "But why are you going now? It's not even close to one yet."

One a.m. is Kat's party curfew. Her older brother, Eric, has a sworn duty to pick her up then, whatever the variables. No one else even offers to drive her home anymore. We all know the drill.

Kat runs a hand restlessly through her wavy black hair as she glares at me. "Please, just help him find it, Mason." Her bottom lip starts to quiver and I instinctively reach for her arm.

"Are you okay?"

"Yeah, yeah," she says, blinking quickly. "I'm fine." She folds her arms under her poncho and looks away.

I toss Jamie a puzzled look. *Could someone please tell me what's going on here?* "Is her brother coming to get her?" I ask. "Where's Hugo?"

Kat strides away, five feet of tension heading towards the door. I follow her out into cold April air, Jamie a step behind me. "I'll find your purse," Jamie tells her. "Stay here with Mason." His face is flushed when he turns to look at me, and I watch him head back inside and shut the door behind him.

"I feel like throwing up," Kat confides, her cheeks in her hands as she sits on the front stoop. "I walked in on Hugo and Monica G in the upstairs bathroom." She stares dejectedly at the suburban street laid out neatly in front of us, a minivan in every second driveway. "They didn't even lock the door."

I drop my head in disgust and make a clucking noise, but Monica G's behavior doesn't throw me a bit. Monica and Kat are more acquaintances than friends; I bet it wouldn't have even occurred to her that she should keep her hands off Hugo. Sometimes it seems almost like she can't help herself. She was totally sexed up the last time we rehearsed alone at my place. Okay, maybe I didn't start discouraging her until a little late in the game, but you'd understand if you saw Monica Gregory. She's the second most popular Monica in my nearly three years at Glenashton Secondary and happens to be even hotter than her predecessor, Monica Trivino. She's also a half-decent actress and ultra-skanky. It's a combo that works for a lot of GS guys, at least in the short term.

Hugo's a different story. Risking his entire relationship with Kat for a few minutes with Monica G is utter insanity. I can't understand why he's not out here right now, down on his knees, begging for forgiveness.

"You're not surprised?" Kat pulls her hands back under her poncho and faces me.

"I'm completely surprised," I tell her. "I don't know what to say."

"He's been trying to get me to sleep with him for weeks." Her chin droops. "He made it sound like he was so into me. That it'd be this special thing between us." She leans down and rests her head on her knees. "I think I'm drunk."

I'm half-drunk myself. I don't have a clue what to say to her. "He's crazy," I mutter. "Did he even see you? I mean, what happened when you opened the door?"

Kat presses her eyelids shut. "I just want to get out of here." Her hands dart out from under her poncho as she stands. "You want to come?" She takes a step away from the house and then swings abruptly around. "I'm sorry . . . God . . . this is your cast party and everything. I'm not thinking." She tucks her ears into her hat and tries to smile. "You were great, by the way. It's like you were totally someone else up there." She said the exact same thing at the start of the party, but I'm fine with hearing it again. "It was almost eerie."

A grin escapes before I can catch it. "You want me to get Sondra or Michelle for you?" They'd know the right things to say. They definitely wouldn't break into smiles.

"No," Kat says decisively. "I'm going to phone my brother and hide out here until he comes." She wrinkles her eyebrows.

"Seriously. I'm not even that upset. The whole thing's just gross, you know?"

"Yeah." I tilt my head and look into her eyes. With her body hidden she looks super-young, practically the same as when we first met. "You want me to walk you home?" I'm not in a hurry to leave the party but it seems like the thing to say. Kat doesn't like the cold but the last of the winter snow melted weeks ago; we really could make it to her place no problem.

"I'm not sure I even want to go home. Just . . ." She shakes her head in aggravation. "Go back in and help Jamie. I'll wait out here for my brother." Her brother, Eric, has no life. I'm sure he'd be here in no time but her suggestion doesn't sit right. Her eyes are miserable, and like a complete asshole Hugo has neglected to even show up on the doorstep. Somebody has to do something.

"We can go someplace else," I offer. "We don't have to go to your house." Kat wants to argue with me. I can see it in her face. "Don't worry," I say. "Just tell me where you want to go, Kat." I rock back and forth on my heels as I stare at her. Truthfully, I'm still half thinking about the party happening behind us. I don't know that I want to go. Maybe I'm channeling Chris Keller, my role in the play, trying to be a better person. Maybe everyone you play rubs off on you a little like that.

"I don't know," she admits wearily. "Let's just walk."

So we start heading south, against the wind, only she won't say a word so I have to do all the talking. It's giving me a dry mouth, and I'm thinking how nice another beer would go down when she stops, hunches over and says, "All this walking is making me dizzy. Can we stop?"

At this point we're, like, twelve minutes away from Yolanda's and maybe ten minutes from my house and I say, "We'll head over to my place, okay? It's not far."

"Seriously, Mason." Her face is turning shades of green and she's forcing her eyes open wide as she stares at a fixed point in the distance, probably in an attempt to stop the spins. "I'm not going to make it."

The girl barely drinks. She had to go and pick tonight to booze it up and make herself sick. "All right, climb on my back." I crouch down and lock my arms around her legs as she hops on. By now I'm starting to get kinda pissed off with the way this is turning out. On any other night I'd be happy to help her out but I'm missing my cast party, the last chance to celebrate the shit out of what we accomplished with *All My Sons,* for someone who could be unconscious in two minutes. Plus, I don't know that I can carry her very far. There's a good chance that I'll be phoning her brother myself in about five minutes' time, trying to explain that Kat's passed-out presence on a generic scrap of lawn has nothing to do with me, despite appearances.

"I wish we brought some pizza with us," Kat mumbles near my ear.

"You don't need to be any heavier," I say irritably. Generally, this isn't a good thing to say to anyone. If I'm lucky she won't remember.

"I'm not that heavy," she protests, releasing her grip on me and jumping down. "Your muscles are underdeveloped." She starts shuffling along next to me and we manage to make it all the way to my house in twice the amount of time it would normally take. The lights are off and the driveway's empty, meaning Dad's still at Nina's.

I fish my key out of my wallet and unlock the front door. Kat brushes past me, kicking off her shoes and collapsing onto the living room couch. "I love your house," she announces. "It feels so lived in." The Medina house is covered in plastic wrap and constantly hosed down with multiple layers of Lysol and Mr. Clean. You could perform surgery in any room.

"You mean messy," I say, smiling as I sit down next to her. Now that we're here I'm back to feeling friendly. There'll be other parties. I did the right thing. "Maybe Nina will fix that." I nudge her arm. "You feeling better? You want some water or something?"

"No, I'm okay. Just don't ask me to walk anywhere else." Kat rubs her eyes and looks thoughtful, her face back to its normal color. "That's going to be really weird with Nina and her kids, isn't it? Having other people in your house, acting like it's theirs."

"I guess." I've been trying not to think of it that way. "Everything's going to change after graduation anyway."

"Yeah, but that's still over a year away."

"It'll go fast," I say, making Kat frown.

"I don't want it to go fast." Kat pulls off her hat and wrestles with her poncho. She drapes it over the arm of the couch and turns back to face me. "All that stuff that happens after is serious. Important life and career decisions."

"You're already worrying about those things," I remind her. She's had this career path conflict going on since at least summer. Her parents are really into the idea of her becoming a pharmacist. Kat's half into the idea herself but she's also hyper-interested in designing jewelry. Personally, I think she's kidding herself with the pharmacy thing. Not that she's not smart enough. I just can't see her in a lab coat counting pills for a living. She needs more than that.

"I know." She pouts a bit when she says that. It's the cutest thing and now's probably a good time for me to admit that I never entirely got over my crush on Kat Medina. Sometimes I almost forget about it. It's like a photocopy of a photocopy of an original that you packed away in an unmarked cardboard box in your attic. The point is, it still exists.

"I can't believe Hugo," she says with a snort. "I can't believe he pulled that bullshit after everything he said to me. The worst part is that he sounded so sincere. He kept talking about how the whole sex issue was a matter of trust between us and that he wanted to do whatever he could to make me feel okay with it." Kat grimaces and goes quiet, and I know she's embarrassed, and it embarrasses me too because we've never really talked about sex. I know she's a virgin but that's about all I know, and she knows even less about me.

"It sounds so stupid now," she adds, her voice hushed.

"He's an asshole," I tell her. "An asshole in disguise."

"Disguised as what?"

Isn't it obvious? *Come on, Kat. Work with me here.* "You always go for that same type of guy. Somebody who looks like Hugo. Somebody who's all about themselves."

"He didn't seem like that." She pulls at her earlobe, plays with her dangly silver earring. "He was always really sweet."

"Except for the last few weeks when he was trying to get you into bed," I point out. And thirty minutes ago when he was giving it to Monica G in Yolanda's upstairs bathroom.

"Even the past few weeks," Kat says. "*Especially* the last few weeks." She strokes her cheek with one hand and taps my leg with the other. "How come you never told me that you don't like him?"

All this weird tension's building in the silence, making the living room shine in a way that you don't need eyes to see, and I stare at her hand, which is now resting on my thigh, and shrug. She's not getting me on this. I'm not admitting a thing. "It's not that I don't like him. I'm just telling it how it is."

Kat looks me square in the eye. There's something so naked

about her stare that my hands tremble. I'd swear she's reading my mind, that she knows exactly how hot she's making me, and maybe, just maybe, that's the point. So I reach out and touch her face with my fingertips. Then we're gazing into each other's eyes, on edge, breathing hard and waiting for the next leap.

I kiss her first. Our tongues push together and I can't get enough. We stretch out on the couch and get serious. She's reaching into my jeans and I'm dipping into hers and it's so out of control that I can't believe it. She's making a quiet moaning noise and looking up at me with hazy, happy eyes and I'm so caught up in it that there's no room for anything else, like thinking.

"What if your dad comes back?" Kat whispers in her tiny Filipino accent.

"You're right." I sit up on the couch. "We should go to my room." This can't be over yet. Neither of us is ready for that.

So we relocate upstairs and I watch her pull her top over her head. Her black bra's next and she looks at me while she's unhooking it, like she's proud of what's underneath. The sight of her bare skin makes my face burn. I kiss her breasts and slip her pants down and she looks so gorgeous on my bed like that, her hair tousled and this sexy-dirty expression on her face, that I have to stop and stare at her for a bit, just to remind myself this is real.

I've spent so many hours imagining different versions of this moment over the years that my brain overheats and melts down to nothing as I watch her. When Kat opens her mouth again, her words are so husky they make my heart stop. "Do you have condoms?"

I almost have a coronary. You'd think it was obvious where this was heading, but this is Kat's virginity we're talking about. I'm stunned.

The thing is, I'm also a pretty good actor. I pull a package of

Trojans confidently out of my dresser and rip one open. I want to tell her this is crazy and that we're both drunk and maybe she'll regret this, but on the other hand, that's not what I want to do at all.

I roll the condom on and go back to the bed without a word. Kat's staring at me with wide eyes and I guess it should feel awkward, because before tonight we'd never even kissed, but the truth is it feels fine. I slide in easy, like we've done it a hundred times, like this is just the latest in a long line of perfect physical encounters. She comes first. I feel it. I mean, *I really feel it,* and I'm thinking, *No way on earth this is actually happening.* This must be some amazing dream. Vivid as hell, beautiful as fuck, but not real. It can't be. It's too good, too natural to be *anyone's* first time, let alone *two* people's first time.

Because, yeah, it's my first time too.

Kat Medina is my first time.

two

KAT'S SPEAKING URGENTLY into her cell phone when I wake up. The light's still on in my room, and I squint at my clock radio, dazed. It can't possibly be one-thirty, can it? Not when my head's telling me I must've been asleep for hours. I stare over at Kat, her eyes flashing panic. She's sitting on my bed in her top and panties, combing her hair frantically into place with one hand.

I roll over and open my mouth to speak but she turns towards me, pressing a finger to her lips. So okay, I'll be quiet. The light's boring a hole into my head, making me clamp my eyes shut. Meanwhile my throat's praying for water and I don't remember what I did with the condom. I pry my eyelids back open and spy it down on the carpet, within arm's length. I pull my jeans and shirt on, pluck the condom off the floor like a piece of litter and shuffle into the bathroom where I wrap it in toilet paper and bury it at the bottom of the wastebasket.

On my way out of the bathroom I nearly collide with Kat, fully dressed, in the hall. "That was Eric," she says quickly. "He went to Yolanda's to pick me up. He said he went to the door and everything and that everyone was searching all over the house for me." Kat turns and hurries along the hall, explaining as she goes. "He said he's been trying to call me for twenty minutes."

I follow her mutely downstairs and towards the front door where she stops to shove her feet into her shoes. "He'll be here any minute," she adds. She's practically vibrating with anxiety and I'm three steps behind mentally, stuck on that amazingly beautiful thing that happened between us upstairs before we passed out.

"It's okay," I tell her. "Don't worry."

"He's FREAKING OUT, Mason." Kat turns to unlock the door. "He'll be here any second."

"Wait," I cry, my mind racing to catch up. "Your poncho."

I rush into the living room and swipe it off the couch. Her hat too. "Thanks," she says, opening the door. And sure enough Eric Medina's pulling into my driveway at the speed of light. I catch one final glimpse of Kat's face before she closes the door swiftly behind her. She looks scared and I want to put my arms around her and hold on to her for a while. I've hugged her lots of times, but this would be different; this is after.

It's too late, though. She's gone.

I amble into the kitchen for water and then slowly back into the living room where I sit on the couch, solo. The cushions are askew but I don't fix them. They're proof something happened.

I sit there, thinking the same things over and over, and they're all about Kat and me upstairs. My mind's in replay mode, doing its best to adjust to this startling new reality, when Dad walks through the front door. "Mason!" He exhales heavily as he crosses the room towards me. "You gave me a fright."

Dad has never stayed the night at a girlfriend's house and

Nina's no exception. He always comes home to sleep. "How was the party?" he asks, shrugging off his sports jacket.

"Fantastic," I tell him. "Outstanding."

Dad sits down on the couch next to me, his feet resting on the coffee table. "Nina couldn't stop talking about the play." His smile stretches into a yawn. "You know, I think this last performance was even better than the other night."

"I think so too." I nod like that's exactly what I've been pondering alone here on the couch. Dad wouldn't be angry if I told him about Kat. It's not like I have to hide it or anything; I just don't want to blab about it either. "You hungry?" I motion towards the kitchen. "I'm gonna make myself some eggs."

Dad glances at his watch and then back at me, furrowing his eyebrows like he can't make up his mind. "No thanks," he replies finally. "I think I'll just head up to bed."

The funny thing is that neither of us moves. Maybe I'm too tired for eggs; I'm definitely too tired for small talk. We're perfectly fine sitting there in silence.

Things were never this relaxed when my mother was around. She wasn't happy unless she was in motion or the middle of a sentence. She hasn't changed a bit since her and Dad split up five years ago but the fact that she's across the country makes it easier to take. She has a boyfriend over there in Vancouver but spends most of her time obsessing over her newspaper column, which means the majority of our relationship happens over the phone.

For the first while after they broke up I missed her a lot. Then it was almost a relief. Breathing space, at last! I mean, there she was driving me back and forth to Toronto, taking me to all these modeling shoots, making me practice natural-looking smiles in the mirror. Sure, I thought I wanted to do it in the beginning. I was a kid. People paying that much attention to you seems like a good thing, and my mother thrived on it. Dad, on the other hand, hated it from the start. It was the first thing he changed when they broke up.

Things have been pretty good with just the two of us these past few years. I don't know what to expect when Nina, Brianna and Burke move in except that it's bound to be noisier around here.

"Okay then," Dad says, jerking his feet off the coffee table. "Past my bedtime."

"Good night," I tell him.

The minute he leaves the room I'm back to thinking about Kat, and the giddy feeling in my stomach tells me I'm nowhere close to finished. So okay, it's time to make eggs after all. I can scramble eggs and think about Kat Medina at the same time.

So far, as life experiences go, the best thing that's happened to me is tonight with Kat. Remembering the event comes in second. Third? The play, of course. Carrying Chris Keller around with me in my bones. It's almost too many incredible things for one night. I'm buzzing like a madman.

It's nearly twelve-thirty when I roll out of bed the next day. Dad's lying on the living room couch with his nose in the paper and a mug of decaf on the table next to him. "Lynn called to ask you about the play," he says, glancing at me over the top of the business section. "She didn't want me to wake you." Lynn's my mother but in most ways she feels more like a cousin. She's way more interested in what I'm doing when it intersects with her idea of cool.

"Okay," I croak. My voice hasn't woken up yet. My neck's stiff too but inside I'm dancing. "I'll call her back later."

"That's what I told her," Dad says. There are no hard feelings between my parents anymore. They communicate with each other like neutral strangers, like you'd deal with a waiter or the person who hands over your dry cleaning.

"Great," I tell him. Right now Lynn's at the bottom of my list. I head into the kitchen, chow down on waffles, shower and then call Kat's cell. I don't have a special speech planned or anything. I'm hoping instinct will take over like it did last night. Really, I just can't wait to hear her voice. The only thing wrong with last night was the way it ended. We never had a chance to talk.

Like I said, I don't have a speech planned. I'm totally unprepared when I hear the beep. "Uh, I guess you're not, uh, in the vicinity of your cell," I stammer. "I'll give you a call on your home phone. Talk to you soon." The anticipation sharpens as I punch in her home number. What do you say to someone you shared such a perfect moment with? What if she suddenly remembers my stupid comment about being heavy?

"Hello, Mason," Mrs. Medina says curtly. Ah, the joys of call display. I've been calling Kat's house for the past three years. This is the first time I've found myself wishing I could be anonymous. After all, I don't know what, if anything, her parents have heard about last night. "Kat's at Sondra's house," Mrs. Medina continues. "You can try her cell phone."

Deep breath of relief. Her parents obviously don't know anything. "Thanks," I say quickly. "No message."

No doubt Kat will pick up my original message any minute now and dial me back. I dig my cell out of yesterday's jeans and plant it on top of my CD rack. *It won't be long,* I think. Not unless she's doing something hugely important. More important than last night? What could be more important than last night?

Yeah, so I'm getting a little antsy waiting. Am I taking this too seriously? Is it possible she wants to treat this casual? But then why make Hugo wait?

Forget it. I'm not doing this. I'm going out.

I call Jamie but the phone rings forever. His parents must be the only people in Glenashton who don't own an answering machine. They won't let Jamie have a cell phone either. They're the kind of people who're always complaining about technology ruining lives but at the same time wouldn't think of depriving their kid of a computer because it'd put his/her education at a disadvantage. Normally at this point I'd IM Jamie, just in case he's around, but the moment I turn to do it, I realize I don't want to talk to him anyway. This is a guy whose mother gives me a hug on my birthday like I'm part of the family. When Jamie's grandfather was dying two and a half years ago, his parents went up north to be with him at the end but Jamie (except for a short visit to his grandfather's because his folks thought anything more would be too tough on him) stayed with us. I remember how quiet he got after his father called to tell him it was all over. And I remember breaking my thumb on the seventh-grade ski trip and how Jamie kept making me laugh through the pain, all the way down the mountain. The point is, if last night involved anyone but Kat he'd probably be the one person I'd tell. Since it *was* her I can't say a word until I know what's going on between us, but talking about anything else will be a lie of omission.

Because of the play I'm in touch with a zillion people and I keep dialing until I catch someone at home. That person's Dustin, and I go over to his house and listen to him riff about how awesome the party was and why did Kat and I take off early, anyway? I tell him I'm not at liberty to talk about it, which makes me sound like a crooked politician. Dustin says his head feels like a bowling ball on account of all last night's beer and that he doesn't want to do much except maybe go to the video store and pick up some movies. So that's what we do, but it's not enough to stop me thinking, and as soon as I get home I ask Dad if there were any calls for me.

"Just Lynn this morning," he replies. "Did you forget to bring your phone with you?"

I'm always forgetting my phone. I've left it in my locker, the public library, Nina's car, assorted people's houses, the counter at Burger King. But not today. It's been in my pocket, eating up battery power all day long.

Kat never called.

three

Y AND Z stop me in the hall first thing Monday morning. They're all smiley and touchy-feely with each other. Normally it's a contagious kind of happy, unless you're part of the Neanderthal redneck crew that can't stand to see two girls together. As it is, I fake a smile and compliment them on the party.

"But where'd you cut out to so early?" Zoe asks. "Kat's brother was fuming. I mean, he was cool with us and all but you could see he was totally pissed with her being AWOL."

Is it me or is everyone I know exceptionally nosy? "There was some personal stuff going on with Kat," I explain. "She just needed to get away from the party. We walked around. . . ."

Yolanda nods at my vagueness. "I've heard some stuff going around about Hugo."

"Yeah, well . . ." I ease my knapsack off my shoulder and lower it to the ground. "I never meant to cut out. It was a great party. I heard Miracle stayed to the end." Dustin told me that last night.

"Actually, she stayed even later and helped us clean up," Zoe says, glancing over my shoulder.

I swing around and catch sight of Jamie approaching. He's staring straight at the three of us and tense vibes spring out in our direction as he nears. "Hey, Jamie," Yolanda and Zoe sing.

"Hey." Jamie stops next to us, but it's all for Y's and Z's benefit. He's giving me the cold shoulder, angling his body away from me just enough to make the point.

"So how was the rest of your weekend?" I ask. Jamie's bad energy's making me extra-aware of everything I've failed to tell him, but whatever's eating him just isn't a priority at the moment. I've got the whole Kat mystery to unravel.

"All right," he says indifferently. "Would've been nice if you'd checked in on Saturday night."

I shoot Jamie an incredulous look. It's like him to worry about his friends but this is too much, even for him. My own father doesn't even ask me to check in on Saturday nights.

Y and Z exchange a coded gaze, say they'll catch up with us later and push on through the hall. Jamie turns expectantly towards me like he's waiting for an explanation. The look pisses me off, kicking my edginess up a notch. So far Monday sucks.

"I didn't know I needed to check in," I tell him. "What's the big deal?"

"I was looking around for Kat's purse for ages like an idiot," he fumes. "And it turns out you guys weren't even there. How am I supposed to know where you went? Her brother shows up looking for her and I don't know shit but I'm holding her frigging purse."

Who cares about the damn purse? "She needed to get away after the Hugo incident," I say. "You saw how she was. I didn't even want to leave. It was her idea. What was I supposed to tell her?" Now he's got me outright lying about the best night of my life.

23

That's not right; it's not something I want to make excuses for. "You're not responsible for me or Kat, Jamie. Relax."

Jamie's nostrils flare. His cheeks redden as he looks me in the eye. "I would've said something to you if I was leaving. You could've at least mentioned it, you know?"

Maybe. I don't know. I'm confused. All I know is I don't want to apologize. On the other hand, I hate arguing with Jamie. Shit, I can't stand arguing with anyone unless I hate their guts, know that I'm never going to see them again or can be reasonably sure they'll get over it within a matter of hours.

"Whatever." I swipe my knapsack from the floor and slip it over one shoulder. "I gotta get to my locker. I'll see you in law later, okay?"

Jamie turns and stalks off. Just like that. I swear under my breath and head for my locker. Next stop is homeroom and then on to double English. We're discussing *Nine Stories* by Salinger and I've read most of them but I can't concentrate. Kat's in my Twentieth-Century History class next period and that's pretty much all I can think about. My mind keeps yo-yoing back and forth between awesome Saturday-night memories and the meaning behind the phone call I never got.

The instant the bell rings I'm sprinting upstairs to history like a superhero on meth. Of course, if I looked like a superhero I wouldn't have this problem. If I was the six-foot-two, six-pack type, Kat would've hooked up with me ages ago. Not that there's anything wrong with me; I just happen to be on the skinny side and not very tall. The thing is, lots of girls don't care about that. I know that firsthand. Kat's the only girl I've slept with but there were a few different firsts before that. Never a serious girlfriend, but some memorable experiences.

Like this girl Brooklyn I met while I was visiting my mother in

Vancouver after Christmas. Yeah, Brooklyn of Vancouver—sounds like an indie movie title but she's a real girl with exceptionally green eyes and a thing for tennis. Her parents' apartment is just around the block from Lynn's and we hung out a little. Somehow, on one of those occasions, her sports bra got mixed in with my dirty clothes and I ended up flying two-thousand-plus miles home with it in my suitcase.

I pass Mr. Echler, my (and Kat's) history teacher, in the hall. He looks like Jesus (if you can picture Jesus in pleated dress pants) but his annoying nasal voice ruins the effect. Whatever he says just wears you out. Anyway, Echler's got a serious Monday-morning drag in his step and I rush past him and into class where two girls are already seated. Perfect. No sign of Kat yet. I back out of the room and stand outside the door like a bouncer.

A minute later I see her. Kat's hair is pushed back behind one ear and her expression's blank. She catches sight of me as I'm look-ing her over and I fold my arms in front of me and try to appear casual. Whatever she says isn't going to faze me; I just need to know what's going on.

"Hi, Mason," she says, edging quickly past me. She turns to look at me from the safety of the classroom and my brain stutters. What. Is. Happening. Here? Can't we even talk about it?

I follow Kat into class and sit down next to her, in my usual seat. And I thought English was bad. Shit. This is insane. I keep glanc-ing over at her, fidgety as hell, images of her naked body plastering my mind. I mean, I know what her breasts look like. I know what *everything* looks like. What it feels like, even. X-rated slides zip through my head, even as the muted real-life Kat refuses to look at me. Jesus. Maybe this would be easier if we weren't such good friends before.

The thing is, she can't avoid me forever. We usually sit together at lunch. We've been doing that on and off for years. Jamie too. And Kat's girls, Michelle Suazo and Sondra. The group expanded to a dozen when Jamie and I started working on the play in January. It's a bit of a mishmash, this trio of cute Filipino girls and assorted members of the *All My Sons* cast and stage crew, but it works. Most of us are so tight now that it's hard to believe that I barely knew some of these people before January.

Only the last thing I need at the moment is the safety of a group dynamic. I need to be alone with Kat and discuss this one thing until I understand it clearly. Because from where I'm sitting it looks like she just wants to pretend the whole thing never happened.

I feel like a stalker when the bell goes. Kat's got me in her peripheral vision but her eyeballs don't move. It's like Jamie all over again, like I turned into a social pariah overnight. Then, just when I think I'm going to have to cut her off in the hall like an angry boyfriend demanding face time, she stops walking and turns to look at me. "Coming to lunch?" she asks.

"Yeah." I stop next to her and bob my head. "But can we talk first? You're sorta freaking me out with—"

"Mason." She bows her head, squinting like I'm giving her a migraine. "I don't want to do this."

"You don't want to do what?" I ask, voice rising. "You don't even want me to mention it?" My reaction makes me angrier. Why should I be insulted? Who cares if it was casual—as long as we're still friends?

Except this could be such a good thing for us. It doesn't need to be an embarrassment.

"Be quiet," she hisses. Her lips are doing their sexy-pout bit again. Believe me, it doesn't help. "I'm sorry," she adds immediately, head snapping up to look at me straight on. "I know how it must seem. I got your message yesterday and I didn't call you back."

Her nails scratch nervously against her chem textbook. "I just don't want to have this conversation, Mason. We both know what happened and I'm not saying I regret it or anything like that." She sips in air and smooths the tension out of her voice. "We've been friends for years. *Good* friends. I don't want this to change anything and I don't want you to be mad but please . . ." Her hair falls forward and she flips it back behind one ear as she looks away. "Let's just go on from there. Just keep it as this separate thing, you know? Something that happened but doesn't affect us."

"So I guess it wasn't as good for you as it was for me?" I kid. The thing is, it doesn't come out sounding like a joke.

"See, this is what I'm talking about," Kat snaps, her right hand clutching at her crystal necklace.

"Jesus, Kat. Give me a break. You expect me to get my head together in the thirty seconds it took you to give me that speech?" She's killing me here. I can't even say that it was my first time. No way I'm sharing that info with her now.

"So you coming for lunch or not?" she asks, teeth scraping against her lips.

"Yeah," I reply, walking alongside her. There's nothing else to say. Sure, I'm pissed and offended, but the naked Saturday-night Kat's still in my head, rocking against me like I'm a good thing she can't get enough of. Besides, I don't want to be the one who cares more. If she can give it up to a friend on some drunken Saturday night without a second thought, I should be able to do the same. It's not like I was even trying to save my virginity; I just didn't want my first time to be with someone like Monica G.

The lunch crowd helps distract me. I grab a seat between Charlie Kady and Miracle and they're both still all about the play. In fact, they remind me of me. Because, yeah, I already miss being up there on stage with them. I miss showing off my skills and admiring theirs. I miss the people we have no reason to be anymore, the Kellers. I even sort of miss the pain that came with that.

Jamie doesn't join in the conversation. He's a few seats away, latching on to Y and Z. On any given day, depending on the seating arrangement, I could go through lunch without speaking to Jamie or Kat. To go through the period without speaking to *either* of them, that's gotta be a Mason Rice first. They're my two closest friends.

Nina drops by on her way home from work. She's cradling a cardboard box in her arms and smiles brightly when I open the door. I take the box off her hands and motion towards her Nissan in the driveway. "Got any more today?"

Nina's been dropping boxes off for the past couple weeks, to cut down on official moving day hassle. She has a key but always rings the doorbell first. Nina's thirteen years younger than my dad, which means she was just nineteen when Brianna was born. She married the guy and eventually they had Burke. Right after they split up, her ex got into a fatal car accident in a snowstorm. You never know what's around the corner, I guess. Just look at Saturday night and this morning. It makes my head spin thinking about it.

Anyway, Dad and Nina work in the same office building. That's how they met. Dad's been a dentist in the same practice since I was, like, five, around the same time we moved into this house. Every time Nina drops a box off, the fact of her imminent move seems a little more real to me. When they first mentioned moving in together I didn't seriously think it would happen, but the stack of boxes in the basement proves me wrong. The house is already changing. Dad's in the process of cleaning out half of his closet, and his home office now stands empty, waiting to be repainted the color of Burke's choice. So far the spare room's untouched. Brianna can't decide whether she wants to keep the futon where it is or sleep on her old twin bed.

"I have two more in the trunk," Nina says, turning back towards the car.

I put the box down in the hall and follow her outside. The two boxes from the trunk are so light that I scoop them both into my arms at the same time. "Looks like you're really on top of the packing," I tell her. "What's left at the apartment?"

"Plenty," she says emphatically. "The place looks like a war zone." Nina swings the front door open for me and watches me set the boxes down. "Thanks, Mason."

"Anytime."

Nina's standing in the open doorway, letting the cold air in, but I know she won't stay. She's got the kids waiting at home. "I'd say I'll see you on Sunday but I have a feeling I'll be back before then," she says lightly.

The engagement shower/housewarming is happening here on Sunday so Nina won't have to move her presents. The wedding itself won't be a major production (courthouse chapel followed by cake and champagne with family and a few close friends at a restaurant down the street) and Dad says Nina didn't want a big bridal shower but that her sister had her heart set on hosting some kind of prewedding celebration. The result is this more laid-back combo party thing and apparently Dad and I are welcome to stick around and hang out with the girls. I'm not sure whether I'll do that or not. I haven't gotten used to having all this free time yet.

"Same time tomorrow?" I kid.

Nina nods like that's entirely possible and says she better hit the road. Once she's gone I haul her boxes downstairs and stack them against the others. Our basement is partially finished and one hundred percent my space. It's where I spent most of my downtime pre-play, stretched out in front of the TV, playing video games or watching movies. Of course, now it looks more like a warehouse than a place to hang out. Maybe I'm better off aboveground.

So I head upstairs, and then I remember that Dad said something about the two of us eating out tonight. We usually do that at least once a week, plus another night of takeout. The rest of the time we grab stuff solo, which was what I was about to do before I remembered about eating out.

Now that I've remembered, going out for food seems like an inspired idea. Any more time to myself and I'm bound to start running Kat details again. I can already feel it happening, and the worst part is I don't want to stop. I'd rather sit here thinking about Saturday night than go anywhere and that's seriously messed up.

I don't want to be that guy.

four

THE REST OF the week pans out pretty much like the Monday that kick-started it. Kat and I pretend we're friends same as always only she won't look at me for more than ten seconds at a time. When my cell rings it's never her and every lunch hour there's at least one person sitting between us. I figure we just need some time to get through it, that things will even out eventually, but in the meantime she's got me. I can't look at her without thinking about it. I can't focus when she speaks. Twentieth-Century History class may as well be in Russian or Hebrew.

On the plus side, Jamie lightens up by midweek and asks if I want to hang out with Miracle, Charlie Kady and a couple other people on Friday night. Miracle's a year older than most of us and fully licensed, which means whenever we go out she usually picks everyone up in the van. She doesn't like to kid around much but she's sociable enough.

There's such a wide range of personalities involved with the play that you learn to tolerate anything. At worst, it's claustrophobic. Like in the past few months I've found out all about Charlie's addiction to Asian girls on the Internet and how Zoe acts bitchy with the entire world when she's fighting with her mother. Miracle had a cold for the first half of February and it made her sound like Demi Moore on two packs a day, like you wanted to ply her with cough drops and beg her to keep quiet. Then, by the time she started to recover, I was totally cool with the new voice. It didn't bother me a bit.

Anyway, that's what it's like with us and why Friday night will probably be the high point of the week. In fact, I feel my energy spike the second Miracle pulls into the drive and I shout goodbye to Dad, who is just about to leave for Nina's to help pack more boxes.

Miracle has Lily Allen on in the van and people are talking over the sound of "Everyone's at It," trying to decide where we should go. As soon as we've picked everyone up—me, Jamie, Charlie Kady, Yolanda (but not Zoe, who's grounded for giving her mom attitude) and Dustin—the Chinese food vote easily sweeps the van. We head over to North Star Chinese Buffet, the cheapest place around, and make ourselves comfortable. I overdose on hot garlic spareribs and listen to Charlie talk about saving the Canadian boreal forest from toilet paper companies.

After the food we head over to the rink arcade but Yolanda hates video games so we don't stay long. We end up in front of Zoe's house where Yolanda dials Zoe and asks if there's any way she can sneak out back. There really isn't and I tell everyone they can come over to my place as long as they don't have an aversion to boxes.

"When're they moving in?" Yolanda asks.

"Next weekend." I've been thinking of it as a future event for at least a month but saying it straight out like that feels strange. Next weekend is no time away.

"And do you like her?"

"Sure, she's pretty cool." I don't have any worries about her. It's just weird how the situation snuck up on me when I've been aware of it for a while.

"I hated my stepfather when he first moved in with us," Miracle confesses. "The harder he tried, the worse it got. He was perfectly nice, perfectly reasonable, but that almost made him more annoying, you know what I mean?"

"You're so stubborn," Charlie says, shaking his head as he grins. "Didn't your mother warn him?"

Miracle's lips poke up into a sharp smile. "I don't think she realized I was such a tough case—which she definitely should've after seventeen years of living with me."

"Not like Mason here," Charlie observes. "I'm sure he'll go easy on her."

Everyone voices their agreement; I'm notoriously easy to get along with.

Once we're settled in my basement Charlie commandeers the remote and starts flicking channels. At first he's the only one interested but then he hits this show on sex toys and amateur erotic videos and suddenly everyone's ogling the screen. It's nothing compared to the hardcore stuff you run into on the Internet, and normally it wouldn't faze me at all, but now my mind's sparking something fierce. I need another chance with Kat. All the things we could do. Unbelievable.

"That one looks uncomfortable," Miracle says, tilting her head as she glances away from the TV. "Weirdly industrial."

"And that's only the low setting," Yolanda adds. "If you're smart you'd take out insurance before plugging it in. How much do you think something like that costs, anyway?"

Y turns to face me and I'm wondering why I'm the resident sex toy expert but I just hunch over, shrugging and trying not to notice that the redhead on the receiving end of the low setting has thighs exactly the same shape as Kat's. *Unbelievable.* Seriously. I'd rather watch back-to-back episodes of *The View* than sit through another ten seconds of this. It's pushing me over the edge. "I'm starving," I announce. "Anyone want food?"

"I'll help you," Miracle offers, following me upstairs. We rifle through the fridge, decide on butterscotch ripple ice cream and carry the tub downstairs with six spoons and bowls. Charlie's switched over to *That '70s Show* and relief leaks into my smile as I kick back on the couch. At the moment, PG comedy is just my speed.

Dad and I do lunch and a movie on Sunday afternoon. It turns out he's not overly into the engagement shower idea himself. He says we can make celebrity guest appearances at the end and then everyone will be happy.

When we pull up to the house later, it's surrounded by cars and there's a collection of white and purple helium balloons floating from the mailbox. From outside I hear a baby wailing. I can't remember the last time we even had a baby in the house, and for the first time I wonder if Dad and Nina will have kids together.

"The boys are home!" someone cries as we walk through the front door.

I glance across the living room and search out the face belonging to the voice—Nina's younger sister, Andrea, who's driven over from Peterborough to play hostess. Aside from Nina and her kids, Andrea's the only person I know in the room. I wave hello to everyone and let Andrea introduce Dad and me to at least twenty women and a handful of kids. "There's plenty of food left in the kitchen," Andrea tells us.

"Great," I say. I'm one of those people who can eat forever and not gain weight. It got me ballistic when I was about twelve and sick of being smaller than other guys my age but now that I've seen some of those guys pack on excess pounds, I like to think of it as a bonus.

"I'm okay, thanks," Dad says. Unfortunately for him, he doesn't have my metabolism. "Any coffee?" he adds as an afterthought. "Decaf?"

"Actually"—Andrea raises her finger—"there is decaf. Let me get you a cup. Sit down next to the guest of honor."

Dad strokes Nina's hair as he takes a seat next to her on the couch. The two of them are surrounded by a fresh set of boxes (partially wrapped this time) and Andrea and I head off to the kitchen together. "Looks like you guys had a good time," I say.

Andrea motions back to the pile of presents on the coffee table. "Nina made a killing—wait till you see all the terrific stuff people gave her."

Inside the kitchen there's a ton of leftovers spread out on the table and counter. Two women are talking by the sink and I smile at them as I grab a purple paper plate and start piling on meatballs. "This is Thane's son, Mason," Andrea tells them. "Mason, this is Patricia and Colette."

I exchange hellos with Patricia and Colette as Andrea heads for one of the coffee machines set up on the counter. "Try the chocolate cheesecake," Colette advises me. "It's *divine*." She throws so much emphasis on that last word that I have to laugh. So okay, looks like I'm trying the cheesecake. I lift a heaping piece onto my plate, right next to the mound of meatballs.

Patricia excuses herself, leaving Andrea, Colette and me in the kitchen. "So how do you know Nina?" I ask Colette, leaning back against the counter.

"Colette's my best friend," Andrea says, holding up Dad's cup of decaf. "How does your dad take it?"

"Lots of cream," I tell her.

"Best friend since fourth grade," Colette elaborates, glancing over at Andrea. "It makes me feel ancient when I think of how long ago that was." But Andrea's too preoccupied with her cream search to agree. "How old are you, Mason?" Colette's gaze settles back on me.

"Sixteen," I say, popping a meatball into my mouth.

Andrea's located the cream and pours it liberally into Dad's decaf. "Voilà," she says, smiling at us as she glides out of the kitchen.

"High school." Colette groans. "Wouldn't want to do that again."

"It's not that bad."

"Well, good for you then." Colette steps towards the coffee machine and pours herself a cup. "It really depends on what kind of person you are, I think. I had no idea who I was in high school. It was utter confusion and chaos."

"Yeah." I nod. "I guess sometimes it is." Utter confusion's a fair description of the past eight days.

Just then Brianna storms into the kitchen. Her hair's piled on top of her head and she's wearing stop-sign-red lipstick and frowning, as usual. "Any more Fruitopia?" she asks.

I shrug and glance at Colette, who moves swiftly over to the fridge and grabs a can from the bottom shelf.

"Thanks," Brianna says unconvincingly.

"So'd you finish packing your stuff?" I ask her.

Brianna shrugs like she can't imagine why I'd ask. "Almost," she says finally.

"What about the bed? You bringing it?" This is what most of our conversations sound like. Sometimes I don't know why I bother.

"No." She stares at the cheesecake on my plate. "The futon's better."

"Double?" Colette ventures.

"Huh?" Brianna says blankly. One of her bottom teeth is dotted with red. I'm not sure if it's her lipstick or something she ate.

Colette sips her coffee. "Is it a double futon?"

"Oh, yeah." Brianna nods.

"It's so much better having a double," Colette continues. "You'll never want to go back to a twin. And futons are great—so flexible."

Brianna nods again, wrinkling her forehead. Then she turns, aims a quick goodbye over her shoulder and leaves us alone again.

"That's not a happy girl," Colette observes.

No comment. With my meatballs finished I launch enthusiastically into the cheesecake. Colette's right; it's divine. You hardly ever hear that word but it's a perfect description. "This is *really* good," I say. And she's pretty impressive herself—one of those people who can talk to you in a way that makes you feel like they already know you, even though you've just met. Good-looking too, with medium-long dark hair, brown eyes and tiny bones.

"Told you." Colette smiles, giving me a peek at her front teeth. I'm not surprised that they don't have any leftovers or smudged lipstick attached to them. "Homemade. One of Nina's friends brought it. Can't remember her name. I'm all right with faces but I'm terrible with names."

"So who am I?" I ask, teasing her. In fact, I might even be flirting with her a little.

"Mason." She smiles wider. "Of course I remember *now*. You're standing right in front of me." She blinks slowly, her eyes twinkling. Is it possible she's flirting back? "But once I walk out that door later today, well, I'm afraid the odds drop dramatically."

I take another bite of cake as I look at her. She has to be something like eight or nine years older than me but it doesn't matter; we're just kidding around.

"I should go mingle," she says, stepping away from the counter in high heels that make her legs look longer than they probably are (but that's okay, I'm enjoying the illusion).

"Why bother? You won't remember anyone."

"Well, maybe they'll remember me," she says lightly.

"I bet," I tell her, the full force of my grin behind the words.

Colette shakes her head at me like she's enjoying this. "I think I know why you don't have a problem with high school, Mason."

What a line to close on. I smile as I watch her go. Then I tilt my head, set my fork down and feel my face heat up about a hundred degrees. I stand there alone in my kitchen, beaming like a madman.

five

KAT COMES DOWN with a bad cold and misses two days of school. I hear the details from Jamie and Sondra and send her one of those cheesy animated get-well e-cards. Kat e-mails me back and says thanks and she'll see me soon. It's the first e-mail she's sent me since the night of the party and I feel pretty good about it, but when I see her at school on Thursday it's obvious we're still at square one.

She stands at my locker in a long white sweater and says, "Can I get your history notes?" Her eyes are sort of glassy, like she's still sick, and her voice sounds strained.

"Sure." I reach into my locker to pull out my notebook. My history notes from the two days she was away are thoroughly intelligible—unlike Monday's or last week's—which is another thing I don't want to spend much energy thinking about. "Are you feeling better?"

Our hands touch as I hand over the notebook and I could swear that she jumps, not enough for anyone else to notice, not even enough for me to notice if it'd happened two weeks ago. "I'm feeling contagious," she says, instantly looking worried that I may have taken that the wrong way, which, let's face it, I have. "My parents didn't want me to miss too much school," she adds hastily. "They sort of turned on the pressure about coming back."

Okay, so she's not feeling better. I thought it was a simple question.

"I got your e-mail," she says, taking one of her obligatory ten-second looks at me. "Thanks."

"Yeah, I got yours too." This is ridiculous. Three years of friendship and now the simplest conversation feels like hard labor. Sure, I miss the Saturday-night Kat Medina but I'm starting to miss the old Kat too, the one I could talk to.

"You know, I think you were right about Nina and the kids," I tell her. "It'll be pretty surreal when they move in this weekend. My dad's office isn't his office anymore. We started painting it last night and it looks completely different. Once Burke's furniture is in there I won't even be able to recognize it." It's this hideous dark green, for a start. It makes the room look half its size.

Kat holds my notes against her hip and I'm trying, I really am, but I can't stop seeing the curve of that naked hip in my head. Also, I feel sorry for her, being back at school and all when she's still sick. Normally I'd act more sympathetic and give her a hug after not seeing her for a few days but now I don't think she'd want that.

"It's a lot to get used to," Kat confirms. "I guess you just have to expect that it's going to feel weird for a while." She flips her hair back, looking tired. "I should go," she says, glancing at my feet. "I'll see you in history?"

"Lunch," I remind her. We don't have history until last period today.

"There too," she says. A smile catches on her lips for a second before disappearing. "See you later."

But at lunch I end up sandwiched between Zoe and Jamie, and Kat barely acknowledges me. She spends the entire period talking to Michelle and Sondra, and I act like I'm cool with it. Hey, I'm cool with everything. She's the one overreacting. I'm not the one who jumped when our hands touched, you know?

"So, Mason." Yolanda leans towards me from across the table. "Any idea what movie we should review?"

Yolanda and I have to do this *At the Movies* style review for Presentation and Speaking Skills next week and we haven't agreed on a movie yet. The class is such a cakewalk that I've been acing it with minimal effort but Yolanda's more comfortable with behind-the-scenes stuff, which is why she's worrying about this on a Thursday when our presentation is scheduled for next Tuesday. "What about something awful?" I suggest. "Something we can totally dis and tear to shreds." Definitely more fun. More distracting for Yolanda too.

"I like it," Yolanda says with a smile. "We can act all outraged."

"Or we can disagree vehemently," I add. "You can throw up your hands and I say '*I can't believe this—did we even see the same movie!*'"

I must be projecting my voice because next thing I know Kat's glancing at me from down the table. She puts one hand to her forehead and looks swiftly away and I'd love to do something crazy like kiss her on the top of the head and stand behind her massaging her shoulders. Everybody would freak. She'd freak. But something about it would feel right.

We should be closer after what we've done together. We should be . . . something.

But the things you want the most aren't always possible. And then again, there are other things I'd rather avoid but can't. Like Burke's dark green room. Maybe he was a slug in a past life. Who else would want a green room? Anyway, I start on the second coat as soon as I get home from school. Dad calls and says he has an emergency, some kid that needs his tooth pulled, and by the time he gets home I'm already finished.

"Great job," he says appreciatively, surveying the room. "Thanks, Mason."

I have green under my fingernails and crusted paint in my hair and my stomach's rumbling from hunger. "You like it?"

"Not my color," Dad says honestly. "But I'm sure Burke will like it." He reaches behind my ear and scrapes at a strand of my hair. "I was going to suggest going out for pizza but maybe we're better off ordering in."

"Good idea."

"We can sit back and enjoy the calm before the storm." Dad smiles, plants his hands on his waist and nods at the green room. "Entirely changes the atmosphere in here, doesn't it?"

"Could be the paint fumes." I feel for my crusty chunk of green hair as we step out of the room. "So what time are the movers going to be here on Saturday?"

"Early," Dad says. "I don't know where we're going to put everything. We might be looking at a summer garage sale."

"You should've suggested that to Nina before she brought all the boxes over."

Dad rolls his head in some kind of nod. "We'll sort it out somehow."

At this point there's not much choice. I shower as Dad calls for pizza but that one lump of hair stays green no matter how hard I scrub. I could dye the rest of it to match and get my tongue pierced. Maybe that would get Kat's attention.

When the pizza arrives Dad and I eat it straight out of the box without bothering about plates. Something tells me that won't be happening again for a while, that Nina would rather dirty a few dishes. It's one of those things that don't really matter but I can't help thinking it just the same.

On Friday night I head over to the local cineplex with Y, Z and Jamie to watch *Creep Forward*. It's a psycho-stalker movie starring the latest Paris Hilton clone, and Yolanda says it's been getting devastating reviews. She takes notes all through the movie, like a true professional, and every fifteen minutes or so I think of something to add and lean over and whisper it in her ear. By the time the movie's finished we practically have our presentation written.

The movers show up around ten the next morning and I throw on my clothes and stumble into the kitchen for orange juice. Two sweaty guys in ball caps trudge by with Burke's mattress. "Know where this goes?" one of them asks.

"Upstairs," I tell them. "First door on your left."

The guy nods thanks and I drink my orange juice fast, expecting Nina and the kids at any second. Besides, it's impossible to sleep with movers banging around the place. A third one lumbers by with a pile of dresser drawers in his arms as I'm rinsing my glass. I'm not sure where the drawers belong but I'm about to direct him to Burke's room with the others when I hear Dad's voice. "Second door on the right upstairs," he says.

Dad strides into the kitchen, a box nestled in his arms. "Morning, Mason."

"Morning," I mumble, still half-asleep. "Anything I can do?"

Dad shakes his head. "Let these guys handle it." He sets his box down on the counter, next to the microwave. "Kitchen gadgets," he explains. "She marked the box."

So there's nothing to do but play traffic controller and cart a couple of ultralight plastic containers into the house. Nina and the kids show up while the movers are negotiating their way up the drive with Brianna's desk. Nina looks tired but Burke smiles energetically as he leaps out of the car. He's got crazy-round cheeks that could star in catalogs if Nina was anything like my mother. "Hi, Mason," he calls, running up the driveway.

"Don't run, Burke!" Nina shouts after him. "Be careful. Stay out of the men's way." Burke shoots a look at the moving guys and stops in his tracks. "Thank you," Nina says nicely. "Just wait there for me."

Burke's good at this. He sways from side to side, keeping himself busy, as Nina opens the trunk. More boxes, of course. Dad tells her to let us take them, and just then Brianna climbs out of the car, holding her cat, Billy. The cat's nearly as old as I am but moves and looks like a panther. Apparently he suffers from a serious attitude problem too. I've already been warned against petting him.

"Maybe you should put him in the bathroom," I advise. "So nobody trips over him."

Brianna tosses me an impatient stare. "I know."

Right. She knows everything.

Nina takes Burke's hand and walks into the house with him. Brianna follows and Dad and I trail behind with the last of the boxes and a collection of plants. "Thanks, guys," Nina says, swiveling to look at us. "I can't believe this is it."

"It's not," Brianna counters. "There's still the *unpacking*." She turns to march upstairs, black cat cradled in her arms.

"Can I look at my room?" Burke asks, hopping on one foot as he peers up at Nina.

"The movers are finished in there," Dad says with a nod.

"Go ahead," Nina says. She starts for the kitchen with Dad in tow and I guess I could go back to bed or battle Brianna's cat for space in the shower but instead I follow Burke up to Dad's old office to catch his reaction.

"You like this color?" I ask.

"Green's my favorite color," he says, showing all his teeth. He darts into the middle of the room and tugs at the tape on the nearest box. It twists between his fingers, folding stubbornly into itself, resisting his efforts.

"It won't open," he complains.

I bend over, yank the tape off in one go and toss it aside.

"You have green in your hair," Burke says, pointing. He begins pulling action figures out of the box and lobbing them onto his mattress.

"I know." I automatically reach for it. "I can't get it out."

"Rub it with baby oil," Brianna advises from behind me.

"That works?" I turn to look at her. She's standing in the hall without her monster of a cat, arms folded in front of her.

"It worked for my friend," she says flatly.

I swear, this is the most constructive conversation we've ever had.

"Mason, can you open some more boxes for me?" Burke asks.

"I'll do it." Brianna walks swiftly into the room, her eyes shrinking as she glances my way. "Don't worry about it." She's wearing this sour expression on her face, like she just caught a whiff of fresh puke, and I laugh as I watch her tear open a second box.

"You're gonna break a nail," I say. I can't help it. If the girl was any more uptight it'd be a medical condition.

Brianna doesn't reply. She just keeps tearing at boxes like she's on a mission. Meanwhile Burke's yanking out anything remotely interesting, littering the floor with superheroes and racecars. It's deep green chaos and I whistle as I back slowly out of the room. If this is what Saturday mornings are gonna be like from now on, I should sleep late.

six

NINA COOKS THIS beef and rice thing on Sunday night. We eat in the dining room because the kitchen table's too small for five. The next night Dad's late but Nina already knows to expect that; she puts his dinner in a Tupperware container in the fridge. Afterwards Nina says that she realizes Dad and I haven't been eating scheduled meals like they have and that she knows sometimes I'll have my own plans.

"I'll let you know if I'm not going to be around," I tell her. "How does that sound?"

"Perfect," she says. "You could let me know some things you like too—or things you don't, for that matter."

Yeah, maybe I could jot some helpful hints down on cue cards. Seriously, though, I know she's only trying to be accommodating. It's just bizarre to imagine Nina making food for me on a regular basis. I mean, I'm not the one she's in love with; I'm just part of the package deal. "Tomatoes," I offer. "Can't stand them except on pizza." Not a big issue really. I'm only saying it for the sake of saying *something*.

Later that night I go over to Yolanda's to practice our movie review presentation. She makes her parents listen to us, and her mother laughs when we start into the bickering bit. I'm not in any hurry to get home so I hang out there awhile watching TV and listening to Y's older brother (temporarily home from university) play drums in the background. I went through my own drumming phase a couple years ago, so I can hear that he's good.

"Is your brother in a band?" I ask.

"Two. He's trying to figure out which one he wants to stick with." Yolanda stretches her legs out in front of her and stares at me thoughtfully. "So what's with you and Kat lately? You two on the outs?"

"What makes you say that?" I run my fingers through my green-free hair (it's true, baby oil works) as I peer back at her.

"Usually you guys talk all the time and lately I never see you together."

"I didn't know we were being monitored," I say. Then, because there's no reason to cop an attitude with Yolanda, I add, "Everything's cool. Same as always."

"If you say so." Yolanda nods. "I'm not trying to get on your case."

"I know, but is this something people are talking about now?" People talk like crazy at GS. Doesn't matter if what they're saying is true or not.

"I haven't heard anything. It's just something Zoe and I noticed while we were *monitoring* you." She smiles at me and I smile back but I'm still a little concerned. Things are weird enough between Kat and me without everyone else noticing. For a second I consider telling Yolanda the truth, just to get it off my chest. I'm sure she'd keep it to herself (or at least between her and Z) but what if just saying it out loud changes things for the worse?

So I don't say anything. I go home, pass Dad and Nina lounging on the living room couch and call out good night. They're both drinking coffee and reading the paper and it's such a cozy little domestic scene that for a second I feel like I must've walked through someone else's front door.

"Good night, Mason," they chime. They sound happy and I'm happy for them. From what I remember Dad was good at being with someone.

Yolanda and I wow everyone with our presentation the next morning. People aren't used to seeing Yolanda act so outgoing, and you can tell they get a kick out of it. They're leaning forward in their seats, grinning and nodding. Some of them have obviously seen *Creep Forward,* and it looks like most of them didn't like it any better than we did. Ms. Courier has this class applause policy—you have to clap whether you enjoyed the person's presentation or not—so the grinning and nodding is a much better indication of what people think of your presentation.

Ms. Courier stops the video camera as we return to our seats. She records all the presentations so we can watch ourselves and become more aware of our body language, voice, etc. I'm pretty in tune with my body language from my modeling days anyway; I don't need to see the video. In fact, it took me a couple years to get over thinking about how I looked all the time. Where I'm at right now is a happy medium. I'm conscious of what I'm doing but I don't obsess about things like the angle I'm holding my right arm at or whether my eyebrows are perfectly neat. Mostly I concentrate on getting the emotion right.

If I weren't so good at that, Kat would already suspect how I'm feeling. Or maybe she does. I don't know and there's no one I can ask.

I'm starting to think about picking up the phone to call her sometime soon. Not to talk about *it,* just to get our friendship back into the groove. Tiptoeing around each other isn't working.

Anyway, I'm thinking about it but I haven't decided yet. Suddenly I'm all kinds of Hamlet. I can't make up my fucking mind.

Take today. I could walk up to Kat in the cafeteria and make a joke. I could lean into the aisle in history and ask her if she'll be home tonight. Then, at the end of the period, I could casually mention that I might give her a call later. It wouldn't be hard.

Unless she goes white, stares down at her desk and stays quiet for so long that there's no need to spell out that she doesn't want to hear from me later. That could happen. Or something worse that I'm even less prepared for. Then what?

This is exactly the kind of thinking that keeps me where I am. At least until after history. I'm two steps behind her in the hall when I surprise myself by reaching out to touch her shoulder. She swings around and looks up at me with suspicious eyes. "You busy after school today?" I ask. "I was thinking we could hang out or something."

Kat's lips disappear inside her mouth as she thinks it over. "Are you okay?" she asks.

"Sure. Why wouldn't I be?" The fact that she's even asking gets me but I don't want to spook her.

"The changes at home." Kat scratches her nose. "I don't know. I just wondered."

"No, I'm fine," I tell her. "It's just that we haven't hung out in a while, you know?"

"I know." She looks tense, like I'm going to jump her right there in the hallway, nine steps from the guidance office.

I'm about to tell her that I wish she would relax around me, that everything would be cool if she'd let it, but Christopher Cipolla cuts between us at that exact moment and says, "Anyone want to ditch last period? I can't deal with French today." He grimaces for effect, instantly sucking up the anxious energy between Kat and me and converting us into an audience. "It's McKenzie's personal mission to crush me—the bitter old bitch."

"You upstage her all the time," I advise. "You can't do that with McKenzie."

"Listen to Dr. Phil here," Kat retorts, her voice biting. She's frowning in disapproval and I don't know what I've done wrong but suddenly I'm just sick to death of this shit with her.

"I'm in," I say, talking over her. "What do you want to do?"

"I'm due at JB at five," Christopher says slowly. He gives us this bewildered look like he's sensed something rotten in the air but isn't sure what it is. "But I'm open to suggestions." JB is The Java Bean, where he started working just last weekend. It's in the middle of downtown Glenashton, surrounded by trendy restaurants with names like Paradoxe and II Mondo. "Kat, you coming too?"

"Actually"—Kat cocks her head in my direction—"I was just telling Mason that Sondra's coming over after class to work on a physics assignment."

"Of course," I say sarcastically. "That's exactly what you were going to tell me." There was never a remote possibility of us hanging out. She's not even comfortable standing next to me.

Kat clenches her jaw as she looks away. I'm positive I could get her pretty crazy if I wanted to. I could crank up the attitude and make her scream at me right in front of Christopher and the guidance office. It'd be one way to get to her.

"Let's go," I tell Chris. "Before you run into McKenzie."

Chris flashes Kat one last look. "Later, Kat."

Kat nods goodbye to both of us and for a second I think I see something besides anger in her eyes. Regret, maybe. I don't know. She's an enigma. Maybe she'll be an enigma from now on. Maybe we're not even friends anymore. I don't know a thing about it.

Christopher and I head downtown and shoot pool in The Windsor Arms. We eat fish-and-chips and then Chris flips through CDs at this jazz music store I've never been inside before. Round about then I remember that Nina will be expecting me home for dinner. I phone Brianna and tell her to let Nina know I'm skipping supper tonight.

"Anything else?" Brianna says wearily.

"Nope."

"'Kay." Brianna hangs up without a goodbye, and because I'm already in a mood I almost call her back and tell her to lighten up. Almost. But she's not the one I'm mad at.

"I should get over to JB," Christopher says, bounding towards me. "You coming for a coffee on the house?"

Sure I'm coming for coffee. I'm not in a frenzy to get home. I walk over to JB with Chris and let him fix me a cup of their coffee of the week: Cinnamania. It's so sweet that two sips give me a colossal sugar rush and I sit at a booth on my own reading one of the house copies of the *Toronto Star*, my foot tapping in time to the Foo Fighters.

"Mason Rice," a woman's voice pronounces. "Looks like the name stuck after all."

My gaze darts up and hangs on Colette standing across from me in a navy blazer and knee-length skirt, her thin fingers wound around a paper coffee cup. The clothes make her look like an official version of the woman I met at Nina's shower. I liked her at the time but Kat's sunk me into a weird mood I can't climb out of. I just want to sit here, sipping my sugar in easy silence.

"Hey," I say evenly. "How are you?"

"I'm fine." She smiles like she's pleased with herself. "How're Nina and the kids settling in at the house?"

"Great." I nod slowly, set down the newspaper and blink at her, searching for something to say. That's not a problem I usually have, and the gap in conversation tips me further off balance.

"Are you all right?" Colette asks, concern in her eyes. "You seem a bit . . ." She makes a wavy motion with her hand. *Seasick?* "Is this a bad time?"

"No." I shake my head and reach for my Cinnamania. "You know, you're the second person that's asked me that today."

"Okay." Colette nods. "That was nosy of me," she says apologetically.

"No, no, it's okay." Somehow her sympathetic tone makes me feel better. At least I'm not in the wrong here. "So you work around here or something?"

"Four doors down. At the travel agency. It's a temporary gig. I'm thinking about going back to school." The fact that she refers to her job as a gig makes me smile. It sounds so laid-back, completely the opposite of how she looks.

"I thought you didn't like school." I smile harder, trusting that she remembers our last conversation.

"Just high school," Colette clarifies. "The horror years." She raises her cup like she's toasting me and adds, "Well, I'm going to hit the road, Mason. Do you want a ride home?"

Do I want a ride? For sure. It's the home part that I'm not big on. The house has seriously shrunk over the past few days. "Okay," I reply reluctantly. "Thanks." I stand up next to her, catch Christopher's eye and tell him I'll see him tomorrow.

"Ciao," Chris sings, looking at the both of us.

Out on the street I gulp coffee and follow Colette's lead. Her Toyota Echo's parked in a lot around the corner and someone's dented the passenger door pretty bad. Colette notices me eyeing it and says, "Condo parking lot scrape. Stupid SUV was hogging the ramp at my friend's place." She shakes her head wildly. "Don't you hate those things? I can't believe anyone's still driving them—it's like wearing a badge declaring yourself an asshole."

It sounds like one of those questions that don't need an answer and I climb into the car and snap on the seat belt. "You remember where the house is?" I ask.

"Sure. Right off Weston."

"Yeah." I nod, and somewhere in that four-second pause my mind leaps back to Kat shrinking away from me in the hall. I mean, how's that supposed to make me feel? It's not like I talked her into something. She was the one who asked if I had condoms. We're supposed to be friends, and the way she's acting, it's as though she can barely stand me. "That's right."

Colette fixes her eyes on me, her lips stretching like she's about to break into a smile, only she doesn't. She sticks the key in the ignition and revs the engine. Then we're pulling out of the parking lot and heading down Kennedy in silence. Don't ask me why but I get the feeling we could keep going like that until we hit my house. I can see it. Not a word, not a sound, not even the radio, until she pulls into my driveway. I'll say thanks and she'll say no problem and that will be the end of it.

Only suddenly that's not how I want this to go. "So what're you going back to school for?" I ask, turning to look at her.

"Law. I'm trying to get some money together first. I have the apartment and car payments to keep up." We stop at a red light and Colette looks over at me and adds, "Lately I've been insanely jealous of all those people that move back home to save money. Seems like everyone is doing that these days."

"And you can't?"

"My parents are big into the *Christian* thing." Colette bends her fingertips around the word, inserting quotation marks. "It's not my scene."

"I get you." I focus on Colette's hands back on the steering wheel. I look at the dark sleeves of her blazer and follow them up to her shoulders. Her neck's long and slender and she's got a single freckle under her jawline. She has a pretty face with sharp, almost aristocratic-looking features, like a woman you'd see playing a young countess in a historical drama—the countess who is smarter, sexier and more intriguing than everyone else in the movie. I'd check out her legs again too but that'd be obvious.

"What about you?" she asks. "Have you figured out what you want to do after high school?"

"Maybe." I smile coyly as I glance at her sideways. I'm all over the map today; I don't have a clue what I'm doing. I mean, the girl is, like, twenty-five but she's really something in this strange, delicate kind of way. It's almost like I can't help flirting.

"Holding out on me, huh?" Her dark eyes shine at me from the driver's seat.

"Nah." I shake my head, point my gaze out the window and try to stay cool. "I'm just not sure yet." I scratch my ear and add, "I've been doing some acting at school."

"That's great," Colette says enthusiastically. "I bet you're good."

"What makes you say that?"

"I don't know. You seemed pretty comfortable with yourself that day at the party."

That day at the party when she flirted back. I'm right about that much.

"I wish I could've been confident like that in high school," Colette continues. "You're so far ahead of the game if you've got it together at fifteen and don't let the stupid things get you down."

"Sixteen," I correct, staring at her boldly. I swear I feel drunk on Cinnamania, like I don't know what I'll do or say next. Maybe it's partly because of how Kat acted today but it's not as simple as that. It's also how long Colette's legs looked in her high heels at Nina's shower and how she keeps saying the right things to me.

Colette stops the car and then I notice we're parked right in front of my house and that in a second I'll have to say goodbye and get out.

"Sixteen," Colette repeats slowly. "Right." She stares steadily back, sizing me up, wondering if she's misinterpreting my intentions.

"I guess it doesn't make much difference." Reality's filtering through my sugar high and I'm beginning to lose my nerve. This is a full-grown woman I'm sitting next to. She's probably been in high heels for as long as I've been in school. "So I'll see you later, Colette." Thing is, I'm still sitting there, waiting for something to happen, my breath vibrating in my throat.

"O-kay," Colette says in a funny voice. "This is the part where you get out of the car, Mason."

"Seriously?" I ask, disappointed. It's stupid but somehow I can't believe she's going to make me get out of the car. Then again, how could I expect any different? "Yeah, sure," I add swiftly, coming to my senses. "Thanks for the ride."

Colette laughs at me, and I blush. "You're so cute," she says, and then, probably because I look embarrassed, she adds, "Don't worry about it, Mason. We're cool." I crinkle up my eyes, wishing I could blend with the upholstery. "Don't worry," she repeats, and I'm sitting there shaking my head, not even trying to hide the fact that I feel like a loser.

In fact, she's being so great about it that I'm almost sort of enjoying this in a weird way. "Okay," I mumble finally. "Thanks."

I turn partway to look at her, red creeping across my face like an allergic reaction, and she looks back at me and says, "Where were guys like you when I was in high school?" She sounds sincere, and we both laugh quietly at the sublime ridiculousness of the situation.

"All right, then," she announces, smiling. "Be good."

I'm still blushing uncontrollably but I smile too. "I don't know about that."

"Just humor me," she says, and before I can say anything else she leans over and kisses me, half on the lips and half on the chin, like she hasn't made up her mind.

I blink incredulously, and in that moment all my manic feelings for Kat start to slip away. It shouldn't be that easy; what can I say? It wasn't even a real kiss but here I am sitting next to Colette in her car, my mind and body humming so hard that the reverberations could cause an earthquake. "Is that some kind of consolation prize?" I ask. My voice is husky; I can't control it either.

Colette eyes me with a look I can't decipher. It gives me goose bumps down my arms, not knowing whether I've made her mad or what. Then her hands spring back towards the steering wheel as she says, "I'd consider myself lucky if I were you." She flashes a smile to let me know she's not pissed. "Good luck with the acting."

"Thanks." You'd think we're never going to see each other again, the way we're talking, but I don't believe that. "Good luck with law school." I bend my head in towards my chest, whip the car door open and tread slowly up my driveway, feeling humble and amazed.

seven

THE NEXT MORNING Hugo and three of Monica Gregory's friends are hanging off her in the GS parking lot, all of them beaming ultrabrite smiles and giving off giddy vibes. Monica's wearing this tiny red plaid kilt that makes her legs look almost as incredible as Colette's and whispering into Hugo's ear. He rubs her back as he nods and I've just shifted my attention away from them when I hear Monica squeal my name across the parking lot.

She motions towards me, urging me to join them. The picture all adds up to something but I don't know what yet, only that Monica wants me to ask.

"Hey, what's up?" I say as I catch up to them. Their sunny group smile (except for Hugo) makes me grin automatically back. The blonde on Monica's left leans in close to her and waits for Monica to answer me.

"I promised myself I wasn't going to spread this around until I knew for sure," Monica declares, eyes sparkling. Then she impulsively grabs my hand to pull me closer still. "But you won't tell anyone, right? Not if I say not to?"

"My lips are sealed," I promise. The group of us heads towards the west doors, Hugo shooting me a hard look like I'm treading on his territory. *You gotta be kidding,* I think to myself. *Monica Gregory is equal opportunity.* Besides, I'm not into her like that; Colette's been taking up most of my mental energy since I climbed into her car last night. I didn't imagine that half kiss or how sexy she looked in a suit. I'm still in a fever nearly twenty-four hours later.

"Okay," Monica says, tapping two fingers quickly to her lips like she can barely contain herself. She explains that she was at the airport with her mother last night, picking up her dad from a business trip, when this talent scout approached them and handed over her card. "My parents researched the agency when we got home and it's one hundred percent legit." Monica's cheeks flush as she continues. "She thought I might be right for a lotto commercial they want to cast a teenage girl for. I mean, who knows if I'll get it but just the idea, you know . . ."

I watch Hugo's eyes twitch as Monica squeezes my arm and loops hers affectionately around it. "That's fantastic!" I tell her. "You scored yourself an audition."

"It looks that way," Monica says happily.

"Fantastic," I say for the second time. "You have to let me know how that goes." Most commercials look only marginally more emotionally challenging than all the department store catalog work I did years ago (if I had to do one more photo shoot where the entire point was sticking my hands in my pockets and staring off camera, looking like I didn't have a care in the world, I think I'd implode) but Monica's clearly hyped about it and I wouldn't turn down a credit like that myself. At least being in a commercial lets you breathe—and maybe even speak—on film.

"Thanks!" she tells me. "I'll keep you posted."

Our group begins to disperse as we walk through the west doors and I'm in the middle of saying goodbye to Monica when I spy Kat outside the cafeteria. She flashes me an urgent *come here* look but I take my time; I haven't forgotten yesterday afternoon's humiliation.

"Hey, Kat," I say finally, ambling towards her. "What's up?"

"This is totally depressing," Kat declares, staring gloomily after Monica G. "Does she need everything handed to her on a silver platter?"

Seems like Monica's secret news isn't so secret after all, but my promised silence on the subject stops me commenting, and anyway, I'm not sure what Kat wants me to say. I tilt my head and shrug my knapsack higher onto my shoulder.

"Where'd you and Chris take off to yesterday?" she continues.

"Nowhere much." *How am I supposed to see Colette again without stalking her?* That's my big concern at the moment. I need another fix. My Kat baggage vanishes without a trace whenever I'm in Colette's vicinity. I don't need to be Dr. Phil to realize that's a good thing.

"You know, I was serious about the physics assignment." Kat gives me an earnest look, does a rapid scan of the hallway and then flicks her gaze back to me. "Sondra and I were working on it most of the night." She runs her fingers through her bangs and adds, "This is so unfair. This Monica thing shouldn't get to me, right? Why am I letting it get to me? It's not that I even like Hugo anymore. I don't even know what it is."

So we're back to Monica G, okay. "It's like she's being rewarded for screwing you over," I say neutrally.

"That's exactly what it's like," Kat says, wide-eyed.

It sounds like Kat's not over Hugo, is what it sounds like.

"I know." I nod and close my fingers tightly around my knapsack strap. "I gotta get to my locker, Kat. I'll catch you later, okay?"

"Yeah. Bye, Mason." She looks straight at me, just like the old Kat would, just like nothing ever happened between us. That could be a good thing, I guess, except that it all comes down to Hugo. I'm not important enough to stress over long-term; he is.

I go to homeroom and listen to the usual collection of announcements over the PA. You can hand in used cell phones, inkjet cartridges, iPods, digital cameras, laptop/notebook computers to Mr. Melesi in room 24 to help raise money for our local food bank. Students are reminded not to park in the designated staff areas in the back parking lot. If you do, expect to be towed. Attention, senior students traveling to Spain with Ms. Acosta: today's lunchtime meeting is canceled. And so on and so on . . .

On my way to English later I pass Hugo again in the hall, which reminds me that Kat's likely having a shitty morning, and at lunch she proves it by coming over to where I'm sitting and planting her ass in the closest chair. Jamie sits on her other side, giving me this fierce déjà vu. He tries to cheer her up in this really subtle way and it works a little but when she stops talking her mouth still looks tense, like maybe she's just pretending for him.

It's so familiar to hear them talk like this that next thing I know, I'm pitching in on the *Distract Kat* campaign, talking about the two Bs at home and how I've lost control over the basement because it has the only TV in the house and Brianna doesn't seem to do anything else. Plus, the girl can't stand me and I'm mortally afraid of Billy (the black cat), which doesn't sound like a very frightening name but believe me, the thing is feral.

"He can't be that bad," Kat says with a smile. "You should try to make friends with him."

"I'm not supposed to touch him," I say with this deadpan expression. "How am I supposed to make friends with him? He doesn't even come near me. He's always lurking in corners, watching me like he's waiting for the perfect moment to pounce. Anyway, Brianna's worse. She's one of those people who make you carry the entire conversation while she sits there scowling at you like you're being an asshole."

"It must be hard for her, though," Kat says sympathetically. "She's just moved into your house, where she probably doesn't feel that much at home since she's living with the two other people that have always belonged there and she's what? Thirteen or something? That's such a weird age in the first place without having to fit into this whole new family."

"Right, but that's not the point. You can make things easy or you can make them hard, you know?"

Kat stares at the table like she's thinking that over, and it feels like a conversation we would've had a month ago, like we're just trying to figure things out generally, without having to watch our step. "Give her some time," she says, that sexy hint of an accent in her voice. "There's no way she can dislike you forever. She just doesn't really know you yet."

Did I hear that right? Once I start to smile I can't quit.

"What?" Kat asks, a crease forming between her eyes.

"Nothing." I put my elbows up on the table as I look at her. "It just feels like things are finally getting back to normal with us."

"Normal?" Kat's voice is tense. Her eyes hurl me a warning.

I've been too deep into the conversation to realize this is something we shouldn't be talking about so freely in front of our friends. Now I lower my voice and add, "Well, yeah, you know. It's like you've been mad at me lately."

Suddenly I can feel Sondra's and Michelle's gazes on me from across the table. Jamie's watching too, and Kat's cheeks are turning deep pink. "Why would I be mad at you?" she demands.

"It doesn't make any sense to me," I admit. "I didn't do anything wrong."

"I'm not mad at you," Kat insists. "That's crazy."

"I don't get it," Jamie cuts in, peering at the two of us. "What's going on with you guys?"

"Nothing," Kat replies definitively.

"Don't worry about it," I say at the same time. "No big thing." And because that seems to demand still further explanation, I tack on, "Something stupid I said."

Kat's jaw has dropped and I immediately know referring to that Saturday night as "no big thing" was a critical mistake, even if I was trying to camouflage my earlier lack of discretion. The last thing I ever want to do is make her feel bad about what happened, and even with everyone watching and listening, I just can't let that situation stand.

"I didn't mean 'no big thing,'" I apologize as she stares down at the table.

But every time I try to fix this it just makes things more wrong. Kat's angry gaze swings back to me and I know I've stepped over the line again. One minute I feel like I can finally relax and the next she's ready to tear my head off. Her entire face is red and her fingernail's digging into her thumb. If we could turn down the cafeteria background noise you'd hear her blood boiling.

I stop talking altogether, drum my fingers on the table and try to look harmless. Unfortunately Kat's not having it. She jumps out of her chair and heads for the exit, Sondra and Michelle five steps behind her.

"What did you do?" Jamie asks hotly.

"I didn't do anything." Jamie's probably never heard me sound more serious but he's shooting me this awful look, like he's caught me torturing his nonexistent pet rabbit.

"She wouldn't do that for nothing." Jamie gestures to the exit. Seconds later a spark of recognition lights up his eyes and I'd rather skip this next part but Jamie's already there. He slumps back in his chair, his mouth slack. "Fuck me," he says quietly. He wraps his hands around the back of his neck and stares at me. "It was the night of the party, wasn't it?"

I don't deny it. I don't speak.

"Holy shit," Jamie whispers.

"We're not going to talk about this, Jamie," I command. Close as the three of us are, this is between Kat and me alone. I should never have opened my mouth about it within earshot of anyone else.

"Why am I the last to know everything?" he snaps, eyes bloodshot.

"You're not." Is that why he's mad? I thought it was because of Kat. "I don't understand why you're so upset."

"Of course you do." Jamie scowls. "You'd be exactly the same in my place."

That's not true. I wouldn't be happy but I'd keep my mouth shut about it.

"Why's she so mad at you?" Jamie continues. His face is contorted into this weird aggressive mask that gets my back up. It's not like he had a chance with Kat; it's not like we fucked him over somehow. "What'd you do to her?"

It's such a nasty accusation that I could almost hit him for it. Who does he think he's talking to?

"What did you do?" he repeats, and this time it's more of a whine but my pulse is racing. The back of my neck's twitching too and I drop my jaw and stare at him. We've known each other forever and I've never been angrier with him than I am at this exact moment.

"You need to calm down, Jamie." My voice has an edge to it that'd cut you clean in half. "You need to stay out of it. Whatever did or didn't happen has nothing to do with you and you should know . . ." I drop to a whisper. "I'd never do anything to Kat that she didn't want."

I shove my chair back and get to my feet. Jamie looks away. Meanwhile Y and Z are pretending not to notice what's going down and I stride out of the cafeteria and along the hall, my right hand clenched into a fist. Out in the fresh air a couple guys are playing Frisbee behind the parking lot and I stand around and watch them for a couple minutes. One of the guys has taken his shoes off and I swear, he's like a frigging Jedi Master with the Frisbee, a complete natural. It calms me down a little to see.

I don't want to think about what Jamie just said to me and I don't want to replay Kat's exit. I don't want to do anything except stand here watching these guys play Frisbee until everything goes back to normal.

Then this senior girl with straight black hair and punk boots stalks out and stands next to me. I don't know her name but she squints at me and says, "You were in that school play a few weeks ago. That was you, right? The guy with the dead brother."

"That was me." It's weird but just the fact of her mentioning it makes me feel like I know her.

"That was a pretty cool play. You were good." She sounds surprised but I thank her anyway. Then I go back inside because I can't concentrate on watching Frisbee with her staring at me and I'm not in the mood to talk. The feeling reminds me of yesterday with Colette and as soon as I start thinking about that I begin to feel like a different person. I don't have to let myself get dragged into this stupid romantic triangle drama with Kat and Jamie. They can play it out without me if they want to that bad, but I want something else. The possibility gives me a rush of adrenaline that I feel all the way down to my kneecaps.

It's the kind of secret you want to be alone with, and after school I head straight home. The TV's on in the basement and I jog downstairs to say hi to Brianna and Burke. Brianna's watching that talk show *The Doctors* and Burke's balancing a book on his knees while he munches away on a potato chip sandwich.

"Hey, guys," I say. "What's up?"

"Hi, Mason," Burke says, grinning up at me. Orange crumbs are wedged up between his teeth. The chips must be barbecue or ketchup.

Brianna doesn't answer. Her eyes barely leave the screen.

"Can he watch this?" I ask her. Isn't *The Doctors* all breast cancer discussions, sex advice and plastic surgery?

"We watch *Yu-Gi-Oh!* in the commercials," Burke offers. *Like that sounds fair.*

"He's not watching it anyway," Brianna says dryly, pointing to Burke's book.

"Yeah, I get it." My eyebrows pull together.

Brianna gives me this lethal look and yanks her feet up onto the couch with her. "Do you want to watch something?" she asks. "Is that what it is?"

This time it's me who doesn't answer. I scratch at my knuckles and tap Burke on the shoulder. "Can I try that?"

A single chip falls onto the couch as he hands over the sandwich. I take a bite, chewing noisily. "Ketchup," I announce. "That's not bad."

"Pickle is good too," Burke tells me, and all the while Brianna's sitting there, fuming like her head's going to burst. It's almost funny. I can't even be mad at her; she's just too obvious.

"Don't worry," I say to her. "I'll let you know when I want to watch something, Brianna." She nods absently, refusing to tear her gaze away from the TV. "I'm going out," I add. "Tell Nina for me."

Brianna nods again and I retrace my steps through the house and into the street. It's a spur-of-the-moment thing, but now that I'm going it seems preordained. Colette's been on my mind all day long. She feels like a compulsion. A day-old compulsion that's already gaining strength. I don't even care if it's crazy; I just want to catch another glimpse of her. I need something to counteract my shitty afternoon.

I keep walking until I hit downtown Glenashton. Colette's travel agency is just on the other side of the traffic lights but that's not an option. She'd be surrounded by coworkers and I'd come off looking like some kind of weirdo. Instead I nip into JB, order a latte, sit by the window and hope Christopher isn't working today.

The latte's cold and all but gone by five o'clock and maybe Colette doesn't stop in every day after work like I'm counting on. The good news is that Chris isn't around either. At ten after, I decide to stick around for another twenty minutes, and five minutes later Colette slips through the front door and walks straight past me, her high-heel shoes making a sticky, clicking noise on the tile floor.

I could take off now and she'd never know I was here. No, she's spotted me. She stares at me from her spot at the counter and she doesn't like what she sees. I flash her a wave but she turns swiftly back towards the counter like she can't make me disappear fast enough. This is the effect I have on the opposite sex these days. Why did this seem like such a genius idea an hour ago?

I gulp down the last of my coffee and stare at Colette's legs. She's wearing pants today and I have to fill in her thighs and calves with my imagination. I'm so nervous that I forget everything I was going to say to her. I've never stalked anyone before; how do people do this?

Colette starts towards me with her coffee, her eyes hardening as they focus on mine. She stands stiffly by my table and says, "Should I be surprised to see you again?"

I relax my jaw as I glance up at her. She's tense enough for both of us. "You want to sit down?" I ask, keeping my voice casual.

Colette bows her head and tightens her grip on her coffee cup. "I don't want to be rude, Mason, but this is getting strange."

"Or I just happen to be enjoying a coffee here where my friend works." Her face falls like she's made a terrible mistake and suddenly I can't take it. If someone has to feel like an idiot, I'd sooner it be me. "Okay," I add abruptly. "That's not entirely true. A friend of mine does work here but running into you isn't a coincidence."

Colette takes a breath as she looks into my eyes. "I don't know what to think of you. Don't you have a girlfriend at school?"

"Not really."

She folds one arm in front of her waist and gives me this crooked stare—angry, sexy and more than a little mysterious. That look makes it hard for me to keep my hands to myself. "You do realize that I'm almost twenty-four and you're sixteen?" she says wryly.

I can do the math. "You think I'm being an ass." Or that I'm being cute with my big-girl crush. I don't know which is worse.

"I didn't say that," she says impatiently. "It's just not workable. You seem like a really cool guy and all." Her hand flies off her waist and settles at her side. "I'm sorry if I gave you the wrong idea yesterday. That was impulsive of me—and stupid." She shrugs her shoulders and glances at the door. "I didn't want you to feel bad but I guess I took things too far in the other direction."

I know I look disappointed. I could put up a good front, but why veer away from honesty now?

"I'm sorry," she says again. She takes a single step away from the table, swivels on her heels and adds, "I can still give you a ride if you need one. We don't need to be awkward about this, do we?"

"It feels pretty awkward to me," I say. "I feel like a complete ass."

"Stop saying that," Colette insists. "Okay, I was slightly spooked seeing you here again but that has a lot to do with me too. I know what I did yesterday could've been construed as encouragement. This is partly my fault."

Maybe. "I don't need a ride," I tell her. "It's okay."

"Man." Colette licks her lips. "Now I feel bad."

"You're a monster," I kid. "You should feel bad." This is the thing with her. The more I see her, the more I want to tease her until we're rolling around on the floor, stripping off each other's clothes. It's a normal enough feeling; I've just never had it this intense before.

We smile at each other and I get that vibrating sensation in the back of my throat, like I can't trust my words to come out right. "I don't even believe you," Colette lectures, eyes gleaming. "You never stop."

"I do," I say. "Don't worry. I'm fine. You've got a hyperactive guilt complex."

"I know it." Colette nods. "So we're okay, right? No hard feelings or future chance meetings?"

"Okay," I say seriously. Colette glances down at my empty coffee cup and before she can change her mind and revoke her offer I add, "I'm done here. Maybe I'll take that ride after all, if it's cool with you?"

"Sure." It could be my imagination but her voice sounds shrill. My legs feel shaky as I walk with her. I'm not at all sure something's going to happen this time but the vibes are sparking something wild. I can hardly think what to say. By the time I figure it out we're in the parking lot, approaching her car. "I didn't mean to make you mad," I tell her. "I just really wanted to see you again." We stop right behind her Echo. "But don't worry; I'm not going to turn into some crazy guy that follows you around everywhere. If you see me around it's just coincidence from now on, I promise." Following her around after this would be creepy, and she's only a twenty-four-hour compulsion, after all. Quitting can't be impossible.

"I know," Colette says. "It's okay, Mason." Her fingers close loosely around my wrist.

My other hand reaches instinctively for her hip and she yanks her body away, instantly creating this gaping forbidden zone between us. "Okay," I say with a nervous laugh. "Do I have to apologize for that now too? Am I getting this all wrong?" I hold my hands up helplessly. "I don't know what you want me to do, Colette."

I'm genuinely confused. And my hand wants nothing more than to zing back into place on her hip. I can't think my way through this. I'm like a caveman trying to figure out crosswalk signals.

"I think you do. I think maybe that's the problem." Colette's headlong stare makes my jaw drop.

I knew it. Jesus. I gaze off into the parking lot, my mind filling up with memories of that night with Kat. I wonder what kind of underwear Colette's wearing; I wonder how else it would be different. She's so much older than me.

Colette drags a hand across her brow and into her hairline. "This is ridiculous." She trudges away from me and unlocks the car doors. "Just get in."

Sure. I climb in and keep my eyes on the dashboard. "Don't

worry," I say evenly. "It's cool." It's better than cool. I have to struggle to stop myself from grinning.

"Of course it's cool for you," Colette says as she starts the car. "You're sixteen. I'd be this lecherous old woman with a boy toy. I'd be one of those cougars—and I hate that incredibly sexist term too—in skintight pants with a pinched face from a cheap face-lift." She exhales frustration, her gaze hurtling over to mine.

"You're only twenty-three," I point out. "It's not a big deal." It's a colossal deal. I feel golden.

Colette glares at me as she squeezes the steering wheel. It reminds me of the way Kat looked at me when she called me Dr. Phil.

"Do you want me to get out?" I ask.

"Of course not," she snaps. "This is really annoying, Mason. Why'd you come back today? Why didn't you just leave it alone like I asked you to?"

I slump down in the seat, unable to answer. How do you put something like that into words? It's never just one thing that draws you towards someone, is it? It's indefinable.

We pull up outside my house in no time and Colette stares nervously up the driveway like she's worried about what Nina will think. I run my hands through my hair and follow her gaze. There's no one out there to see us and no one would suspect anyway. "Don't be pissed," I tell her. "I can't have another person mad at me."

"Another person?" Colette echoes, meeting my eyes. "Who else is mad at you?"

I sit there telling her about Kat, Jamie and me. The entire story takes two minutes and when I'm done I absolutely feel sixteen. Most of it sounds ridiculously immature, except for that night with Kat. You can't tell me there wasn't something real in that.

"Your friend Kat sounds really weirded out," Colette says. "Maybe she's not used to hooking up with people so casually."

"She's not." I don't explain about both of us being virgins; I don't want to sound any more like a sixteen-year-old than I already do.

Colette nods, winding a finger into her hair. She's got more elegance in one finger than most people have in their entire bodies. It's impossible for me to stop staring. "I'm not pissed with you, Mason," she says. "I just don't like the way I've been acting with you—you're a kid." I shake my head and she repeats herself, studying my eyes.

"Are you going to tell me to get out of the car now?" I ask. It's the last thing I want to do but I can't push her. It's incredible enough that we've gotten this far. Honestly, she's sexier by the second. My mind's on a rampage.

"Mmm," Colette hums thoughtfully. "I guess you should."

I unbuckle my seat belt and obediently reach for the door but Colette grabs my shoulder before I can open it. I swing around, immediately collapsing back into the passenger seat, my heart thumping like a wild thing. I'd say something but it feels like her turn. She already knows where I stand.

Our eyes lock in silence. We sit there watching each other for too long. "Am I going to see you again?" I ask finally, my fingers scratching at an imaginary clump of green hair.

"Sure," Colette says. "We'll do prom together." She fiddles with her watch strap as she stares at her fingers. "I'm sorry. That was bitchy." Her eyes soften a little as her hands settle back on the wheel. "How about you come over to my place right now and we get this entire thing over with?" Before I have a chance to wonder if that's an all-inclusive deal, she adds, "And I'm not getting into it with a sixteen-year-old, so purge every porno movie you've ever seen from your mind. We're just going to talk it through and I guarantee by the end of the conversation this will seem like an extremely bad idea."

This is the weirdest thing I've ever heard—going home with someone to talk yourselves out of hooking up.

"Are you in or not?" Colette asks.

"Definitely," I say soberly. "I'm in."

eight

COLETTE LIVES IN a basement apartment in this mammoth new subdivision on the east side of town. The tiny trees are as thin as matches; it's a wonder they made it through the winter. Her private entrance is through the side door, and as soon as you walk in you land up in a box-shaped laundry room with a beige dress shirt draped over a clotheshorse. "This way," Colette says, leading me towards another door.

So far we haven't said much. This is her idea and I'm fuzzy on the details.

She unlocks the door and we head downstairs. The steps are plush carpeted and everything looks professionally finished. It's exactly the kind of place I'd expect her to have. "This is nice," I say as we step into the living room. Neat without being antiseptic. Fashionable but not flashy.

"The worst thing about this apartment is the lack of light." Colette points up at the undersized windows. "Winter here felt like a dungeon in Moscow." She unbuttons her suede jacket and doubles back to the closet to hang it up. "Are you hungry?" she asks.

"I could eat." I follow her into the open-concept kitchen where she spritzes a tiny potted plant.

"Good." Colette swings the freezer open and slides out a box of jambalaya. I stand around watching as she sets a head of lettuce down in front of me on the counter. An oversized tomato, red pepper and box of croutons appear next. "Cut this stuff up for me, would you?" She crouches down by my legs and pulls a cutting board out of the cupboard beside the sink.

Everything feels different between us than it did in the parking lot. It's like she's trying to teach me a lesson or something. I slice up the pepper, though, and act like I feel at home in this apartment where I've never been, with this twenty-three-year-old woman I barely know. What's the worst thing that can happen?

Colette doesn't speak. She's whisking ingredients in a measuring cup. "It's really quiet down here," I say.

"The people upstairs must be out," she tells me, and continues whisking.

I'm done with the salad ingredients and Colette hands me a salad bowl and set of tongs. I toss the salad and then walk around her living room, checking out her coaster set, candleholder collection and the framed photographs that line her bookshelf. Two zombie cheerleader girls are laughing into the camera in the first one. Between the greenish foundation, blood stains and blackened eyes it's hard to recognize either of them but my guess would be that I'm looking at Colette and Andrea when they were about my age. In another a more mature Colette's standing between two middle-aged people, the three of them dressed for a special occasion. They must be her parents. There's a picture of their younger selves in front of a trailer, the two of them holding hands.

74

"How long have you been living here?" I ask, staring over at Colette in the kitchen.

"Since November." She plonks the whisk into the sink. "Andrea and I were roommates for a while, before she moved in with her boyfriend in Peterborough. And after that I had a bigger place on my own, in one of those apartments on Wagner, but I'm trying to save money for school."

"Your parents won't help with that?" She said something about that last time she drove me home but I want to know more; I want to hear whatever she'll tell me.

"Maybe," she says. "I wouldn't want to ask them." Overhead I hear the reckless thump of small feet. The owners must've just walked through the door with their kids. "Can you come here a second, Mason?"

More dicing. Maybe this time I'll graduate to the blender. I saunter back to the kitchen and lean against the counter, awaiting further instructions. Colette pulls her body flush against mine and kisses me fast. The shock jolts through my limbs in a microsecond. It's the purest craving you can imagine. Stronger even. I savor the briefest taste of her tongue before she pulls away and says, "You see, it's no different than kissing somebody your own age."

Of course it is. I put my hand on her shoulder and squeeze. My fingers touch her hair. I don't know if she's just screwing with my head or what. I feel like a science experiment. I want to run my hands over her body but at the same time I don't want to mess up. What if she tells me she never wants to see me again?

Colette moves away from me and starts plucking plates out of the cupboard. I stare at her pointy little breasts as they strain against her top. This is the best look at them I've had yet and honestly, I don't know how much more of this I can take without losing my cool.

"We have another thirty minutes or so until that's ready," she says, motioning to the stove. "Why don't you sit down?"

"Is this an audition?" My voice tightens around the words. "What're we supposed to talk about, Colette? I don't have a clue what I'm doing here."

"Sit down," she says patiently. "I'm sorry if I'm making you uncomfortable. This isn't the easiest situation for me either."

"You're completely in control," I say, still standing. I cock my head at the kitchen. "What was that?"

Colette edges by me and sits down on her leather couch. "You wanted me to kiss you, didn't you? It's a classic teenage guy fantasy. You don't even know me. You're just hanging this cliché idea on me—the sexy older woman."

"And what's it for you? Some kind of psychology experiment?" I feel like a lab rat on Viagra or Levitra. I think I want to go home.

"Not at all," she claims. "I like you. I shouldn't have brought you here. I thought if we talked it over we could get past it. For one thing, I'm already involved with somebody. For another, Andrea and Nina would have my head on a platter if they ever found out about this."

Since I'm sixteen there's nothing illegal about us, no matter what we do, but pointing that out to Colette would just underline the age gap, and besides, I'm stuck on something else she said.

Colette rubs her cheek with her palm and adds, "And it sounds like you have your own set of complications you need to sort out."

"I thought we could just get to know each other," I mutter finally. "I didn't know there was somebody else."

"There's always somebody else." She combs her fingers slowly through her hair. "You see what I mean? It's already sounding complicated. The more we talk about it, the less appealing it seems. You just want somebody you can bonk without it getting

76

complicated like it did with Kat. *This* isn't anything close to what you want, Mason."

I don't know what I want. She's got me reeling.

Just then the doorbell rings and Colette darts upstairs to answer it. Alone with the homemade salad dressing and the smell of jambalaya I start thinking about that second kiss and how Colette's been trying to tell me what I want but hasn't once said what she wants.

I hear two voices at the top of the stairs, one of them Colette's, both of them female. "At least let me say hello to him," the other woman chirps, bounding downstairs. "Oh—hi there," she sputters, a queasy look stretching across her face as she reaches the kitchen. "I thought you were someone else."

"This is Mason," Colette says from behind her. "He's a friend's stepnephew, I guess you could say."

Yeah, I guess you could say that. I extend my hand—ready to follow Colette's lead—and blink warmly at the nameless person in front of me. "Nice to meet you."

"This is my friend Leslie," Colette continues cheerfully. She smiles at me as she says it and I realize it's the first time I've seen her crack a grin today. It changes her entire face. Makes me feel almost like I'm with the teenage girl from the Halloween photo, minus the cheesy gore.

"I really just dropped by to say hello," Leslie says, looking faintly guilty. "I'm sorry to barge in on you unannounced."

"It's not a problem," Colette says. "Mason and I were just about to shift some of the living room furniture around but it's nice to see you."

Leslie nods uncertainly, tells us both goodbye and bolts for the staircase. Colette follows, acting normal. I'm surprised she's handling this so smoothly, and I strain to hear their conversation, something about Ari and Saturday night. I wonder if this Ari person is the boyfriend Colette mentioned and if he's the type to appear out of the blue, instantly grasp the undercurrent and swing a punch at me. That doesn't particularly scare me on a physical level—Dad made me take karate for two and a half years; I can handle myself—but it's not a scenario I'm in a rush to experience.

"Wow, that was weird," Colette declares, reappearing. "She's so pushy." Colette rolls her eyes as she sighs. "She had to come in and see what was going on. There was no stopping her. Thank God she doesn't know Andrea. That could've been a disaster."

"You were good," I tell her. "That stuff about the furniture—you're a good liar."

"I'm not," Colette says. "She just pissed me off being so bossy."

"So who was she expecting?" I curve my hands around the edge of the counter. "Your boyfriend?"

"He's not my boyfriend." She tilts her head and scratches her neck. "I didn't say I had a boyfriend. I said there was someone else." She tugs off her high-heel shoes and tosses them into the hall. "But, yes, that's who she was expecting."

"Ari?"

"Yup." She half smiles as she looks at me.

"This is screwy." I'm in over my head.

"Yes, I know." Now she's full-out grinning and I can't help it; she's contagious. "I told you it was."

"Okay," I tell her, fighting a smile. "I think I'm beginning to get it, but you know you never said what you wanted. I mean, okay, you're this hot older woman and I'm looking for someone to *bonk* without it getting complicated." Her words, not mine. "But what's in it for you? What's your angle?"

"Mason, come on. I'm not going to stand here and tell you how beguiling you are." My cheeks are sore and I bow my head so I won't have to look her in the eye. Would asking for clarification on the beguiling issue damage my case much? Because I'd give my left arm to hear that. "So are we close to getting this worked out?" Colette continues. "Are we good or do we have to stick with this discussion?"

"I guess we're good." I stifle a sigh. "I still think it's too bad." Between feeling flattered, let down and steadily in lust with the incredibly revealing nature of Colette's thin-fibered top, that statement's a half-decent approximation of what I'm thinking.

"I know," she says, "but come on, seriously. You're only sixteen. You're practically operating without a brain."

"What?" I throw my head back and roll my eyes. "First off you're saying how together I am and now I'm operating without a brain. You can't have it both ways, Colette."

"Okay, okay," she says. "Let's just eat and then I'll take you home, all right?"

She sets the kitchen table and we sit down to eat together, almost like a real date, except where Colette's considered, I bet a date usually means wine, and she's basically just told me to get lost. It's uncomfortable and acutely confusing for a long while but then she gets me talking about acting and the play. I tell her about missing Chris Keller and how sometimes I'll be in the middle of a situation, like this one for instance, and find myself wondering how he'd handle it. His words pop into my head from some other place.

We talk a bit about Brianna, Burke and Nina too and then I tell her it's not fair because I'm doing most of the talking and she's hardly said anything about herself. "What do you want to know?" she asks.

"Anything. The story of your life."

She smiles again. She has the kind of smile that instantly softens her face. Like one minute she's sexy in this edgy unpredictable way and then she smiles so warm and pretty that you want to say something that'll freeze the expression a couple seconds longer. She starts telling me about tenth grade and how she was in this club called SAC (Student Activist Club) that wanted to change the world and how that was really the best part of high school and she wants to get back into "the struggle to change things for the better" and be less self-involved because she used to hate people like that so much when she was in school. Then she talks about how conflicted she used to be back then because at the same time she secretly admired the people who seemed like the center of their own universe.

"So you're saying right now you're too much the center of your own universe?" I sum up.

"Pretty much," Colette replies. "I think it's a reaction from being the opposite for so long but it's also incredibly easy, you know? It doesn't give you time to think about anything else. Why worry about issues like global warming and human rights when you can spend your evenings weaving twisted romantic webs and shopping for your new summer wardrobe?"

"You can't be that bad."

"Not that bad," she clarifies, "just mind-numbingly ordinary. Anyway, that was the old me. The shameless, soulless early-twenties one that I'm trying to put behind me."

I don't think she's trying to put me off anymore. I think she means all that. I'd like to hear what she's planning for her mid-twenties but we're finished with dinner. Colette tells me to just leave everything where it is and she'll take care of it after she drives me home.

"Don't worry about that," I tell her. "I can get home on my own." I'm not sure how but I'll figure something out. Having her chauffeur me back across town would just emphasize everything she said about me being a kid. That's not the impression I want to leave her with; I'd rather she remember our conversation.

"How?" she asks.

"Don't worry about it. I'll take care of it." Maybe I'm being pathetic. It doesn't matter. I'm not letting her drive me home.

"Okay," Colette says, like she understands. "I hope I wasn't too overwhelming. I know this was weird but at least you'll remember me."

"Of course I'll remember you." I bite my lip and peer into her eyes. At this point I have nothing to lose. "You know, we never had a real kiss." I didn't see the earlier one coming. It was finished by the time my mind caught up to the event.

"Okay, Mason," Colette says somberly. She stands in the kitchen in her bare feet, waiting for me to do it. My arms are numb and my fingers are tingling like I've got frostbite. I step slowly towards her, holding my breath. We don't touch. My mouth is sloppy on hers: too fast, too hard. I should know better but I've been waiting for a second chance all night.

So I slow down the pace and follow her lead. She teases me with tiny jabs of her tongue. I suck her bottom lip. We play-kiss until it turns hungry. Then it's raw and deep and relentless and I have to yank my head back to make it stop.

Colette looks at me in surprise, her dark lashes blinking slowly. I do a fast scan of the room, searching out a pen. It's so quiet in her apartment that I'm afraid of the sound of my own voice. I snatch a pink highlighter from her coffee table, flip over a stack of unopened mail and print out my phone number on the back of an envelope. The scrawl looks childish because my hand is trembling.

"This is my cell number," I mumble, setting it down on the kitchen counter. "In case you ever want to get a hold of me." I turn and walk towards the stairs, taking them two at a time. I have heavy footsteps for my frame. She could be thinking that down in her apartment with the dirty dishes. She could be tossing my telephone number into the trash along with the unfinished lettuce. She could've let me kiss her like that only because she knows she never has to see me again.

The possibilities are endless and my right hand, it's still shaking as I step out onto Colette's street. I don't notice a thing. The driveways, houses, passing cars, anorexic trees. None of it registers. The beat raging in my chest is the only thing I know. That and the one possibility my mind keeps rushing back to and smacking up against like it materialized out of nowhere.

Maybe . . .

Maybe that kiss was exactly what Colette wanted too.

nine

THE FIRE ALARM wakes me up during homeroom. I was thinking about us in her apartment again—or dreaming it maybe; my brain is too tired to know the difference. "Move it, people!" Mr. Stafford booms from the front of the class. "You want me to burn to a crisp because you didn't get your eight hours last night? Come on! Let's go!"

In the hall behind me two girls are talking about Monica G and the talent scout at the airport, confirming that if the incident was any less of a secret you'd be able to watch it on YouTube. I shuffle outside and squint into the morning sun. Usually I like fire drills but having one this early is a waste. There's nothing to interrupt.

"Okay, roll call, people," Mr. Stafford shouts. "Listen up!" He fires off a series of names, including mine and Michelle Suazo's (who happens to be in my homeroom). Then there's nothing to do but stand around and wait for the all clear. Normally Michelle and I would stand around together but instead she's obsessing over her iPod, keeping herself hyper-busy. Lately Michelle and Sondra don't have much to say to me. I wonder what Kat told them. Did she turn me into the bad guy?

I scope out Jamie by the bleachers with Yolanda and decide to get this over with in one go, like Colette wanted last night. I shouldn't have to do this, but otherwise Jamie will stomp around avoiding me indefinitely and the truth is I feel a little sorry for him. He's been into Kat for so long and this can't be doing his ego any good. It was okay when we could mouth off about her shitty taste in guys together. Now everything's been whacked off balance because even though Kat doesn't want to hear about it, she remembers that night and it was me there with her. More than that, it was good.

So I walk over to the bleachers, say hi to Yolanda and ask Jamie if we can talk a minute. Jamie tries to look bored. He tells Y that he'll catch up with her later, his voice weary like he's doing me a favor. Once she's gone he folds his arms in front of him, freezing his eyes on me. "Look, whatever, okay," he says cynically. "I don't give a shit anymore."

"Bullshit."

Jamie blinks but his eyes don't move. "Say whatever you want, Mason. It doesn't change anything." His fingers dig into his sleeves. "You could've at least told me, you know?"

"You know what really pisses me off about this?" My molars clamp down as I look at him. "You accuse me of getting her loaded or something and then . . ." My right hand slices through the air in frustration. "You think I'd do something like that?" I'm aggravated all over again. He should've been the one to start this conversation. Why did I come over here?

Jamie gives me a James Dean squint and drives his fingers through his hair. "You're not flipping this over on me," he says unapologetically. "Don't even try. You know you should've said something. All these years the three of us have been friends and you think you can just—"

"I wasn't going to tell anyone," I cut in. "This wasn't about you, and I know it sucks because we're talking about Kat but the truth is it sucks for me too. She's hardly spoken to me the past few weeks. It took Monica Gregory getting *scouted* to get her to look me in the eyes."

Jamie squeezes his eyes shut, short on sympathy. "Man, sucks to be you," he says sarcastically.

"Apparently not as much as it sucks to be you," I shoot back. "Shit." I glance down at the overgrown grass under my feet. "This is stupid. It didn't mean anything in the first place, except that maybe she wanted revenge on Hugo, and now it's over and she obviously wishes it never happened."

"But it did happen," Jamie says quietly.

"I know. But it's done. It's over with. It feels like it happened about a hundred years ago." My apologetic tone comes as a shock. Why am I still trying to justify myself? I don't regret what happened and I have nothing to be sorry about.

"I hate when you get like this. Can't anyone ever be mad at you?" Jamie kicks at the grass with his shoe. "You get the girl and I'm still supposed to feel sorry for you? What the fuck is that?"

Get the girl? Is he kidding me? I'm treading water here, getting nowhere. He doesn't understand that my night with Kat is history.

"Forget I came over here this morning," I mutter, beginning to back away. "Bury your head in the sand and feel sorry for yourself if that's what you want."

Jamie shifts his weight and stares blankly. "You crossed a line. You know it."

I'm not even sure whose line he's talking about—Kat's or his—

but we're done talking it over. "See you later, Jamie," I say, and this time I don't sound sorry or mad. I'm finished butting my head against a brick wall and Jamie knows it. He shrugs and turns his face away.

I'm walking off in Mr. Stafford's direction, my thoughts drifting away from Jamie and Kat and back towards Colette, when Miracle grabs hold of my arm.

"I've heard a lot of crap that I don't even want to repeat," she says breathlessly. "I just wanted you to know that I'm in if you want to bail on lunch today."

"Thanks, but I'm still going to the cafeteria." Otherwise I'll feel like I'm advertising a guilty conscience.

"Cool," Miracle sings approvingly. "See you then."

It turns out Kat, Sondra and Michelle aren't at lunch anyway. Kat was late for history earlier so we never got the chance to talk and now Jamie sits between Y and Z in the cafeteria, pretending that I'm an empty chair. It's exactly what I expected of him after what happened this morning, but I don't let on that it bothers me. Zoe's nearer to me than Yolanda and she talks to me in spurts, zipping in and out of the conversation to rejoin the parallel one happening on her other side. She tells me that her mother advised her to start watching what she eats because her thighs and breasts are starting to get big.

"Isn't that called puberty?" I ask, glancing quickly at her chest. I'm tired of defending myself—it's a relief to be able to talk about anything else.

"I know, right?" Zoe pulls her top tight across her back and juts out her breasts for me. "They're not even C cups. She says she's looking out for me because she was fat in high school and it was horrible, but I've seen her photos and she wasn't anywhere close to fat." Zoe rakes her Caesar salad, the moody Z hovering overhead, preparing to take possession.

"Don't listen to that bullshit," I tell her. "Your mom is psycho, Zoe. She'd criticize a dentist for not brushing his teeth right."

I picked that up from my dad, and Zoe smirks and says, "She wouldn't, actually. She's not like that around other people."

After lunch Yolanda and I have Presentation and Speaking Skills together and on the way she tells me she's so frustrated with Zoe's mom these days that she doesn't even know what to say to Zoe about it anymore. "When her mom answers the phone it takes all my willpower not to scream at her that she's toxic, selfish and emotionally retarded. The only thing stopping me is that Zoe and I would never be able to see each other again but I swear to God, if we ever break up I'll do it in a second."

Z's mom doesn't know the truth about their relationship, not because she's homophobic but because Z's afraid her mom's criticism would suddenly sharp-focus on Y and that would be harder to deal with than keeping their relationship under wraps.

Our conversation gets me thinking about Colette again, not that I ever really stopped. She's like a movie constantly running in the background. I keep seeing her face, that strange look in her eyes after I kissed her. I wonder how much difference it would make if we didn't have to worry about Andrea and Nina. What if I was just some random sixteen-year-old guy she met at the mall?

Miscellaneous Colette-related thoughts loop through my mind all afternoon. I'm so lost in my own head that I don't notice Kat coming at me in the hall after final bell. She's six feet away before I jolt back into the real world. Her wide brown eyes seek out mine as she says, "I wanted to catch up with you before you left today."

"Okay," I say, surprised. Seems to me she's been trying to

achieve just the opposite lately. "But if it's going to be anything like the discussion I had with Jamie this morning I'd just rather skip it, all right?"

"He's being weird with me too," she says hurriedly. "Can you come outside with me? There're some things I want to say but it's not going to be like your talk with Jamie, I promise."

We slip out the nearest set of doors and edge away from the buses until we're standing by an unclaimed patch of brick wall.

"So what did Jamie say to you, anyway?" Kat asks, looking worried.

I throw one of my hands up into the air as if to say it doesn't matter, but she doesn't understand—this still feels like life and death to her. "He's really pissed with me," I reply. It's hard to feel the least bit generous towards him today, but when it comes down to it the one thing I genuinely care about in all this is my friendship with both of them. Maybe getting things out in the open will do some good. "Because of what happened between me and you," I continue. "Basically it seems like . . . like he thinks I manipulated you somehow."

"That's not what happened," Kat says, chewing her fingernail.

I push my left foot against the wall so my knee juts out into the space between us. "So you noticed that too."

"Everybody knows about us now," she says fixedly. "It's going around the whole school."

"Does it really matter? People hook up all the time, Kat. This is just the latest thing to hit the headlines. In a few days it'll be something else and no one will give a shit."

"I will." She's pouting so bad that I want to pinch her cheeks and tell her not to worry. "I've been horrible about dealing with this, I know, but it wasn't in the plan." A wisp of hair falls forward as she bends her head. "It's not about you. I mean, if it had to be someone I'm glad it was you because I know I can trust you." She grabs the stray strand and holds it in place against the wind. "I know I should be able to get it together and deal with it maturely and that it shouldn't be a big deal but the fact is, *it is a big deal for me.*" Her cheeks suck in sharply as she flicks her hair back behind her ear and then drops her hand. "The only reason that night happened was because I felt so comfortable with you, and I really messed that up in a big way because I don't anymore. Now I'm panicked anytime you're around—and you're always around. I sit down to lunch and there you are across the table. Then you're sitting next to me in history or coming up to me in the hall and I'm all confused, like I'm into you or something—but I don't want to be."

She sounds defiant and I try to interrupt but Kat keeps going, her eyes glued to mine. "So I'm sorry I can't deal with this the way you want and pretend like nothing ever happened, but it's not that I'm mad at you. It's all just too close and sudden for me right now."

"You're the one who wanted to skip past it like it never happened," I remind her. "Not me." She's got me so wound up that I can't think straight. *Into me?* Why does she have to make that sound like the absolute worst thing in the world? Why can't I even be happy about it for two seconds without her squashing it?

Kat focuses on the wall behind me and shakes her head, looking pained. "I didn't want you thinking about us like that. Next time we're alone you could be wanting a second helping, thinking 'Why not, we've done it before.'"

So that's what trust sounds like. The thing is, she could be right. I might've thought that.

"And anyway, I didn't want to talk about it," she adds. "Even talking about it is too weird. We've been friends for so long; I can't change the way I think that quickly. It just feels wrong. We should've just stayed friends. That's what we're best at."

"I know that. That's why yesterday was so cool for a while. It was like the old us." My stomach twinges as I tear my gaze away. I don't even know what I want most from her anymore and I guess it doesn't matter. She's already decided what she wants.

Kat groans and scrunches up her face. She's so embarrassed that it's uncomfortable to look at her. "I can't do the old us anymore. I'd like to but it's different, Mason. Especially now that everyone else knows. It's like it's official. There's no going back."

"We just need to relax." I rest my hand on her shoulder without giving the motion a second thought. "It doesn't have to be like that." Kat stands ultra still, careful not to react, but I can see the proof in her eyes. It's not the same when I touch her anymore. For her, it's all about that single night.

"As soon as you're with someone else everything will go back to the way it was," I insist, snatching my hand back and dangling it at my side. "We're just in this awkward in-between stage." Our entire relationship's slipping through my fingers and practically all I can do is watch. I wonder if it would help to tell her about Colette, but the words don't come.

"Maybe," Kat says doubtfully. "But in the meantime I think it's better if we take a breather. I've been having enough trouble dealing with you lately and now there's Jamie being jealous too. Maybe we were all too close to begin with." She shivers, folding her arms hastily in front of her chest. "It's sort of incestuous."

"We've barely even been talking lately," I point out. "How would this be any different?"

"Before we were trying to act like everything was normal. And it's not. The three of us need breathing space. I don't think we should hang out at lunch together for a while and maybe next time there's a history project or whatever we should try to work with other people."

"That's not going to make things any less weird, Kat. How're we supposed to get past it if we're never around each other?" She can't mean that. The last three years must count for something.

Kat sighs and tells me she's sorry but that she just doesn't feel right with things the way they are. She says she doesn't want me to think that means we're not friends anymore and that she will absolutely be there for me if I really need her.

"Yeah, me too," I say slowly. I almost can't believe it. I know things have been strained between us lately but this is extreme.

"Thanks," she says earnestly. Relief settles onto her face but I feel like she's reached in and twisted my guts sideways. I remember the first time we slow-danced together at Leslie Alvarez's fourteenth birthday party. I was almost afraid to put my hands on her, convinced she'd be able to read my feelings through my palms. The thing is, I think she's known all along anyway. Maybe it just didn't matter much before.

"Okay." My voice is low. "I guess I'll see you around."

Kat squeezes my hand quickly. She heads for the door but I'm way behind. I've been miles behind since I woke up in bed next to her that night.

Then I realize that on top of everything else she lied to me. Our conversation wasn't any different than the one I had with Jamie this morning. Neither of them wants me around.

ten

IN THIS CRAZY new world where my friends are not my friends and a twenty-three-year-old girl kissed me like I was a twenty-three-year-old guy, I don't know what to expect next. I go running (something I dipped into last summer but haven't gotten around to much lately) and then start my law homework. Miracle calls to remind me that *The Grapes of Wrath* is on cable tonight because I mentioned, months ago, that I'd never seen it. She starts raving about Henry Fonda's "mesmerizing performance" all over again but I can't watch it anyway; Burke and Brianna are ensconced in the basement for the night.

"Burn me a copy," I tell her.

"I'll bring it in tomorrow," she says.

I spend the rest of the night finishing my homework and IMing Chris Cipolla, Dustin and Charlie Kady. At first they want to talk details but I tell them it's noyb and they leave it alone fast, except that Dustin says Jamie seemed mad at lunch.

nmp, I say.

It's after midnight when I sign off and go down to the kitchen to microwave some popcorn before I brush my teeth. In this crazy new world where my dad and I are no longer alone in the house, I walk in on him and Nina making out in front of the refrigerator. He's fondling her ass and kissing her neck rough and she's tugging at his hair, her eyes squeezed shut and her lips parted.

It's wild and I freeze for a second because although I know they sleep together it never occurred to me that they sleep together the way other people sleep together.

I back silently out of the room and creep upstairs, Billy slinking by me in the hall, giving me the evil eye. Inside the bathroom I brush my teeth and wet my face, wondering how much longer they'll be steaming up the kitchen because now I can't stop thinking about popcorn. Are they actually going to do it down there or what?

"Mason?" Dad says, rapping gently at the bathroom door.

I grab a towel and open the door.

"I believe we got in your way just now," Dad says apologetically.

"It's okay," I tell him, wiping my face.

"I don't want you to feel that you can't walk around your own house." He leans against the door frame and adds, "We won't be making a habit of that."

"I was just going to make some popcorn," I say, to let him know we can drop the topic. "But actually there's something else I think we need to straighten out."

"All right." His voice registers surprise. "What's on your mind?"

"Brianna's practically living in the basement these days. I don't want to throw my weight around but we only have one TV." I used to be the only one who watched it; Dad prefers listening to the radio or reading the newspaper.

"Nina and I were talking about that the other day," Dad comments. "How about you and I head over to Best Buy together next week and pick one out for your room?"

"Okay." But it's not just the TV. Sometimes I want to stretch out on the couch with my cell attached to my ear or stride into the house with my friends in tow without worrying about where we'll park ourselves. Brianna and Burke haven't even been here a week yet and I'm already starting to feel like a caged animal.

"It's an adjustment for all of us," Dad says. "I guess we'll just have to come up with solutions as we go along."

During the play I'd barely have noticed a few extra bodies around the place. Maybe I'm just spending too much time at home these days. This is a bad time to fall out with Kat and Jamie—we share all the same friends.

It's a frustratingly crappy situation that occupies most of my weekend. Jamie's determined to guilt-trip me for something he would've done in a heartbeat and, yeah, I have some hard feelings about that. I don't want to obsess on what Kat said about staying away from each other but how exactly do you cut yourself off from someone that you've thought of/seen/spoken to every day for the past three years? I understand that she's confused but her cure hurts worse than the disease.

It's obvious that I'm better off concentrating on Colette, so in the midst of all that I start thinking about that white-hot kiss from the other night too. The whole thing leaves me in this bizarre half-hungry, half-distracted state and the only time I shake it is when I'm out on Saturday night. Charlie Kady and I cruise around in his dad's LeSabre, trying to decide what we should do. We hit Wendy's for burgers and then Charlie lets me drive awhile. In the end he decides we should look up some girl he met at Whole Foods last week. When we get there she tells us her shift ends at nine, so we have to go back and pick her up then. The three of us drive over to her friend's father's condo where she and Charlie disappear into the bedroom for almost an hour and a half.

The abandoned friend and I watch *Supernatural* and make jokes about their absence. She seems relieved that I don't try anything but when Charlie and I leave she offers her phone number anyway.

In the car Charlie tells me how much he likes the Whole Foods girl and how mind-blowingly fantastic the sex was. He shoots me a furtive look, and for a second I think he's going to pump me for details about that night with Kat again. "She told me it was only her fourth time," he says instead. "She said it always hurt before."

He's on a postsex high; he thinks he's gifted. I know what that's like.

"What'd you think of her friend?" he asks.

"She's okay." I can't figure out why she handed over her number, but it doesn't matter; it's not like I intend to call. That's probably what Colette thought when I gave her my number. So why do I expect to hear her voice every time my cell phone rings?

Okay, I'm semi-obsessing but at least I'm not stalking her anymore. I'm just not the dangerous type. No doubt she already knows that about me.

Billy the cat must sense it too because during the week he brushes up against my legs for the first time. It feels like a compliment; I've never seen him do that to my dad and they've been around each other a lot more.

Unfortunately that's the high point of the week. Jamie refuses to say more than three words to me at a time—even over lunch when we're all sitting together (minus Kat and her girls, who've defected to the other side of the cafeteria). It's glaringly obvious but everyone does their best to ignore the amped-up tension.

Every day the situation gets a little more tired but I don't do a thing about it. I'm through trying to convince Jamie of anything. I don't want to argue. I don't even expect him to apologize. I just want him to stop blaming me for something (a) the two of us directly involved in felt pretty happy about at the time and (b) that I'm suffering more fallout for than anyone realizes.

In private Y confides that she thinks Jamie's acting like a twelve-year-old girl. She also tells me that she saw Kat talking to Hugo in the parking lot that morning and that they were so focused on each other they wouldn't have heard an atomic bomb detonate.

A savage pain grips my ribs when I hear that. I know I'm not supposed to care anymore but the thought of them getting back together seriously throws me.

"Can you find out what that was about?" I ask, feeling desperate.

"I think I can do that," she says reluctantly. "Give me a couple days to work on it."

So this is how my week goes down: nightly family dinners, homework, running, stilted lunch hours, waiting for Colette to realize just how beguiling I am and harassing Yolanda for the results of her detective work. It's not a good scene.

Finally, on Friday, Y pulls me aside on our way into Presentation and Speaking Skills and whispers, "I talked to Kat and everything's cool. Just Hugo being stupid."

"What do you mean?" I take another two steps away from class so no one will overhear.

"It's moronic." Yolanda bunches her eyebrows. "He wanted to know why she did it with you when she wouldn't do it with him." The GS gossip mill has been very specific about us, maybe because Kat's been different with me for weeks. No one is willing to buy into the idea that we did anything less than have full sex together.

Y folds her arms in front of her breasts and adds, "Honestly, you guys are such dickheads sometimes. Like the universe revolves around your swollen membrane."

"Hey," I say defensively. "*Way to lump us all together.*"

"Sorry. I just think the sex thing is better when you're on an equal playing field—not worrying about what you can *get* from someone."

"You're still doing it," I point out. Yolanda doesn't make a habit of running down straight guys but lots of them gave her a hard time when she first came out in eighth grade. I guess some of it stuck.

"Okay, end of lecture," she says resolutely. "Anyway, there's nothing going on between them. Apparently they got into a shouting match because Hugo said he wouldn't have hooked up with Monica Gregory in the first place if Kat had been giving him some *home loving.*" Y tacks a smirk and thick Southern accent onto those last two words.

"He's so full of shit," I growl.

"Yup."

"Thanks for letting me know." I'm way too relieved to feel good about it.

"Yeah." Yolanda smooths down her sleeve and grasps her elbow. "I'm not really comfortable with reporting back to you like this, you know?"

"I won't ask you again," I say. "Thanks. Really. I feel better." It's amazing what two minutes' worth of secondhand information can do for you.

That night I sit in the basement with Burke watching *Lemony Snicket's A Series of Unfortunate Events.* Brianna's at a sleepover and I don't think either of us misses her. Burke's afraid of Count Olaf and this worried look crowds onto his face whenever Jim Carrey's on-screen. It's hilarious and I have to suck back a laugh every fifteen minutes. The other funny thing is that he's all-out crushing on Violet Baudelaire but in complete denial about it.

"Hey, she's cute," I tell him. "There's nothing wrong with liking her."

"Stop talking about me liking her," he says, exasperated. "*You* like her."

"Yeah, but I don't have a problem with liking her," I tease.

Guess what? Six-year-olds are unpredictable. Burke roars and lunges towards me on the couch. His scrawny six-year-old hands struggle to pin my arms back while his bony knees dig into my leg. "Chill, buddy," I say with a laugh. "This isn't *Jerry Springer*."

"Who's Jerry Springer?" he demands, easing off.

So I guess that's not one of Brianna's shows. Looks like she prefers the intellectual challenge of *The Doctors* or *Oprah*.

"A crazy guy with a TV show," I tell him, my lips relaxing into a smile. "You can't just jump people like that, buddy. You could break my old-man bones."

"You're not an old man," Burke says, grinning back at me. One of his bottom teeth is missing. He looks like a hockey player.

"Compared to you I am."

Burke sits with his back against the couch and says, "No more talking about Violet, okay?"

Because he *luvs* her, obviously, but sure, whatever. The kid is breaking me up. "Okay, fine," I agree, grabbing the remote and rewinding the last sixty seconds. We watch the movie in peace until Nina comes down and announces that it's Burke's bedtime.

"Ten more minutes," he pleads.

"I think the movie's almost over," I add.

"As soon as the movie's over then." Nina turns to go, then swings abruptly back towards Burke. "I almost forgot, Jerome called me at work today. They have a place for you this summer."

Burke kicks his feet in the air and grins in approval. "That sounds like good news," I say.

"I'm going to camp," Burke explains, still wiggling with happiness.

Nina gazes fondly down at him. "Don't miss your movie, guys." She heads upstairs, closing the door behind her.

"It's not a camp with bunk beds," Burke tells me, turning to face the screen. "It's only during the day. They take you places and you play sports and eat lunch outside. Last year Mrs. Bartlett came over every day but camp is better."

"Who's Mrs. Bartlett?" I ask.

"An old lady." Burke scratches his knee as he glances over at me. "She could do card tricks but she didn't like to go outside when it was hot." Suddenly Billy the panther cat appears out of nowhere and meows up from under Burke's outstretched feet. Burke's hand casually grazes the top of Billy's head, a reflex action that I've been careful to avoid.

"Hey, you think I can pet him now?" I ask. Burke shakes his head, giggling like I've made a knock-knock joke. "I think he's starting to like me," I add, dropping my hand and leaning forward. Billy darts across the basement like a bolt of lightning while Burke hunches over and laughs so hard that he burps.

"Okay, so maybe he doesn't like me that much," I say, laughing too.

"He doesn't like anybody except us," Burke proclaims, showing off his hockey player grin. "That's just the way he is."

"What about Mrs. Bartlett? Did he like her?" In my mind she's pear shaped, probably because of her name, and wears long sleeves all summer. She's the type of person who'd admire an antisocial cat, even if it didn't like her back.

"No." Burke rubs his eyes and jiggles around like a lunatic on the couch. "Mrs. Bartlett only likes birds," he gasps between giggles. I swear, he's laughing so much that I half expect him to wet his pants.

"You're a maniac," I tell him. It's impossible to keep a straight face with him howling away next to me. "You're missing the movie." I rewind it a second time while Burke struggles to catch his breath.

It takes nearly twenty minutes to finish the movie and then Burke gets up, without Nina having to remind him, and tells me good night.

"Night, buddy," I say. "See you tomorrow."

"See you tomorrow," he echoes, running upstairs. He's got those frantic little-kid footsteps that I heard at Colette's place and I realize this is the first time I've thought about her or Kat all night. Maybe I need to hang out with Burke more often.

eleven

CHRISTOPHER CIPOLLA PHONES early Saturday afternoon and asks, in a keen Cockney accent, if I want to catch a play in Toronto tonight. My accent isn't half as good as his but I do my best to keep up with him. "What's the story, guv?" I say. "What's this 'ere play about then?"

The play's called *Spin Cycle* and his cousin's part of the stage crew. He can only get two free tickets but his cousin might be able to score a discount on the rest. Miracle, Dustin and Jamie have already decided to go and Christopher plans on calling Y and Z too.

"You in, mate?" Chris asks.

It's impossible to avoid Jamie. Why even try? "Absolutely, mate," I tell him. "Sounds bloody brilliant."

Chris wants to take two cars so Miracle won't have to chauffeur for once but Zoe just got her license six weeks ago and her mother won't let her take the expressway, and everyone else either doesn't have their license yet or can't get hold of a car. We all kick in for gas and parking and Miracle says she doesn't mind driving anyway.

"I can drive next time," Jamie announces in the van. "I have my road test on Tuesday."

"I didn't know that," I say. For a second I forgot that he's not really speaking to me. His presence is so familiar.

"Yeah," Jamie says out of the side of his mouth. "Tuesday."

This is the first time I've seen him outside of school since the cafeteria meltdown, and the tension between us feels out of place in the real world. "Good luck," I tell him.

"Thanks." Jamie nods to himself and looks away.

He hangs back when we pile out of the van, like he's trying to put some distance between us, and I let him. A big part of me wants to sit beside him in the theater and talk at him until he caves and talks back. Instead I slide into the seat next to Miracle's and watch Chris lower himself into the chair on my other side. It's better this way. For once I'll let someone stay mad at me for as long as they have in them. Why should I bend myself out of shape for something I don't even regret? The truth is I still wouldn't take that night back. I'd change a couple things, yeah. I wouldn't say Kat was heavy and I wouldn't let her leave until we talked about what happened but that's it. The rest was too perfect to mess with.

Spin Cycle's uneven but intense and I get this swell in the pit of my stomach, like I can see how good it could be if the entire cast measured up to the guy who plays Tom. He's so mean sometimes that it's hard to sit still and watch. He's dangerous and magnetic and when you least expect it he says something really funny and you can't help but laugh, even though you don't want to.

There's some nudity too and it's jarring to have this guy striding around the set with no pants on, completely different than seeing someone naked in a movie. If I really want to act it's something

I need to consider. From my safe place in the audience the possibility feels terrifying but I also know that it's different when you're up there. The work gets inside you. You don't think the way you normally do. You flow with the scene the way Tom's doing; you let go of the person you normally are and just let it happen.

Anyway, Tom's more toxic by the minute. You almost feel contaminated watching him. An underlying threat of violence pushes closer to the surface and the tension builds and builds until there's only one place for it to go. After that you just want to get it over with and we clap in relief when the actors take their bows. Miracle, Chris and I give the guy who played Tom a standing ovation and when the lights are back on I check his name in the program: Ian Chappell. He graduated from York University in 2004 and has been a Shaw Festival company member for the past five years. Half a dozen other plays are listed in his credits.

I'm only getting started at this but I think that's what I want my bio to look like when I'm his age. Meaty three-dimensional film or TV roles would be great too, but acting for the audience right in front of you, feeling them boost your adrenaline with a personal kick of their own, not much can touch that electricity.

Afterwards Christopher's cousin Julian comes out to talk to us. He wants to know what we thought of the play and Miracle and I start raving about Ian Chappell straightaway. Then I remember that Julian's part of the stage crew and start commenting on the set and stuff. "Do you want to hang around awhile and meet some of the cast?" Julian asks.

"Absolutely!" Zoe and Yolanda exclaim. "We'd love to."

But Miracle's full of surprises. "Maybe another time," she says hurriedly. "I need to get the van back. Thanks for letting us come, though. It was fantastic."

I give her a puzzled glance and wince as she pinches the back of my arm. Jamie witnesses the painful exchange, steps forward and starts talking to Julian to fill the gap in conversation. Meanwhile Miracle pushes her head close to mine and says, "I don't want to meet anyone."

"Why?"

"I just can't." Her voice is hushed so only I can hear it. "After seeing someone put all that into a performance, it's too weird. What do you say to them? It's . . . it's completely overwhelming."

"I don't think you really need to say anything," I whisper. "There're so many people here that he'd never notice." Obviously we're talking about Ian Chappell. That much is understood. No one else was good enough to awe her that way. I didn't even know she got starstruck. She doesn't seem like the type.

"You guys go ahead," she says, bunching her arms up in front of her corduroy jacket. "I'll wait in the van. Although that looks odder, doesn't it?" She drops her program on the floor in front of us and I bend down to pick it up for her.

"Thanks," she says, pinching the program between unsteady fingers. "Okay, I'm being ridiculous." She takes a long breath, the classic antidote for a case of nerves. "I'm fine. I'll be fine. This is stupid. Let's go."

"What? You mean meet him?"

"Yeah," she says firmly. "Let's just do it."

"Really?" Given another ten seconds she could change her mind again.

"Yes." Miracle nods boldly and straightens her jacket. "Um, Julian." She cranes forward and interrupts his conversation with Jamie, Y and Z. "You know, I think we have a bit of time after all. If it's no trouble for you, that is."

"No trouble," Julian says agreeably. "A few of us usually hang out awhile after the show. Let me go talk to them. I'll catch up with you guys in a second."

The theater's right down at Harbourfront and we go outside and stare at Lake Ontario. It's too early for mosquitoes but it's a pretty mild night and I roll up my sleeves and feel that swell in my stomach again. I'm not even positive what it means. There's a universe expanding around me and in some ways I'm almost impatient, but then again I'm happy enough in the moment with everyone analyzing *Spin Cycle* in excited voices.

"Can I use your cell phone?" Zoe asks, waving her hand in front of my face. "I have to check in with my mom."

"Sure." I smile as I hand it over. "Go ahead."

"You have a message," Zoe says as she turns it on. "You want to check it first?"

"Nah. Go ahead."

It's probably Charlie Kady. He was supposed to hook up with the Whole Foods girl again tonight. If they're going to be together awhile I guess I should start remembering her name.

Z talks to her mom for a minute and then presses the phone into my hand. Behind her Miracle's rocking on her heels and listening to Y describe this state-of-the-art ten-tier wedding cake she saw on the Food Network last night. I speed-dial my voice mail, push the phone against my ear and jerk back in shock.

"So I've had your number for a while now." Colette sighs and starts over. "I hate leaving messages. I'm the queen of the anonymous hang-up but I guess in this case that would defeat the purpose. I wanted to talk to you about what happened when we last saw each other. Maybe bringing you to my place was a bad idea. I thought for once in my life I'd be completely direct with someone but it still ended up the same way. Funny how that works."

I tighten my grip on the phone and breathe in fresh air blowing in from the lake. "Anyway, I've been thinking about you," she says slowly. "Give me a call tomorrow if you want to talk." She recites her phone number and promptly hangs up.

I listen to the message twice, my pulse speeding. I'd play it a third time but Julian steps out of the theater with two of the *Spin Cycle* actors plus some guy with a shaved head and goatee. Ian Chappell isn't with them and Miracle instantly lights up with relief.

It's crazy. My body's all over shaky, same as if Colette was beside me. I churn out a smile as Julian introduces us to his friends but I can't think. I stick close to Miracle, who is doing enough talking for both of us now that it's clear Ian Chappell isn't going to show. The group of us walks over to Queen's Quay and eats burgers and I swear, I miss the entire thing. I can't even finish my food.

"Was it okay?" the waitress asks, pointing to my plate. The fries are doused in ketchup but I can't have eaten more than a handful.

"Yeah, it was fine," I tell her. "I'm just not that hungry." Jamie glances at me from the other end of the table and I automatically start to grin. His gaze leaps stubbornly past me but I can't work up the slightest resentment; I'm up to my neck in anticipation, gratitude and shock. *She's been thinking about me.*

"I'll take your fries," Y volunteers.

"I'll help," Dustin says.

"Knock yourselves out." I pass Y my plate and wonder what Colette's doing right this second and why I can't call her tonight instead of tomorrow. Is she with Ari? Let's face it, his existence won't stop me from calling. It's not a matter of *if*, but *when*. I drum my fingers against the table and gulp in oxygen tinged with the taste of mustard and vinegar. A bolt of lightning knocks around under my ribs, charging out through my nails, my lips and my teeth. The last time I felt this alive was the night we finished *All My Sons*.

I'm up early Sunday morning and Burke and I eat bowls of cereal together at the kitchen table. He's into Lucky Charms; I'm more of a Cheerios kind of guy. These are the tolerable kinds of differences that I appreciate—not like Brianna stumbling into the room with her hair on backwards (hey, I can't help it if that's how it looks), scowling and asking why the empty milk carton's sitting on the counter.

"Good morning," I say, fixing her with an extrawide smile. She reprises her scowl, throws last night's chili into the microwave and pulls up a chair across from me. "You're not eating that for breakfast?" I ask. Leftover pizza, sure. Chili, now that's revolting.

"It smells like farts," Burke complains, smiling at me.

I laugh, almost choking on my Cheerios.

"You ate it last night," Brianna reminds him. "I don't remember you telling Mom it smelled like farts then."

"It didn't smell like farts then," Burke says, shoveling in a spoonful of blue moons, pink hearts and green clovers.

"Oh my gawd," Brianna says under her breath. "You are *so* retarded."

Whatever sibling rivalry they have going is none of my business, but Burke is six and a half, which puts him at an automatic disadvantage. "Just ignore her, little B," I say.

"*Little what?*" Brianna screeches. Honestly, her voice makes the hair on the back of my neck stand on end. It's that bad, especially in combo with her tangled devil-woman hair. "He's not your little brother, you know. Just because we're living here now doesn't make us related." The microwave bell dings and she flies across the kitchen and yanks out the chili.

I plunk down my spoon and stare at her. She completely misunderstood me. I meant *little buddy*, not *little brother*, but that's not the point. "What's your problem, Brianna?" I'm careful not to use the F word in front of Burke, but my tone implies it.

"What, like you guys are all bonded now after watching one stupid movie together?" she says bitterly. Her gaze switches to Burke. "Don't think he really likes you just because he laughed at your stupid joke. You're still retarded."

Nina strides into the kitchen in her robe and slippers before any of us can react. "That's enough, Brianna," she says sharply. "Stop badgering your brother."

Brianna glares down at her chili. It stinks worse now that it's been reheated, and she flips it over, dumping it swiftly into the sink. "He's being a pain," she protests. "They're both being obnoxious."

"It sounds like you're the one being a pain," Nina says in a flat tone. "I hope you plan on cleaning that mess up." She motions irritably to the sink.

"I'll clean it up," Brianna mumbles. "It's your smelly chili but fine, I'll clean it up."

"Watch it," Nina warns. "You're on thin ice."

Brianna shrugs like she doesn't care.

"Wait for me in your room, Brianna," Nina commands. "I'll be up in five minutes to talk to you."

"What about the chili?" Brianna asks, further testing her luck.

"I'll take care of the chili." Nina grits her teeth and turns towards the counter. "Just give me a minute to grab some coffee and then we'll talk."

"*Fine.*" Brianna storms out of the kitchen. We hear her footsteps on the stairs, heavy and deliberate.

Burke digs back into his Lucky Charms, unfazed, while Nina plucks a mug from the shelf above the stove and switches on the coffeemaker, looking harried. "How're you guys doing this morning?" she asks.

"I'm finished," Burke announces, tapping his spoon against the bottom of his empty bowl. "Can I watch cartoons?"

"Of course." Nina smiles thinly. "Might as well bring me your bowl. It seems I already have some cleaning up to do." Burke hands her his cereal bowl and heads off to watch TV and I know by the rigid way Nina's holding her arms that she has something to say to me. I wish we could fast-forward through it because whatever it is won't fix Brianna's attitude in a hurry, and besides, I've already stopped caring. Brianna can be as bitchy as she wants. I just need to make it to noon without picking up the phone to call Colette. I don't want to seem overeager.

"Sorry about Brianna," Nina says, leaning against the counter. "I, for one, am glad you and Burke are getting along so well."

"He's a cool kid."

"Yes, he is." Her eyes are pensive. "Brianna is too. She's just going through a bad patch. Everyone says girls are tougher at this age. It's not about you. I hope you don't take it personally."

I take another bite of Cheerios and listen to Nina's coffee gurgle. She turns towards the sink and starts scooping up steaming chili with a wad of paper towels. I throw the rest of my soggy cereal into the garbage after it and go back to my bedroom, wondering why it's not even ten o'clock yet and how I'm going to make it through the next two hours.

But I don't. Of course I don't. I punch in Colette's number at eleven and hang up when her machine answers. I don't let myself call again until after eight that night and by that time I have a pounding headache behind my eyes from the weight of anticipation. I should know better because of Kat but I don't. Of course I don't.

"Hello," Colette says smoothly.

"Hi, Colette," I fire back. "It's me—Mason."

"Mason, hi." Her voice changes when she says my name. I don't know whether that's a good or bad thing. "You got my message."

"Yeah." I lie on my bed and think of Ian Chappell's stellar performance in *Spin Cycle* last night. This is the easy stuff; I shouldn't give it a second thought. Besides, if I'm twitchy over the phone she may not want to see me again. "I was at the theater with some friends last night."

"The theater?" she repeats keenly. "What did you watch?"

I give her a quick recap of the play, careful to stay loose. She follows up with questions about themes and performances and I answer a few before panicking that we'll never get to the important part and interrupting her in midsentence: "You said something about wanting to talk."

"I did," she says faintly. "It's a good phrase, isn't it—we need to talk. It pretty much fits every situation." She pauses for a second. "I wasn't going to call you but my problem is, well, I suppose I should've thrown your phone number away, for a start."

"I'm glad you didn't." My head doesn't hurt anymore. I could run a marathon. I might have to. All that excess energy charging through my veins needs someplace to go.

Colette laughs. The sound makes me smile. I'm in so much trouble here. I don't know what I'll do if she says we shouldn't see each other again.

"Are you going to make me do all the talking?" she asks. "Do I have to do all the grunt work—climb out on a limb for you?"

"Poor you," I tease. "What do you even see in me?" Okay, so I feel a little better now. This isn't so difficult. This is fine.

"It's a mystery," she says. "Maybe you're my final fling as a shameless, soulless early twentysomething."

"I thought you'd already turned over a new leaf." I sit up with my back against the wall. I can't believe we're having this conversation. The undercurrent's giving me a massive rush. "I thought you were going to save the world from SUVs."

"You know, you're right," Colette says, mock-serious. "I think you've stopped me from making a major mistake here. Thanks, Mason. I owe you one."

"No problem." I'm gonna do it. I'm gonna dive into the deep end and ask her. *This is where it's all meant to go.* "So do you think we can see each other again sometime?" I say that with complete sincerity. I don't want there to be any misunderstanding.

"It's kind of late right now," Colette says, matching my tone. "What about tomorrow?"

"Tomorrow's cool." Tomorrow's incredible. I stand up, fold one arm across my ribs and pace back and forth between my bed and desk. "I can meet you at The Java Bean if you want."

Colette pauses like she's thinking it over. Maybe she's worried about meeting in public but I don't want to risk sounding sketchy by suggesting her place right off the bat. If anyone's going to suggest that, it should be her. "It'd be, you know, just like bumping into each other," I add. Translation: No one would have a clue what we're up to. Then I suddenly remember about Christopher. "My friend's not working tomorrow," I say. He's doing Tuesday and Friday shifts this week; he told me that yesterday.

"All right then," she says. "I'll see you after work."

I pace some more after I hang up, my hands crammed into my pockets and the skin on my face tingling. Then I get it together, change into track pants and run for over an hour. I'm wired, like in the final days before *All My Sons,* but somehow this is different—maybe because whatever happens between Colette and me depends more on her than it does on me.

twelve

IT'S POURING RAIN when I wake up, and Dad knocks on my bedroom door and offers to drive me to school. In the car I'm too tired to talk, but not to think. We listen to details of the latest national political scandal involving the minister of the environment and drunk-driving charges while I picture Colette, in bare feet, her breasts spiky against her top. "We should get that TV tonight," Dad says. He apologizes for not getting around to it earlier, but the truth is I forgot too.

"I'm hanging out with some people tonight," I say. Television's the last thing on my mind, despite our conversation.

"Maybe later this week then," Dad offers.

"Sure." But I can't think past tonight. It's the same all day long. Not even Kat next to me in history distracts me. I couldn't give you one accurate detail about her appearance today. The only person that gets my attention, even a little, is Monica G, and that's only because she rests both hands on my shoulders outside the cafeteria and frowns with her mouth open like she's trying to be a menace.

Of course she's way too hot to succeed. She looks more like a frustrated porn star.

"I can't believe you went to a play without me," she complains, a thick line of disapproval popping up between her eyes. "You never even tried to call me, did you?"

The play was Christopher's idea. I didn't phone anyone. "I guess everyone just assumed you'd be busy with Hugo." As far as I know they're still together.

"We're not with each other twenty-four seven," she snaps.

"I didn't realize you'd care that much," I say apologetically.

"I don't exactly know a lot of people who are interested in theater." Monica rubs her finger under her chin and hooks her thumb through the belt loop on her jeans. "I thought someone would've at least texted me."

"Next time for sure, okay?" I touch her hand. "Any news on the commercial?" Last I heard she'd gotten some head shots done and read for the part. "When am I gonna see you on TV trying to sell me lottery tickets?"

Monica pushes her hand into my chest and smiles reluctantly. "Now you're just sucking up to me so I won't be mad at you."

Nope, it's because she's gorgeous. But seriously, I don't mean that either. I guess I feel bad about excluding her, even though it was unintentional.

"No news," she continues, her smile fading. "But I don't think I got it. All the other girls there looked more, like, seasoned. And my voice wouldn't cooperate. I sounded fake."

Kat would be happy to hear that but I tell Monica that I'm sure she's being overly critical and that I bet she did fine. Over lunch

I tell everyone what Monica said about wanting to be asked along to *Spin Cycle*. They confirm that no one even considered inviting her, and Zoe says what everyone is thinking: "I know she was in *All My Sons* with us, but I guess it seemed like most of the time she was more interested in being a sex kitten."

"I guess the two aren't mutually exclusive," Jamie comments.

Round about then I crawl back into my own head and resume concentrating on tonight. It makes the hours go by slow, until about four-thirty, when I sit on the end of my bed and decide I should sink a Trojan into my back pocket. Stranger things have happened, right? Kat was a virgin and this girl is twenty-three and joked about me being her final fling. So I do it. I slide a condom into my pocket and walk out the door.

It's bright and warm outside, like the weather got a memo that we just hit May, and my ego's bloating up like a sumo wrestler but I'm edgy too. At JB I order a latte and sit facing the front door. I'm a few minutes early, which is a good thing, because I see Jamie and Dustin the second they step inside.

"What're you guys doing here?" I ask anxiously.

"Same thing as you," Jamie replies, all ironic. "Imbibing the local java." He's still hauling that anti-Mason attitude around, grimacing at me like I'm a rung beneath him on the evolutionary chain, but I don't have time for it today.

"I have to talk to you." I struggle out of my chair and motion for him to follow. Dustin sidles over to the counter while Jamie reluctantly trails me back towards the door. "I need you guys to do me a favor and get out of here," I tell him. "I'm meeting someone and she won't come in if she sees me with anyone else."

"Who?" Jamie probes. "Who're you meeting?"

He's so easy to read that I feel sorry for him. It would cut him into pieces if I said Kat's name. "Nobody you know. She's older.

Don't say anything to Dustin or anyone." It doesn't matter that Jamie's angry with me. I know I can still trust him to keep a secret.

"How much older?" Jamie asks, raising his eyebrows. "Where'd you meet this girl?"

"She's twenty-three," I whisper. "I don't have time for details. She could be here any minute."

"Twenty-three!" Jamie exclaims. He looks like he's just seen the ghost of someone he's not sure he likes and he squints past me as he says, "What the fuck happened to you anyway, Mason?" Indignant confusion hangs on Jamie's features as he refocuses on me. "You're turning into a regular chick magnet." He ambles towards Dustin at the counter and two minutes later they're gone.

I drink my coffee and wait and when Colette comes in she smiles at me before heading for the counter. She's wearing a black skirt that comes down to just above her knees and a burgundy silk shirt. I think about her breasts under the silk and mentally feel for the Trojan in my pocket. I know I brought it. I'm safe.

Colette crosses over to my table with her coffee and it's like a déjà vu from the times before, only I'm way more nervous, which doesn't make much sense because this time I know she wants to see me. Anyway, Colette stands with her knees against the table and says, "I'm not feeling very well. I wasn't sure what you'd think if I canceled."

"You want to cancel?" I hate that I sound little-boy disappointed.

"I thought if I did that you'd think I was chickening out," she says, looking into my eyes. "The truth is Andrea called last night after I spoke to you and I kept thinking about what a bad idea this is. But . . . I'm still here."

I run a hand through my hair and focus on my coffee cup. "So you're actually sick?" My gaze zooms up to meet hers again. I want this to happen so bad that I can't keep my eyes off her for two seconds.

"Just a cold," she says, and I notice that her voice sounds slightly scratchy. She fishes a tissue out of her purse and wipes her nose. Even the way she wipes her nose is sexy. If she does have a cold I think I want to catch it. I look at her knees pressed up against the table and imagine wrapping my hand around one and stroking the back of her thigh. Would she like that or would she ask me to stop? The thought alone has me paralyzed midbreath.

"I really don't feel up to doing much," she adds. "I just want to put on my sweatpants and laze around in front of the TV for the night. I know it's not very exciting, but if you want to . . ."

I remind myself to act like this isn't a matter of life and death. No more of that desperation garbage; that doesn't impress anyone. "Yeah, sure," I say evenly. "We could pick up some takeout."

So that's exactly what we do. We stop at Mr. Greeks on the way to her place and I insist on paying. I get pork souvlaki and roast potatoes and she orders the shrimp dinner. The food nearly taps me out and it occurs to me that I can't wait until summer to get a job; if I'm going to spend any more time with Colette I need one now.

It's quiet back in her apartment. No one's home upstairs; we're completely alone. That relaxes me for a second but it doesn't last. I wish I could read Colette's mind. Then maybe I'd calm down some. Then again, the anticipation's part of the thrill.

"Do you drink beer, Mason?" Colette asks as she reaches into the fridge.

"I'll take one." She flips the top off and hands me the bottle. I sip some down and stand with my weight on the kitchen counter as she starts to unpack the food. She has to stop in the middle of it to grab another tissue from her purse and I take over the unpacking and watch her at the same time. "Time for more hardcore cold

116

medication," she says. "Did you ever notice that only the nighttime stuff works and that just knocks you out anyway?"

"Maybe it doesn't work. Maybe it's just a sleeping pill disguised as cold medication."

"That's what I'm thinking," Colette says hoarsely. She swallows a mouthful of beer as she looks at me. "If I felt better I'd be nervous," she confides.

"I'm nervous now," I say with a laugh. "I hate that."

"Don't be nervous." Colette sniffles. "I'm too sick to prey on you much tonight."

"Okay," I say. "So you'll just prey on me a little. I can handle that." I'm so relieved she didn't cancel that I don't care what happens. Just being here is enough.

Colette smiles and touches my face. Her fingers are cold but I don't jump. "God, your face is so smooth. Do you even have to shave?"

Sure I shave. Twice a week without fail.

Colette leans her face in and kisses me sweet. She tastes the same as last time, despite being sick, and I run my tongue along hers and touch her hair. Her hand's light on my neck, almost a tickle. I'd laugh but I don't want us to stop. I skim my fingers along her shoulders and splay them out on her back, pulling her close. Her chest crushes against mine and I drop my hand and rest it against her breast.

I stroke it until the nipple aims into my hand. Colette laughs and buries her head in my shoulder. "And you said you were nervous."

"I was." I stop to peer into her face. She's all severe angles, perfect skin and these stunning almond-shaped eyes that are so dark they're almost black.

"Past tense," Colette says into my neck. She pulls back and

slides her hands into my back pockets and I stiffen, knowing exactly what she'll find.

Sure enough her fingers reach for the condom and dangle it gleefully in front of my face. "You couldn't have been *that* nervous," she says, setting it down next to my souvlaki. "You obviously thought you were getting lucky tonight." Her tone doesn't give me any clues. I don't know whether she's kidding around or if she's trying to teach me a lesson like that time with the dicing.

My shoulders sink and Colette cups her hands around my neck and says, "Don't worry, Mason. It's okay. God, you can be really funny sometimes. I didn't know you were so sensitive."

Maybe she doesn't mean to but she makes me feel inexperienced. That's what she's picking up on. Also, I'm so turned on that I'm not thinking in layers like I usually do. It's all black and white—she's laughing at me and I don't know why. I must be guilty of something. I must be an ass.

Colette turns her head away and sneezes in the direction of the living room. I hand her another tissue and she blows her nose into it. "This is such a pain," she groans. Then she rubs my chest like we've been a couple for years. "I don't think this is going to happen tonight, Mason. Trying to kiss you right now feels like holding my breath underwater."

"It's okay," I tell her. "Let's just eat."

Nothing turns out the way I imagine with this girl. Every moment seems unconnected from the last.

"I'm going to dig out that cold stuff and change into my comfy-ugly clothes," she says. "I won't be long."

She leaves me in the kitchen and I carry our takeout over to the coffee table, shoving away a collection of pamphlets and magazines to make room. I eat in front of the television whenever I'm sick; I'm guessing Colette's the same. I find the cutlery and bring that over with our beers. I don't feel weird about being here anymore and I'm done feeling awkward about the condom too. Knowing nothing's going to happen between us tonight goes a long way in cutting the tension.

The pamphlets, now that I look at them, are mostly about saving various animal species—pandas, seals, orangutans. But there are ones from Amnesty International, UNICEF and United Way too. I guess she hasn't decided which cause she wants to get involved in yet.

A couple minutes later Colette shuffles into the living room in track pants and an ancient concert T-shirt that says Lunatic Fringe on the front. She looks like that more-cute-than-sexy younger version of herself I got a glimpse of last time I was here, but that cuteness hooks me too. When I ask her about the shirt she tells me a friend of a friend was in the band and they split up years ago but she still listens to their music. "They were one of those bands that you're positive are going to be huge—massively talented, fantastic stage presence and true to themselves, the whole package. Then, about four years ago, they just sort of imploded. It was almost tragic."

I've never liked a band enough to refer to their demise as a tragedy. Maybe I haven't been listening to the right bands.

We sit on Colette's couch, watching crime shows and working our way through our food. Colette complains that she can't taste much and I try not to think about how much money I wasted on this shrimp dinner she can't even taste. Not that I obsess about money, but I don't have a whole lot of it to begin with.

It gets later and later and neither of us throws away the leftovers so they're still sitting there and I pick at her shrimp while she mumbles something about making coffee. Her head nestles into my shoulder while her hand rests on my thigh. The way she snuggles up to me reminds me of Billy the panther brushing against my legs. She breathes deep, almost like she's asleep, and I start to think she might be but then she asks how things are going with Kat lately. I stroke her hair and explain how Kat says we're still friends but she needs space. I tell her about Jamie's monosyllabic communications, Ian Chappell's mesmerizing performance in *Spin Cycle* and how I listened to her phone message twice Saturday night and haven't been able to think about anything else since.

She's so sleepy and soft next to me that I don't mind admitting that. She smiles into my face and soon we're kissing again. I touch her over her T-shirt and then under it. I fall in love with that pre-historic T-shirt with the tragic backstory and crusty lettering. I fit my hands around her teardrop breasts and brush my lips against her mouth. I pull her T-shirt down to cover her up and then search her nipples out all over again. I can't stop touching her like that, can't quit looking. She lets me do that for a long time, her eyes half-closed and her voice midway between a whisper and a laugh.

Sometimes we talk about what's happening on TV in the background or tiny details about each other and what we're doing. *Am I heavy? I love your eyes. I can never tell what you're thinking. Yes, you can.*

We could go on like that forever. At least I could. Mostly she's just lying there, smiling at me with drowsy eyes, letting me do whatever I want.

"You look so tired," I murmur. "I should go home and let you sleep."

"I'm tired," she agrees, "but it's okay." She runs her fingers tenderly through my hair. "I can't believe I'm doing this. What would people think?"

I don't want her to worry about that. There's nothing wrong with this. We both know what we're doing.

"Are you going to work tomorrow?" I ask. "Maybe you should call in sick."

"Are you kidding? I don't want to waste a precious sick day on actually being sick. That's the difference between work and school. At work they stick you with an outrageously low number of allowable absentee days and then complain when you actually take them."

I squeeze Colette's leg and sit up next to her. "That sucks." There she goes making me feel like a kid again. Or am I just being oversensitive? It's hard to be objective about somebody as beautiful as Colette, especially when she's the type of person who wants to save the world from itself and smiles at you when you touch her, even though she has a cold.

"I'll drive you home," she says, sitting up too.

"That's okay. You should get into bed, before your cold gets worse. I haven't exactly been letting you rest."

"It was sort of restful." Colette smiles. "We were lying down."

Can I just say that it's ridiculous what they make you do to get a driver's license here? I'll be practically seventeen before I can go anywhere alone. Clearly I don't have that kind of time. I need a job and a car. *Now.* I can't get by on being beguiling.

"I can get home on my own," I tell her.

"It's late," Colette points out. "It'll only take a couple minutes. Don't be silly."

I let that go too. The back of my neck twinges but I let it go.

"You can drive if you want." Colette tosses me the keys and that makes me feel better.

I drive her Toyota Echo back to my house. Colette listens to the radio and leans against the window like a kid on a road trip. As soon as we roll onto my street, she says, "Stop here. We don't want anyone to see us."

I park down the road from my house like she wants. "Take care of yourself," I say, unbuckling my seat belt. I push her hair out of her eyes and smile at her. "I'm glad you didn't cancel."

"Yeah, me too." She reaches out to hold the tip of my finger. "You're very sweet. Kat doesn't know what she's missing."

I blush in the dark. This is as vivid as life gets. It doesn't matter that we're not lying on her couch with her weight pinned under mine anymore. I still feel the same.

"Call me when you're better," I say. "Or if you just want some company."

"You too." She pecks me on the mouth and watches me climb out of the car.

It feels perfect, despite her cold, the sneaking around and Ari (who we didn't mention). Even walking away from her feels perfect because now I can think about it all in a way I couldn't while it was happening.

I stick my key into the front door and start from the beginning.

thirteen

DAD TRIES TO wake me up when I sleep through my alarm. I'm very convincing. I sit up in bed, eyes alert, and tell him that I'm absolutely getting up and can I have a late note for the school secretary? After he writes the note I climb back under the covers, just for a second. This particular second turns out to be an hour long but it's cool; I have my note and now I'm actually wide-awake buzzed again.

I have to check out Lunatic Fringe and find out if they're as good as Colette says they are. I have to find a job. Maybe Chris Cipolla can put in a good word for me at JB. There's so much to do.

First I shower. Then I eat a huge container of yogurt and a waffle. Billy winds himself around my legs under the table as I gulp down orange juice. He meows loudly in complaint when I ignore him. Either he's forgotten snubbing me or we've unexpectedly graduated to a whole new level of camaraderie. I lean back in my chair and glance down at my feet. Billy stares back at me with his eerie cat eyes and meows more.

"You're just going to run off," I tell him. But I can't help myself; I put my hand down to pet him anyway.

Smack. He slaps me with his paw, his claws drilling mercilessly into the middle of my right hand. "Fuck," I scream. "Holy FUCK." Billy tugs me towards him like a dead thing. If I pull back my entire hand will rip open like some gruesome horror movie special effect. "Fucking cat," I repeat, glaring at him. "Fucking homicidal psycho cat." Then I realize I have to be nice. Calm. I need my fucking hand back in one piece. It's fucking killing me and I need it back. I'm not a piece of string or a fucking dollar-store chew toy for Christ's sake. This is too fucking ridiculous.

"Let it go," I whisper, gazing down at Billy with benevolent eyes. "There's a good cat, Billy. Just let it go."

Billy eyes me with a cold expression. He only has one expression and he's definitely mastered it. For a few seconds he doesn't do anything but stare up at me with his fucking malicious paw hooked into the back of my throbbing dead hand.

Then he suddenly releases me, as though he doesn't want to waste any more precious energy—he has better places to be, more important people to mutilate. He slinks away, leaving me to deal with the blood. Now that the claws are gone there's so much of it. Red drips down my fingers and I rest my injured hand gingerly on my lap and stare at it, mesmerized. Weirdly, it doesn't hurt much anymore. It just looks like the biggest fucking mess imaginable.

After a couple seconds I get up to run my hand under the kitchen sink. The gashes don't look quite so grisly once they're clean. Maybe I don't need stitches after all. Maybe I can just play field medic and pile on a bunch of bandages. I disinfect the wound, wincing as I do it, and apply pressure with a wad of paper towels. Fifteen minutes later it stops bleeding enough for me to stick a slew of Band-Aids on and leave for school.

I'm not quite as happy as I was an hour ago and I want to strangle Billy with my bare hands but I still have my late note. The secretary gives me a pass and I head over to Twentieth-Century History. Mr. Echler doesn't comment on my late pass. He just coughs and motions for me to take my seat.

Kat glances over at me with the tiniest smile as I drop into my chair. She reaches out and sets a small square of folded paper on the corner of my desk. I open it and a happy face beams up at me.

I don't know why Kat's sending me happy faces now, after we've spent nearly two weeks staying out of each other's way, but I guess it's cool. It's not like I've stopped missing her during the past two weeks. I still want us to be friends again.

I draw three lines under each of the happy face eyes, fold the paper back up and plonk it on Kat's desk. Now it's a tired happy face.

The note bounces back to me twenty seconds later, the tired face unaltered. Under it she's written: *r u ok?*

My head snaps up and we take a good look at each other for what feels like the first time in forever. She's wearing a striped polo shirt I don't remember having seen before and her eyes are purposeful, like she genuinely wants to know how I'm doing. That familiar Kat feeling slips under my skin, warm and aching, and I nod to say, yes, I'm fine. Her eyebrows twitch in curiosity as she points to her hand, silently requesting the whole story.

The gesture flashes me back to eighth-grade geography, when our fresh-out-of-college teacher was determined to be everyone's friend. You could get away with anything in that class and Kat and I got away with writing a semester's worth of notes. Simple stuff mostly, like *what'd you do last night?* or *if you could be anywhere right now, where would you be? (and don't say anything dirty because you know I don't want to hear that!).*

I guess those notes are landfill now. No one thinks to save stuff like that. I probably won't save the happy face either.

Or maybe I will.

I pick up my pen, rip a page out of my notebook and start to explain about Billy, the savage cat that lives to taunt me. Hairy fingers reach across my desk and snatch the paper out of my hand before I can finish. *Shit.* Mr. Echler crumples up my note and pitches it into the garbage next to his desk without a word. Kat and I exchange stealthy glances, sure that Echler will have his eye on us for the rest of the class.

Sure enough there are no more opportunities to pass notes, but Kat stops me in the hallway afterwards and says, "That was so boring. His voice was putting me to sleep."

I rub my eyes with my able hand. "I know. Me too."

"So what happened?" Kat motions to my bandaged hand.

"Crazy fucking cat thinks I'm a scratching post," I say, smiling despite my words. Then I yawn so wide that Kat can probably see my tonsils. Let's just say I didn't sleep much last night. I'm lucky I made it in this morning at all.

"Ah, you tried to make friends with it." Kat grins back at me. "It looks like you were right about that being a bad idea."

"Disastrous," I say emphatically. I'm feeling pretty good about having an actual conversation with Kat again and I'd love to give her the gory details but unfortunately we both have classes to get to.

"I get it now—so the picture was an angry face."

"A tired face," I correct. "I was out late last night. Totally

126

overslept. Hence me being alone with the cat and making this incredibly bad decision to—"

"I bet you wanted to kill it," Kat interrupts. "The cat, I mean. So what were you doing last night until all hours?" She smiles like this is an entirely normal question and it is, but I don't know how to answer.

Kat raises her eyebrows when I don't answer straightaway. Silence is a reply in itself. She has a pretty good idea what it means and now she has this dazed look on her face, like she's not sure how she should feel about it. I completely understand. I don't know how she should feel about it either.

"I'm going to make you late again," she says quickly. "You should get to class."

"Yeah, right." My gaze drops to her beige-and-navy-striped shoulder. "I'll see you later." We shuffle away without looking each other in the eyes—at least I do; I can only guess about her.

The conversation leaves me with a raw, restless feeling but I don't let it stick. I can't let Kat scramble my priorities with a dazed look. We've been there before and it doesn't lead anywhere that we can both agree to go. So I sleepwalk through the rest of the morning and at lunch I decide to catch a quick nap out by the track. It's summertime warm and I'm not the only one out there. A bunch of ninth-grade girls are sitting on the bleachers, painting their toes. Some couple I don't recognize is running around the track, Frenching each other every twenty feet. There are people pretty well everywhere you look and then there's me, lying on the grass with my arms under my head.

"Wake up," a voice says.

Freshly painted toes line up near my head. "You're gonna be late," one of the girls continues. "The bell rang."

"Thanks." My throat's dry from falling asleep in the sun like that. I'm starving too. "Does anybody have any food? Anything at all?"

"I have some rice crackers," a skinny girl with gold toenails says. "You like rice crackers?"

I eat her sesame seed rice crackers as I head towards English class. I feel a lot better after sleeping through lunch, except that I'm ravenous. After school I bum money off Charlie Kady and head straight for Domino's to pick up a cheeseburger pizza. I finish off a slice along the way and immediately start in on a second but there's plenty left so I tell Burke and Brianna to help themselves.

Brianna stares at me like I have five heads but she takes a slice. "Thanks," she says.

I hold the box out to Burke. "What about you, buddy?"

"He doesn't eat it," Brianna says.

"No pizza?" I ask skeptically.

Burke gives his head an energetic shake. "It's sticky."

"He doesn't like the way the mozzarella stretches," Brianna explains, and I wonder what it's like to have your own personal translator. Burke could sit there with his mouth shut and she'd probably still be able to provide subtitles.

"You know, your cat is frigging vicious," I tell her, showing her my bandaged hand.

"He doesn't like people touching him," Brianna says. "We told you that." And how insane is it to have a pet that doesn't like to be touched? He should be out in the wild, mauling baby birds. "He didn't bite you, did he? That's a scratch, right?" Brianna's eyes look vaguely worried.

"It's one hell of a scratch."

"A scratch is better than a bite," she says knowingly. "With a bite you're more likely to get an infection." *Am I supposed to be relieved?* "You want me to look at it? I took first aid last fall."

"No, it's okay," I tell her. "I took care of it."

The phone rings and Brianna stares at me like she's waiting for me to pick it up, so I do. "Hello?" I cram the cordless between my ear and shoulder and pick up another slice.

"Mason?" That's Colette's voice and I grin into the phone. I didn't expect to hear from her so soon and that she's calling my landline doubles the shock. Today's full of surprises.

"Yeah, hey. You sound better." Brianna faces the TV but Burke's eyes are on me. I back out of the room with the phone in one hand and my slice in the other.

"That's my medication talking," she says.

"Let me guess—the nighttime formula?"

"Of course."

"Are you at work?" By now I've closed the basement door behind me and am safely out of earshot.

"I'm on break and I'm calling on your *home line*—which you should know was giving me a heart attack and a half because I was sure one of the kids would pick up. But then, I didn't have much choice since you left your cell at my place last night."

"Shit," I mutter, setting my slice down on the kitchen table and patting my pockets, which is completely unnecessary seeing as Colette just told me she's in possession of my phone. "I didn't even notice it was missing."

"Do you want me to drop it in your mailbox tomorrow? I'd do it later tonight only I need to crash, for real this time. This nighttime crap has me exhausted."

"I can swing by your place tomorrow and get it." The thought of her driving over here to dump my cell phone in the mailbox is too weird. Besides, I want to see her again. I want to know what happens next.

There's a noticeable pause in the conversation. "I have plans to-morrow," she says. "It's probably easier if I drop it off." She hesitates again before adding, "This doesn't feel right, does it? All these furtive meetings and phone calls."

"It'd be easier if you didn't know Nina."

"All the other facts would be the same."

True. There's nothing I can do about that. If she decides it's too risky, we're over. This could all be finished in about ten seconds. The thought makes me frantic but I play it cool and say, "I had a really good time with you yesterday but if you're that worried maybe it's not worth it."

At first Colette's quiet. Then she says, "You're really logical about this."

"Not really. I just don't want us to spend all our time asking ourselves whether this is a bad thing or not. If it's not clear that it's a good thing, what's the point?" This isn't a lie exactly; it's what I *would* think if logic had any place here.

"Things are never as cut-and-dry as that." She sounds pretty rational herself. "I don't know what you expect but I can't switch off my concerns at the drop of a hat. Liking someone isn't necessarily just a good or bad thing. It can be both."

"Okay, I know that. You're making my head spin here. Can we at least appreciate that we had a nice night yesterday?"

"It was very nice," Colette confirms. "*You're very nice.* There's no question of that, okay? We had a nice time but right now I need to get back to work so please tell me what you want me to do with your phone."

"I'll pick it up tomorrow," I say. Then I remember that she has plans tomorrow. "Sorry, you're busy—Thursday then, okay?"

"I have some things to do on Thursday," she tells me. "But you can drop by for a while beforehand if you want."

That's how we leave things. I don't ask what her plans are and if they involve Ari. There's more than enough for her to worry about without me dragging him into it and maybe I really don't want to know anyway.

I pick up my slice and carry it downstairs to watch TV with the two Bs. I'm tired of being accommodating. It won't kill Brianna to miss *The Doctors* for once.

fourteen

A STRANGE THING happens to me in the cafeteria the next day. Jamie drops into the chair next to mine, whacks his unwrapped samosa down on the table and says, "You kept a low profile yesterday." His eyes shift to my freshly bandaged hand, his anti-Mason attitude conspicuously muted. "What happened? She bite you or something?"

"The cat took a swing at me," I tell him, popping a french fry into my mouth. *That reminds me, I should ask Nina to add waterproof Band-Aids to this week's shopping list. The others can't survive a vigorous hand washing, let alone a shower.*

Jamie rocks in his seat. "So how'd it go on Monday? Were you serious about this girl being twenty-three?"

"Keep your voice down," I say.

"Sorry." Jamie puts his elbows up on the table and tilts his head towards me. I know it's mostly curiosity that has him there but the fact is, I need someone to talk to about Colette.

"Thanks for splitting the other day," I tell him. "It's kind of awkward. She doesn't want anybody to see us together."

"Seriously, wow." Jamie rubs his knuckles against the table. "How did that even happen to begin with? How do you get into a situation like that with a twenty-three-year-old? And what is that *like*?"

"What's it like?" I repeat. Confusing, weird and wonderful. I think of her Lunatic Fringe T-shirt with the scratchy faded letters. I remember scooping her breasts into my hands and kissing her short and sweet so she wouldn't have to hold her breath too much. But that doesn't explain what I felt. You could do that with lots of different people and it wouldn't feel like much. With her, it was pure magic.

"It's complicated," I tell him. "I don't know if it's actually happening with us or not. She has a lot of doubts—the whole age thing—and to make it worse she knows Nina."

"Are you serious?" Jamie says. "That's a little close for comfort."

"Yup." I rub my hair. "And she's got a boyfriend too. Well, not a boyfriend but she has another guy."

"Jesus, Mason." Jamie's head jerks up and I catch a glimpse of underlying irritation that reminds me we aren't quite done with the Kat stuff after all. "What happens if he finds out?"

"He's not going to find out. Anyway, barely anything's happened between us and they're not a couple."

Jamie scratches his forehead as he considers this. I don't expect him to understand. He's only hooked up with two girls in the past two years and even then I got the feeling he just did it because he thought he should. A tenth of my current complications would easily be enough to put him off—even with the possibility of sex thrown into the mix.

Of course, if Kat was interested in him, that'd be different. He'd jump through flaming hoops and suffer the risk of third-degree burns to his genitals but I don't want to think about the three of us in the context of this senseless romantic triangle anymore.

"So what happened with your driving test yesterday, anyway?" I ask, because we're not having the Kat conversation again if I can help it.

"Aced it." He mangles a smile. "I even nailed the parallel parking. I already have the keys to my mom's car and a promise of Saturday-night usage." He digs his key chain out of his pocket to show me and I can almost see the battle going on inside his skull—he's not sure he's through being mad at me.

"Beautiful," I say, smiling back. "I'd kill for a license. Shit, I'd kill *you* for a license."

"Yeah, I bet you would." His tone is oddly reflective so maybe he knows that he's been a pain lately.

I take a couple of seconds to digest that and then I'm ready to confess more Colette details. "I'm dropping by her place again tomorrow night," I tell him. "I left my cell phone there."

"Sounds to me like you guys are still a happening thing." Jamie casts a sideways glance in my direction as he sinks his teeth into his samosa. Hearing that from someone else is a hundred times better than telling myself. I push another fry between my lips and chew on my growing grin.

The next day Jamie throws me another curve when he catches up with me on my way out of the cafeteria and tells me to have a good night. I say thanks and mutter something about feeling like an idiot having to ride my bike over to her place, and that's when he really gets me. He scrunches up his eyes, like he just remembered why he's pissed with me, and says, "I'm not going to get roped into being Mason's Booty Call Taxi Service for however long this thing with you two lasts but if you don't have any other way to get there I guess I can drop you off."

"Seriously? You can get the car tonight?"

"I think I can swing it," Jamie says. It's obvious that he doesn't want me making a huge deal out of the offer so I don't. I'm not entirely done being pissed with him for being mad at me either but it'd be tremendous to show up on Colette's doorstep without my bike. The fewer things around to remind her of my age, the better. Getting home's a separate issue. I can figure that out later.

So I tell Jamie to come by around seven-thirty and he shows up at my house later as planned. Dad answers the front door, observes Jamie's car keys dangling from his fingers and offers his congratulations. I hear him from halfway down the stairs where I'm sticking one of those sadistic mint breath-freshener strips in my mouth. My eyes water and my tongue burns but Jesus, I'm fresh.

"What're you guys up to tonight?" Dad asks with a smile as I show up at the front door. This isn't Dad keeping tabs (he doesn't do that); he's just making conversation. Dad and Jamie get along really well, just like I do with Jamie's parents, and if Dad wasn't so busy adjusting to our new roommates I'm sure he'd have noticed that Jamie hasn't been around much lately.

"Just cruising," Jamie says after a split-second delay. Neither of us is used to sneaking around or lying to our parents. I guess that makes us lucky.

"Newfound freedom," Dad notes.

Newfound something. We tell him goodbye and climb into the same Honda Civic I rode in a thousand times as a kid. Jamie's mom has had this car for years and it's strange to sit in the passenger seat with Jamie driving but mainly I'm thinking about Colette and what she'll be like this time.

"So can you ask her if she has any friends who're interested in younger guys?" Jamie jokes. "What's her name, anyway? You never said."

"It's Colette. Colette Fournier." I only know her last name from spying it on the mailing label on the United Way leaflet.

"French?" he says. "Is she from Quebec?"

"I don't think so." I shrug and look out my window. "Her parents live here." Truth be told, I don't know much about her when it comes to factoids like that. We've kept ourselves busy talking about more important things.

Jamie doesn't have much to say after that. His presence next to me in the Honda feels like a bitter blend of admiration, loyalty and disapproval and I wish one single thing in my life could be simple, but then again, I'm just happy for the ride. My last conversation with Colette was on the rocky side. Anything that helps tonight go smoothly is a bonus.

Soon we're turning into her subdivision and I give Jamie directions to her door. He pulls into her driveway and we sit in the car staring at two little boys in soccer shorts darting across the front yard after a Nerf football. Their father sits on the front stoop, alternately watching them and casting a suspicious eye on us.

"This sucks," Jamie says with a groan. "What're you gonna do?"

"What choice do I have?" I unbuckle my seat belt and open the passenger door. The father stares openly as I approach the house.

"Hello," he calls. "What can I do for you?"

"I just came by to see Colette." I say that as calmly as I can. No big thing, right? There are a thousand reasons someone like me could want to speak to Colette Fournier. *Sure.* My spine is shivering. If he has a follow-up question my voice will crack.

"Around the side," he says, pointing to his left.

I nod thanks and walk around to the side door, questioning for the first time if I'm crazy to get involved with someone like Colette, who has a career, an apartment and some other guy to bonk, while I have a whole other year of high school, a seven-speed bike and the promise of my own TV. We barely even live in the same dimension.

Five seconds later she answers the door and hurriedly motions for me to come in. I stand in the laundry room as she slips her bare feet into blue flip-flops and says, "My appointment got moved up. You can wait here while I'm gone if you want—or come along and keep me company. Your choice."

"What appointment?" I don't sound happy.

"Mason, what's the matter?" Colette searches my face. She's wearing light capri pants and a sleeveless yellow top that reveals an inch of skin around her midriff when she reaches up to skim her fingers through her hair. She looks great but the circumstances suck. I just got here and now we have to leave again?

"Your landlord is outside with his kids," I say.

"That doesn't matter," Colette says confidently. "He's just the landlord, Mason. I could be your math tutor for all he knows." Go figure. Now that I'm rattled she's all smiles.

"Monday I had to park a mile from my house but this guy's sitting in your front yard and it's all good?"

"I know. But the landlords don't involve themselves in my life. It's purely a business arrangement." Colette leans her weight pensively against the washing machine. "I can drive you home if you want. Just let me get your phone, okay?" She stares into my eyes, waiting for an answer.

"Your jumpiness is rubbing off on me," I tell her. "I don't want to go yet—I just got here." I take a step towards the washing machine. "I just had the feeling this was all supposed to be a big secret."

"It is." She takes a long breath and rubs the back of her neck. "I'm not very good at this."

"Me neither." I rest my palms flat against my jeans. "Every time I think we're getting somewhere you change on me."

"Where is it you think we're getting?" Colette asks. She moves hastily away from the washing machine and adds, "Honestly, we don't have time for this now, Mason. If you want me to drive you home I can take you on the way but I have to go now."

"On the way where?" She warned me that she had plans tonight but I'm angry anyway. I want her to invite me downstairs and lie on the couch with me. This is bullshit.

But I'm not ready to go home, so I get in the car with her and we drive out to the country to check out a litter of Malti-Poo puppies that she saw an ad for in the paper. Two of the puppies are already spoken for and Colette wants the remaining girl. This farmhouse with spotted cows roaming around in the background is the place she had to be in a big hurry. A bearded middle-aged guy in a Blue Jays T-shirt and his blond wife let Colette and me play with the pups and ask questions. They don't have any questions themselves and they don't seem suspicious of our relationship. Maybe they think she's my sister. Maybe they don't care who we are to each other as long as they sell their puppies.

The important thing is that they get us acting all gooey, these insanely adorable scruffs of white and brown that lick at our faces and scamper around like this is the best moment in the history of the world. Colette's eyes light up in a way I've never seen and I'm glad I came along, even if she's wasting my time and giving me the runaround, never really intending for us to get to know each other any better than we do now.

Colette gives the farmer couple a down payment because the puppies aren't quite old enough to leave their mother yet. She says she'll be back in a few weeks to pick up her puppy, and when we get back into the car we're both sublimely happy. We talk about the puppies and their mother, Elsa, who has the sweetest temperament you've ever encountered, and I complain about Billy the bastard cat going terrorist on me and why couldn't Nina have had some kind of terrier instead?

Colette glances at my hand like she hadn't noticed the bandage before. "That cat gives me the creeps," she says. "Listen, Mason." Her voice drops. "What did you mean before when you were talking about us getting somewhere? Did you mean physically or something else?"

Her bluntness out of nowhere like that startles me. What's the right answer?

"Because you know about Ari and I don't want you to get the wrong idea that this is going to turn into something serious and exclusive. We're just enjoying each other and having a good time, right?"

"I know." I didn't think she was going to be my girlfriend or anything, but at the same time I don't appreciate her throwing Ari in my face. "That's not what I meant. It's just that so far it doesn't feel like you've relaxed into the idea of us being together at all, in *any* way. Monday was great, but when we talked on the phone the next day you were oozing guilty vibes, like you didn't think we should see each other anymore." I scratch my bandage as I continue. "And to be honest I don't want to hear any more about Ari. Maybe you're cool with me talking to you about other girls, but as far as I'm concerned we can skip those kinds of details, okay?"

"Okay," Colette agrees. "Does this mean I shouldn't ask about Kat anymore?"

"You can ask about her if you want. I just don't want to hear any more about Ari."

"You know we never talk about Ari." Colette presses her lips together. "I only wanted to make sure that we're clear what we're about."

Sex and good times, I get it. So shouldn't we at least be having sex? Incidentally, I have another condom in my back pocket. I'm ready to go when she is.

As soon as we get downstairs I back her up against the wall and kiss her. For the first few seconds she seems surprised and then her body leans generously into mine, like this is the moment she's been waiting for. This time I don't have to worry about breathing breaks. We ram our mouths together like wild things. I suck on her neck and shove my hands up under her bra. Ari can wonder where the hickey came from—or maybe he already knows about me.

Colette slips her hands under my T-shirt and onto my back. "Let me look at you," she says, pulling off my T-shirt.

I smile at her but I feel ferocious.

I tug her top off and stare at her pink nipples, my mind throbbing with sensory overload. She's wearing this lacy beige bra thing but now it's hanging around under her collarbone, not covering anything. Colette reaches around her back, unsnaps it and lets it fall to the floor. "Come on," she whispers, taking my hand.

I follow her into the bedroom. She has one of those beds with a hundred pillows on it and she sits on the edge and unbuttons my jeans. I watch her do it, feeling my skin blaze while simultaneously wishing I had a build like Hugo's. Maybe then I wouldn't feel like such a kid with her.

"Did you bring another one?" she asks, reaching into my back pocket. She tears open the condom, slides it on like an expert and sucks me off.

My face is drenched in sweat and I come so fast that it shocks me senseless. I peel off the condom and clean myself up in the bathroom, breathing so hard that the entire neighborhood can probably hear it. When I go back to Colette's room she's lying on the bed, naked, with half the pillows pushed onto the floor. She's so skinny that her pelvic bones jut out. Her pubic hair's trimmed short and she has a tiny bruise on one of her knees that you'd hardly notice only she's so white. I'm in absolute awe and I start to sweat again as I look at her.

"You look like a sculpture," I say, my voice low.

Colette smiles that smile that turns me golden. "You know you're beautiful, don't you? That day in your father's kitchen I couldn't take my eyes off you. I felt so evil." She laughs this deep sexy laugh that I've never heard before, and I stretch out on the bed next to her and touch her skin. The sight and feel of my fingertips on her bare skin seems like fantasy.

We kiss, our bodies jammed up tight together and our hands greedy. She's two hundred degrees of blistering hot and it's so much better, and different, than I was expecting. I lick her everywhere, like a cat lapping milk—a feverish, deliriously ecstatic cat that only scratches if you want him to and Colette knows exactly how she wants it. I want to give it to her too but it takes so long that we have to break and talk because I'm worn out. "Sorry," she says with a hint of self-consciousness. "It always takes a long time when I'm getting to know someone new."

"So it seems like we're just the opposite," I say, smiling as she tucks her hand into my armpit.

She laughs that voracious, sexy laugh again and I can't believe how incredibly, colossally lucky I am. I smooth my hands over parts of her anatomy I'd only been able to imagine up until now and I guess I should feel nervous, given the gap in our experience level, but I'm too deep in the moment for that.

We talk about our favorite movies and songs and the first

guitarist she ever had a crush on when she was thirteen. I tell her about mastering the perfect smile when I was ten and how I thought I wanted to be a drummer for a while but that I just never clicked with music the same way I did with acting.

"I wish I was like you," she says. "I'm really interested in law and I think I have the right kind of mind for it, but it's not like with you and acting. It's not a passion."

By now I've built up some energy reserves and I dedicate myself to working on her again. Colette breathes heavy and plays with my hair. She coughs as she comes and we drift slowly off to sleep, my arm draped across her ribs. I stay most of the night and we keep waking up and rediscovering each other, sometimes frenzied and sometimes half-asleep. It's not like anything else that's ever happened to me. It feels like another life in a parallel universe where my sole purpose is to touch and taste Colette in between snatches of sleep. In some ways I honestly can't believe I'll eventually have to leave this room.

The funny thing is that during all that we never straight-out fuck and I don't even notice until I'm alone in my bedroom later, changing my clothes.

What can I say? It didn't feel like there was anything missing.

fifteen

LYNN CALLS AS I'm stretched on my bed, watching *Relic Hunter* after school the next day. Dad and I picked the TV up two days ago and I'm so tired that *Relic Hunter*'s as much complexity as my mind can deal with. Actually, it turns out the show's *more* complex than I can handle. Tia Carrere's kicking some army guy's ass and I've already lost track of who he is and what he's done to piss her off. Exhaustion's fast becoming a recurring theme in my life.

Lynn wants to know about my summer plans. Honing my craft? More theater? Shakespeare perhaps?

"I need to land a job that pays more than minimum wage," I say with a yawn. "Increase my cash flow." I don't expect my dad to sponsor this thing with Colette. Truthfully, I'm not sure what he'd make of our involvement. He doesn't interfere with my life much but this feels different.

"Well, you know you could still pick up some modeling jobs for extra money," Lynn suggests. "Only, I know you don't want to do that anymore." If she knows, then why bring it up? But that's Lynn for you, always pushing. "It's a big crossover area, though, isn't it? It could bolster your acting career. Do you still take care of your skin?"

"Don't worry about my skin," I tell her. "I'm not doing any modeling. That dream is over." *Her* dream. And I remind her that it's finished with pretty well whenever she brings up modeling, which isn't often these days.

"I know," she sings. "I'm all for the acting, Mason. You're a rising star."

This is the short version of what my childhood sounded like. No great sob story, I know. It's not the worst thing in the world to have someone fawning over you and trying to turn you into something perfect but it's not the best thing either. Lynn's faults are just a bit more transparent than lots of other people's.

She can be really cool at times, though. Like, she'll try anything once. The last time I was in Vancouver we went snowboarding together and she never complained, even though she kept wiping out. Plus, she's turning into quite a good writer. Sometimes I check out her opinion column online to chart her evolution.

I get more of a kick out of her from a distance than I ever would if she lived around the corner. Some people are better in small doses. That's just life.

Anyway, I say goodbye to Lynn and lie there listening to my stomach rumble over Tia Carrere's dialogue. I close my eyes and silently debate whether I'm more hungry or tired and I guess my stomach wins because I get to my feet and stumble down to the kitchen.

Brianna's microwaving something garlicky, and two girls with long hair, one redhead and the other a blonde, are sitting at the kitchen table leafing through a glossy magazine. "Hey," I say sleepily, scratching at my neck.

The blonde looks up at me with a smile. "You're Mason, right?"

"Yep, what's your name?"

"Merilee." She motions to her friend. "And this is Jane." Merilee cranes her neck over the table to look at Brianna. "You never said anything about how cute he is." Jane blushes the way only redheads can and I go over to the microwave to sneak a peek inside.

"Is that garlic bread or pizza?" I ask Brianna.

"Neither," Brianna says, doing her best to ignore Merilee's comment.

"Technically it's garlic bread," Merilee confirms, grinning at me. "It just looks like pizza."

Brianna turns to face the microwave. "So you want some?"

"Yeah, sit with us," Merilee pleads, closing her magazine. "Give us the heads-up on GS. We're all going there next year, you know. Is it as bad as they say? Like that story about a girl running a blow job lottery and blowing guys in the janitor's closet. Is that true?"

Brianna looks mortified and this Merilee person's staring at me like I could walk on water. "I never heard that," I tell her. "It's a good school as long as you don't get messed up with the wrong people."

Merilee wants to know who the wrong people are and what kind of people I hang out with, but it's pretty clear that what she really wants is to keep me in the kitchen. "Where's Burke, anyway?" I ask as Brianna offers me a square of melty garlic bread.

"He has a playdate," she replies, setting the rest of the garlic bread on the table in front of Merilee and Jane. "You can watch TV in the basement if you want. We're not watching it."

"Why do you keep trying to get rid of him?" Merilee asks.

"Why don't you just go upstairs with him if you like him so much?" Brianna snaps.

"We're just talking." Merilee fixes a vicious death grip stare on Brianna while Jane glances helplessly up at me. "Why don't you take a pill or something?"

"I'm *so sure* that's all you want to do—talk to him." Brianna swings around to face me at the counter. "Just go already, Mason. *Gawd.*"

The kitchen's tension level has already spiked to epic proportions and now I'm smack in the middle of it. "I'll go when I'm ready," I say. I don't particularly want to hang around but I'm not taking any more shit from Brianna. That attitude has to go.

"You see," Merilee says triumphantly. "He wants to stay."

"Gawd, Merilee." Brianna scowls and reaches for Merilee's magazine. "Talk about throwing yourself at someone."

"Talk about being a bitch," Merilee retorts.

"Sounds like your friend knows you pretty well," I say, staring intently at Brianna. "Can't you ever be nice? Even just for two minutes? Seriously, Brianna, what's the problem?"

Brianna pales as she stares back at me. "You don't know me," she says grimly. "And you don't know my friends."

"Whatever." My voice oozes sarcasm. "Thanks for the garlic bread." I flash her the biggest, cheesiest grin my lips can manage and walk off with a mouthful of garlic. The girl's personality impairment isn't worth my time.

Burke's home in time for dinner and we have another one of those traditional family meals where the five of us sit around discussing our day. We're coming up on the three-week mark but I can't say this communal-dinner thing feels any more natural than it did on day one. Maybe I'm just too old to get into the idea of siblings and place settings. All I know is that every time I sit down at the table with them I feel like I'm showing up for Stepfamily Integration 101.

Burke's chin is covered in spaghetti sauce, even though Nina cut his noodles into inch-long mini-strips. Half the time I cut mine up like that too. It's a lazy way to eat but who cares?

Dad and Nina are talking about this glow-in-the-dark mini-golf place where one of his hygienists held a birthday party for her son. The hygienist was full of good things to say and Dad and Nina want to head over there with Burke and Brianna tomorrow. "You too if you're free, Mason," Dad says.

Brianna glances at me from across the table, the tension from earlier hanging in the air, thick as L.A. smog. "Don't worry," I say to her. "I'm not planning on going."

"I don't care where you go." Brianna focuses on her spaghetti.

"Brianna!" Nina's head swivels sharply. She gapes at Brianna, her nostrils flaring. "That's rude."

"He started it." Brianna twirls a long strand of spaghetti expertly around her fork. Her face is expressionless, like she's trying not to care.

"It's fine," I say. "This is her specialty."

"What?" Brianna drops her fork. Bolognese sauce splashes onto her wrist. "What's that supposed to mean?"

"Being a queen bitch."

Brianna's shoulders sag. She picks up her fork and mashes into the spaghetti like it's a pile of potatoes. She's speechless and the satisfaction spreads from my fingers all the way up to my cheeks. I sit there grinning wildly to myself over a plate of steaming spaghetti. I'm a hero.

"Mason!" Dad rarely shouts but he's shouting now. "That's unacceptable. Apologize to Brianna."

Burke's eyes pop wide open. He turns in his chair so most of his body's facing me. Brianna hasn't finished pulverizing her pasta. Her face is blotchy and I shouldn't say it but you know I will. Why step out of the line of fire now? "Sorry you're such a bitch, Brianna. It must be a tough haul. I mean, it's pretty well twenty-four seven, isn't it? You never take a break."

Dad's fist pounds the table. "Mason, I want an apology out of you this second and let me tell you, it better be good."

Brianna drops her fork for the second time. She tears out of the room as Dad glares at me. "Good job, Mason," he says. "Are you happy with yourself?"

"You don't understand," I tell him. "She's impossible."

"I don't care," Dad yells. "You're three years older and you know better than to treat someone like that!"

You know what? I'm not hungry anymore. "I'm done," I say coldly. "Thanks, Nina. It was really good."

Nina nods and I notice her elbows aren't on the table anymore. She doesn't look angry with me, just discouraged. "I'm sorry," I tell her. "We've been having some problems."

"I know," she confirms.

"Leave the table, Mason," Dad commands.

Gladly. I leave my unfinished spaghetti sitting in a heap on my plate and go upstairs. Billy scurries towards me in the hallway, his eyes glowing with malevolence. If he lays into me now I'll fight back, swear to God.

I pass Billy first, then the bathroom. I stand outside of Brianna's bedroom, listening at her door. If I heard her crying would I apologize? I don't know the answer to that but I don't hear anything anyway, just the distant sound of plates clanking as they're loaded into the dishwasher.

sixteen

I never do apologize to Brianna but glow-in-the-dark mini-golf isn't optional anymore. Dad reserves a one o'clock tee time and I pile reluctantly into his Ford Taurus along with everyone else. The black-lit mini-golf place spews out thunderous pop-punk tunes as we play, making it easy for Brianna and me to blend into the background. Burke, on the other hand, careens around the fake coral reef and kaleidoscope-colored UFOs like he's on crack.

It's cool, though; he's having fun. He doesn't even mind about coming in second-last. (Nina's officially the worst golfer I've ever seen.) Being the youngest, I guess he's used to it.

Afterwards Nina supervises him in the video game room while Dad, Brianna and I head for the snack bar. Dad veers off to look for the bathroom and Brianna and I grab munchies and a table for six. "The lighting in this place is really throwing me," I tell her, holding out my open bag of M&M's. I was still pissed with her when I fell asleep last night but this morning the anger seemed pointless; we still have to share a house together. "It could be midnight out there," I continue, "or the middle of February." Brianna shakes her head at the M&M's and slurps her soda. "Next thing you know they'll be packing us off to Disney World and taking family snapshots with Mickey Mouse."

Brianna nods dully and gnaws on her straw, hamster-like. If she's impressed by my sociability you'd never know it. "How's your hand?" she asks, staring at the single remaining bandage.

"It's okay. No sign of cat scratch disease or rabies yet." Before she can contradict me and say that rabies takes a lot longer to show up or that her cat doesn't have any diseases or whatever the hell she intends to say, I add, "Listen, Brianna, what's your problem with me, anyway?" Believe me, I say that as patiently as I can. I'm tired of the animosity.

"I never said I had a problem with you."

"You gotta be kidding," I say. "It's like you and your cat are in a frigging contest to prove who hates me the most."

"That's not true." Brianna presses her fingertips down on the table until they turn white. "Does everybody automatically have to like you?"

Pretty much, yeah. But I scoff at that and scoop up a handful of M&M's. "I just thought if there was a problem we could talk about it."

"You know, you don't have to do this," she insists. "Nobody's even around to hear it."

"That's not why I'm—"

"Anyway, I don't hate you," she says, interrupting. "Merilee can be a real pain. I thought I was doing you a favor." Her voice is calm but her vibes are as defensive as ever. Frustration ripples through me as I scrutinize her. I don't want to spend the next fifteen months in constant conflict with this girl I barely know. There has to be a solution.

Just then Dad pulls up a chair and sits down between us. "It's hot in here," he says, wiping his brow. "Is anyone else warm?"

"I'll get you a drink," Brianna volunteers. "What do you want?"

Dad reaches for his wallet and tells her he'd love a lemonade or iced tea. As she walks away he gives me this funny smile as if to say *You see, she's not as bad as you think.* Maybe. The fact is, she does act a notch or two less hostile with me for the rest of the afternoon. Maybe that's as good as it gets with her.

The remainder of the weekend is taken up with a Saturday-night movie with Charlie Kady (the Whole Foods girl has a family wedding), various homework assignments that I don't get around to finishing and an endless Sunday-night session with Colette. We heat up chicken korma and fool around on her couch and then her bed. It's every bit as hot as Thursday only less surprising so she takes a little less time and I take a little more and somehow by the end of it we still haven't fucked and I don't even mind.

That's how it goes with us all week—warm mouths, naked skin and these bits of time that seem like forever while they're happening. It's utterly fantastic except for three minor things. One, Colette's habit of barging into the bathroom to brush her teeth while I'm taking a piss. Two, my eternal and embarrassing transportation problem. Three, the prescription made out to Ari Lightman on the bathroom counter next to her soap dish.

Spending so much time alone with Colette has strange side effects. Virtually everything that happens while we're apart seems disjointed, like raw documentary footage that needs editing. I'm restless during my Presentation and Speaking Skills debate on cloning and rush through my rebuttal (because I know it doesn't matter) but get angry when Ms. Courier criticizes my performance (because I know she's right). Kat watches me during history when she thinks I'm not looking but doesn't try to speak to me or send me any more happy faces, and Jamie spends lots of time talking to me now but only while we're at school.

Then there's Brianna, who passes me in the hall one evening and catches me off guard by saying she's about to watch a Reese Witherspoon movie with Jane in the basement and that I probably don't like Reese Witherspoon anyway but if I do I can come watch because they're about to start. So I watch half this Reese Witherspoon movie in the basement with them, assuming that this is our pseudo-sibling version of a truce, and then Colette calls and I spend the other half on the phone in my bedroom with the TV volume up high so no one can hear what I'm saying.

With Colette even silly ten-minute conversations about nothing feel larger than life. Sometimes I wonder if that's because we're this dirty little secret and maybe if everyone knew, our relationship wouldn't feel so important. *Sure.* Who am I kidding? Every time she calls I feel like Burke tearing around the mini-golf course with electric eyes and infinite energy.

Seeing her is an even bigger rush. We can't pretend to run into each other at The Java Bean forever so we do this thing where we meet in the parking lot a few blocks from her work. I stand a couple rows over from her Toyota in case a coworker walks into the lot with her. It hasn't happened yet but if it does she'll meet me outside Hennessy's pub with the car. On this particular Thursday the coast is clear again and she smiles at me as she unlocks the doors. The weather's too amazing to spend the entire night indoors (like we have for the past week) so we drive to Toronto where we can blend into the crowd.

I like the idea of walking around outside with her (and knowing that we'll still have plenty of time alone in her apartment later). We buy fully loaded hot dogs from a street vendor and stroll across Queen Street West looking at vintage-clothing stores, juice bars and eclectic cafés. Antiques shops and independent bookstores huddle between hip bars and tattoo places. In fact, with every step we're surrounded by tattoos and food—The Bishop and the Belcher, Tiger Lily's Noodle House, the Queen Mother Cafe—an endless jumble of sizzling aromas and tribal art. I tell Colette we should get matching tattoos and we search through pages of designs (from Sanskrit symbols to skulls to Celtic knots) before she says, "You're not serious about this, are you?"

"Were you?" I ask in surprise. Here I thought we were both kidding but all of a sudden I know I'll go through with it if she wants to.

"Definitely not," she confirms. "We've just been looking at so many that I was starting to wonder." We close the book of Chinese symbols we've been scanning and cross slowly towards the door. "I'm a big coward when it comes to things like that," she adds. "I get faint whenever I have a blood test. Just seeing the needle pierce the skin . . ." She shudders and I grab her hand. Then we're outside, walking down the street holding hands like any regular couple. It's not the smartest idea but it comes so naturally that neither of us stops to question it.

"So how do you handle the dentist?" I ask. My dad has a reputation for putting his patients at ease but I'm sure Colette wouldn't want to see him. We don't need to add any more layers of complexity to our relationship.

"I only go every couple years," she says guiltily, as though I'm about to lecture her about gingivitis in the middle of Queen Street. "Whenever I can work up the courage." She squeezes my hand. "What about you, what are you phobically afraid of?"

Phobic is a strong word. The idea of bats flapping around my head freaks me out but I've never seen one outside of the zoo. I'm trying to come up with a better answer when Ian Chappell's face jumps out at me from the crowd. He's walking towards us in a white tunic and skinny black pants, looking just enough like his *Spin Cycle* character for me to notice him.

Jesus, that's Miracle on his right. Dread sweeps across her cheekbones and jaw but she's quick to fix that. By the time we're standing in front of each other she looks like a girl in a soap commercial: springwater clean and in perfect emotional balance.

"Mason," she says, smiling. "How're you?"

"Good," I reply quickly. *And still holding Colette's hand.* "You guys doing the Queen Street circuit?" My goal is to get through this conversation without commenting on either of our bizarre pairings. I guess you could call it improv.

"Yeah, it's a great evening, isn't it? No humidity. I love it down here." Miracle blows me away, as usual. She's exuding calm in the middle of our chaos, her hair moving gently in the wind as she holds my gaze. Is it possible she has nothing to hide?

"Beautiful. I should come down here more often." I let go of Colette's hand and motion towards Miracle. "Colette, this is Miracle."

"Miracle," Colette repeats. Her posture's wooden but her voice is casual. "That's a beautiful name."

"Thank you." Miracle slopes her head a little, almost like a miniature bow. "I didn't like it at all when I was younger but I'm doing my best to grow into it." Miracle switches her gaze to Ian

154

Chappell. "Mason, this is Ian. You remember we saw him in *Spin Cycle*?"

I nod. "Of course." I didn't think she'd bring that up but it gives us something else to talk about. "You were *outstanding*," I tell him. "You had me on edge until the very last second. You were like one of those guys with wild eyes you see in the street, you know? The kind where you wonder if they're going to start swearing at you for no reason and then they say something smart that makes you wonder if maybe they're not so crazy after all." I might be babbling. Why am I so freaked? Miracle isn't going to tell anyone. And what is she doing with Ian Chappell, anyway? We need to have a private conversation ASAP.

Ian Chappell stares at me with fiercely observant eyes. "Exactly," he says. "That's really my feeling about Tom too. Always on edge. Never misses a beat. Very compelling guy but I can't say I'll miss him. That's a heavy load of tension to carry around."

Miracle glances down at her watch. "You know, we should probably get some food before you have to head over to the theater, Ian."

"You're right." Ian touches a strand of her hair, only for a second but that's long enough to answer my question about their status. "You two want to come along? There's a terrific Thai place not two minutes from here."

So Ian isn't in hiding after all. He has to be close to thirty and it doesn't bother him that Miracle's only seventeen. Or maybe he doesn't know.

"We can't," Colette says, feigning regret. "We have to get moving too."

Past my bedtime. Shit. I can't believe Miracle's hooking up with this thirty-year-old professional actor she couldn't even speak to a couple weeks ago. I don't know whether I should be happy for her or if I should plan a one-man intervention. Does she know what she's doing? Do I? Does anyone?

Apart from all that I wish I could talk to Ian Chappell about acting awhile longer. There's so much he could tell me. "Yeah, we have to go," I say.

"All right." Ian drapes his arm lazily around Miracle's shoulders. "Have a good night." He lifts his hand to flash us a wave.

Colette and I continue in our direction, our bodies hunching like they want to melt into the sidewalk. "Who was that?" Colette whispers urgently. "An ex or a friend? Can you trust her?"

"She's not going to say anything," I say. "You know that guy is, like, thirty years old. I don't think she wants anyone to know about him either." Colette casts an impatient look in my direction and I know that sounds stupid coming from me, of all people, but it's different, right? That's a thirteen-year age gap.

"So you think we can trust her?" Colette asks.

"Don't worry. I'm positive she won't say anything. Even if she wasn't with Ian."

Colette folds her arms across her midriff and digs her fingernails into her skin. "So much for thinking there's anywhere safe we can go together."

"Yeah." I'm disproportionately disappointed. She didn't say we couldn't see each other. We just have to keep it indoors.

"We should go back to the car." Colette looks over her shoulder, as though Ian and Miracle or any one of a hundred other people we know could be trailing us through Queen Street, snapping photos on their cell phones.

"It's okay." I stretch my hand across her back. "It's nothing. I'm more worried about her."

"Why are you worried about her?" Colette's brown eyes peer at me in suspicion. For a second I think she's jealous.

"We're pretty good friends. When we saw that play she was so intimidated by his talent that she didn't even want to speak to him afterwards. I'm not saying that he took advantage of her or anything but—"

"That sounds exactly like what you're saying," Colette counters. "She seemed pretty capable to me. Or is it only okay when the guy's younger?" She sighs and leans into my arm. "I'm getting defensive. Can we skip this discussion?" She stares distractedly at a trio of girls with dyed black hair begging in front of a convenience store. "I wish we'd at least had time for coffee. I think I'm in caffeine withdrawal."

"We can get coffee," I say. "What're the odds we'll run into them again? You heard them—they were getting food."

So we go to this funky little coffeehouse we spotted earlier and there's no sign of Ian and Miracle but Colette orders takeout. We drink our coffee in the car, on the way back to her place, and I know better than to say I wish we could've stayed in the coffeehouse, but for the first few minutes I'm definitely thinking it.

seventeen

TWO THINGS WEIGH heavy on my mind Friday morning—my run-in with Miracle the night before and my history essay on the United Nations. The essay is typo-free with comprehensive footnotes and credible arguments. It's at least a B-plus paper and I've left it on the kitchen table—or maybe the counter. I explain that to Mr. Echler at the start of first period history but he balances himself on the edge of his desk and says, "You're well aware that late papers lose ten percent a day, Mason."

"I'll get it at lunch," I tell him. "Will that cost me anything?"

Mr. Echler nods like that's fine with him and I sit down, ultra-aware of Kat's eyes focused in my direction. They give me a guilt pang, like they always do lately, and I wish that she'd stop but then what would be left between us? "What's up?" I say, turning to look at her.

"Not much," she says quickly. "You?"

"Same."

She blinks her thick eyelashes at me and grips her pen. It's like a code that I'm not meant to decipher and I glance back at her as nonchalantly as I can. "You didn't finish your essay?" she asks.

"I did," I tell her. "It's at home." I don't know how to have a natural conversation with her anymore. I sound like Dustin before he started working on the play. It's painful.

Kat almost smiles. "I thought you only did that with your phone."

Me too. I'm tired and distracted. Summer will be easier. At least then I won't have to worry about how to deal with Kat staring at me and the gnawing feeling that I've let her down. I still need to find a job, though. According to Christopher, The Java Bean is overstaffed. Some ex-employee with a humanities degree and heavy student loan came back last week. Maybe I should ask Charlie Kady to find out how much Whole Foods pays.

I smile at Kat but she's already looked away. There's a big possibility we'll spend the entire summer apart, for the first time in three years. With her and Jamie avoiding each other too, there's no reason to think our paths will cross much.

That feels wrong, but then most everything about us has felt wrong since that night. Maybe I'd take it back if I could. One night can't be worth all this awkwardness. Technically it wasn't even a night, more like two hours. A couple of hours shouldn't have the power to cripple our friendship.

This is why I don't like to think about Kat; it doesn't go anywhere. I just get messed up and there's no reason for that when I'm in a totally different situation now.

On my way to the cafeteria later (to beg someone with a car to make an essay run with me) it happens again when I spy her walking by, shoulder to shoulder with this guy named Sanjay. He's not her usual type. His build's kind of similar to mine and he won the tenth grade Media Arts Award last year. Sanjay has a reputation for being funny and Kat's smiling when I see them. It gives me a chill, even though I know they're not together (not yet). If it's not him, it'll be someone else. It's only a matter of time.

Kat drops her gaze when she sees me and I hope I look normal enough but I'm not so sure. I'm not Miracle. I don't have enough talent to cover all the cracks.

Anyway, I go into the cafeteria and head for our regular table, edging Kat out of my head with thoughts of the here and now—or more specifically, here, now and yesterday. Miracle's sitting next to Y and Z and she's the perfect person to chauffeur me home. We can discuss our Queen Street encounter on the way. "Hey, Mason," Yolanda and Zoe chime, looking up at me.

"Hey, guys," I say. "I have to borrow Miracle for a while."

Miracle bugs her eyes out at me. "Borrow me for what?"

I explain about my abandoned United Nations essay and she grabs her sandwich and brings it out to the parking lot with us. So far neither of us has brought up yesterday and I start to wonder if I should let it go. But like I said, I'm not Miracle. I can't pretend I'm not curious.

"Thanks for doing this," I say as we get into the van. "I'd never have made it back in time." I stare out the window and lick my lips. "So you guys had a good time yesterday? You and Ian?"

"We didn't have much time together. He had an eight o'clock performance." Miracle glances over at me with her razor-sharp Meryl Streep eyes. "You want to ask me about it, right? You want to know the story of me and Ian? Did you really forget your essay?"

I laugh and say, "Yes, I forgot my essay. We don't have to talk about it if you don't want to. I just couldn't believe running into you guys like that. You never mentioned anything about him."

"Just like you never mentioned Colette," Miracle notes. "You want to talk about that?" I laugh again and this time she says, "Are you getting giddy on me?"

"Maybe," I admit. "You went back to see the play again, didn't you?"

"Obviously. What about you? Where'd you find her?"

"My kitchen." I tell her about Nina's shower and give an abbreviated version of what happened after. We pull up outside my house and Miracle, still listening, follows me inside. There's leftover stir-fry in the fridge and she helps me eat it as we talk about Colette. This time I don't bring up Ari. Lately his existence gives me a bad feeling, and besides, there are plenty of other things to talk about.

"So Ian Chappell," I say, finally steering the topic back to Miracle. "Is he as cool as he seems? All actorly and clever?" I can't ask for the juiciest details, like the difference between a sixteen-year-old and thirty-year-old in bed. Miracle and I don't have that kind of relationship.

Miracle rinses her dirty fork in the sink as she stares at me. "He's not like anybody I've ever met," she confesses.

"And is it serious? Are you going to see him again?"

Miracle's expression tells me I've gone too far but she says, "Whenever I can, but no, I wouldn't say it's serious. He has a kid in Montreal. He meets people all the time, you know?"

"You mean he's seeing other people?"

"Not now." Miracle's eyebrows spring together. "You think I'd hang around if he was hooking up with other people? I just mean he's not the type to settle down at twenty-nine. He's got this amazing energy, like he's in a constant state of evolution." Her eyes shine as she talks about him. "It's inspiring to be around someone like that who's willing to take risks just to be able to find the truth in something."

"That sounds cool," I say. It's good to see her excited about something real for a change. If I didn't know better I'd think we were stuck inside a musical and she was about to belt out a torch song.

"Yeah, well . . ." Miracle nods and rinses her fork a second time. "You and Colette looked good together. She's really pretty—in that classic, sophisticated way."

"Thanks." We both know this conversation stays between us. That's understood. "She's really cool too." I smile as I remember Colette that first day in my kitchen, raving about cheesecake. Miracle smiles too and it's a nice moment, this secret between us, but I feel like I lied somewhere along the way. Miracle's story had a kid in Montreal but mine didn't have an Ari.

I don't have a clue who Ari Lightman really is. I wouldn't let Colette tell me anything about him so now I just wonder. Maybe he's an ex-member of Lunatic Fringe, one of those lean guitarist types with dirty hair and agile fingers. Maybe he's some rich guy that can't stand to see his middle-aged wife naked anymore. Or maybe he's an intellectual sex symbol, working on his PhD on pastoral poetry. I don't know. The only thing I can be sure of is that come Sunday his prescription's no longer in Colette's bathroom. I check the garbage, her drug cabinet and the collection of bath oils and body butters that surround the bathtub. I try to remember how many pills were left in the bottle the last time I looked. Has he been coming around enough to finish them off? Have they stopped seeing each other?

The scenarios could make me ballistic if I let them.

I could ask Colette for the truth but I won't do that either. It feels too late. So I stand in her kitchen, put my arms around her and whisper something dirty in her ear. She laughs and lets me spread my hands over her breasts but her eyes look distracted. I assured her about Miracle again the last time I was here. It can't be that.

"You want to go out?" I ask. "Drive somewhere?"

"How about California?" Colette quips, one hand on my chest. "Go west, young man!"

"Now you're talking. I'll take the first shift at the wheel." I curl a hand around her waist and squeeze. "We can learn to surf—get jobs selling sunglasses and Che Guevara T-shirts on Venice Beach."

Colette smiles as she pulls away. "You'll end up there eventually, you know, making movies and getting laid by a succession of blond starlets."

"So you've got my future all plotted out," I say with a grin. "How about you? What happens to the future hotshot lawyer?"

"Who knows?" Colette says mysteriously. "That's a long way off." She taps her foot against mine and says, "I saw my parents the other day. Did I tell you?"

Nope. She must've told Ari. I fight the temptation to give in to jealousy. If I can't beat it, Colette and I won't work. That's the deal. She's been pretty clear about it.

I shake my head and she continues: "It was my aunt Rachel's funeral and of course—"

"I didn't know your aunt died," I cut in. "I'm sorry."

I stroke her arm and she says, "I'm okay, thanks. It was sudden, a heart attack, so my mom was pretty much in pieces but the weirdest thing is that it looks like they'll be raising her daughter, Shan."

"What about your uncle?"

"No one knows where he is. They went through this long, complicated adoption process to bring Shan over from China and then he disappeared when she was five—didn't leave a note or anything, just packed his suitcase one night three years ago and that was it. But the really funny thing is that he would've hated for my parents to take Shan. He used to be part of my parents' church too but he couldn't stand it. He and my aunt got out."

"You make it sound like a cult."

"I guess it feels like that if you don't believe in it," she says. "Maybe all religions feel like that if you don't believe them. I don't know." She shrugs and fits her fingers between mine. "It was just so weird being back in the church with all these people I used to know. They seemed the same as ever and I felt like a totally different person."

"I've never even been to a funeral," I say softly. "That must be really hard." I know there's nothing I could've done but I wish she'd told me about her aunt sooner.

Colette skims her fingers slowly across my cheek and looks into my eyes. "Sometimes I forget about how young you are and other times that's all I can see."

I get that she's in a contemplative mood but I hate when we talk about this.

"Imagine this little girl coming all the way from China and ending up with my conservative, evangelical, suburban parents," she says. "It feels like a cheat. I mean, what happens if she turns out to be a lesbian or gets pregnant at fourteen?"

"Life is crazy." Suddenly I'm thinking of Nina's dead husband, and Burke and Brianna sprawled out on my basement couch. "Are your parents really that bad?"

"No." She sighs into her hand. "They just make so many things harder than they have to be."

"You turned out okay."

Colette's cheeks swell until she erupts into laughter. "That's debatable, right?" She motions towards me as evidence. Then she grabs the bottom of my shirt and pulls me towards her. She kisses me wetly on the mouth and says, "I'm picking up the puppy next week. You want to come?"

What? Ari doesn't want to go? "You mean actually go out in public together," I tease. "I dunno."

"It's a farm." Colette twists my arm around my back, pretending to be impatient. "I'd hardly call it public."

"Sure, I'll go. You pick out a name for her yet?" The last time I was here she was highlighting suggestions in baby name books. Allie. Molly. Sadie. Pretty much anything ending with an *ee* sound.

"I was thinking of Gracie," she says. "Not too cutesy but pretty."

What did I just say? "It's nice," I tell her. "Not trying too hard." Unlike me. I'm still struggling to get past the mystery of the disappearing prescription bottle. I kiss her again to quiet my head. She's wearing a thong and my fingers dip into her pants and stray back to the string. *Incredible.* The feel of her skin is exactly what I need right now. I unzip her pants and cup her ass in my hands. I'm amazed that she never gets tired of me grabbing at her, never tells me to stop. Maybe that's why I haven't pushed things along and asked her about sleeping together.

Colette touches me over my jeans. She has this fierce-concentration look on her face and I know exactly what she's about to do but this time I stop her. "Let's lie down," I tell her, my voice projecting testosterone. I brush her hair back behind her shoulders. "I want to be inside you." Our eyes gulp each other in. The stare's so intense that it makes my face burn. Before, everything else was enough. It's not like that anymore.

"Do you want that?" I ask, not quite whispering. For a second I feel like your typical hormonally driven sixteen-year-old guy trying to sell a generically reluctant girl on the idea of sex. Only, I don't think there's anything generic about us and I know better than to think I could push Colette into anything.

"It sounds *fantastic.*" Colette's mouth transforms the word into undiluted longing. The tone makes me ache deeper. I'm the lucki-est guy on the planet. My ego has swollen to Marlon Brando dimensions.

Colette licks expertly at my ear. "But are you sure?"

My face tingles with embarrassment. Jesus, I've got this all backwards. I thought I was giving her the space and time to come around to this moment. But all along she's been waiting for me. "You know it's not my first time," I tell her. I don't say that it'll only be my second.

"I know." She looks into my eyes. "I just don't want to feel like I'm influencing you one way or the other." If she keeps talking about my age I won't be able to do it. Would she notice if I covered my ears? "Pervert that I am, I don't want you to blame *all* your future sexual kinks on me," she jokes.

Fine. Okay, that's fine. I can handle the kidding around. It's bet-ter if we don't take this too seriously.

"Do you have a room and position preference for this?" she asks slyly and my brain stalls. I gawk at her flawless lips and un-zipped pants, racking my mind for something halfway clever to say.

Colette doesn't wait. She grabs my hand, leads me into the bed-room and throws every last pillow onto the floor, like we'll need more space on the bed than usual. Then she strips off everything except her thong and stares at me with glowing eyes. I yank off my shirt, feel for the condom in my pocket and toss it onto the bed-spread. Colette reclines on the bed, her weight on her arms. I tug off my socks and jeans and meet her stare. The excitement's almost too much to take. I feel like a virgin, despite Kat.

"Come here," Colette murmurs, beckoning me forward. Her lips arch into a heady smile as I step towards her. "What are you waiting for?"

I climb on the bed with her and finish what we've started.

eighteen

I park three doors down from my house and kiss Colette goodbye. The two of us smell like sex. I didn't notice that back in her apartment. "I wish I didn't have to go," I tell her. "I wish I could stay the night." I imagine what it would be like to sleep with my body curved around hers all night and wake up with the morning sun in our eyes. We could have breakfast together. We could have morning-sunlight sex.

"It's okay," Colette says sensibly. "We should get some sleep. We both have to be up early tomorrow." She pecks me on the cheek and rests her hand against the back of my neck. "I'm really sleepy. Aren't you?" Probably. But I'm too wrapped up in her to have much awareness of myself.

I get out of the car and listen to her drive off. Inside the house I wander along the hall and into the kitchen, my brain gorging on details from earlier tonight, oblivious to the present. A male figure's hulking at the counter in the darkness, his back towards me. I jump out of my skin, crying, "Jesus, Dad, you scared the shit out of me! What're you doing creeping around in the dark like that?"

Dad swings around with a jolt. "Mason!" Now I can make out a bottle of water in his hand. His fingers clutch it tightly as he takes a step forward. "You almost gave me a heart attack. I thought you were in bed."

"Dustin and I were out with Yolanda," I lie. "She and Zoe had a fight. She was pretty upset."

Dad peers at the microwave clock. The luminous blue digits read 3:14. "It's so late," he says, coughing into his empty hand. The last time we had a conversation about me being out late on a school night I'd just turned fifteen, and so far Dad hasn't mentioned anything about school but his tone implies it.

"I know." I yawn like I've had a tough night consoling a friend. Is that sex smell as potent as I think it is? Maybe I should've just told him I was with a girl. "I'm exhausted. I don't know how I'm going to get up tomorrow." I say it before he can. "What're you doing down here, anyway?" I point to his water bottle, shifting the emphasis away from me. "You look like a serial killer down here in the dark."

"A serial killer in a bathrobe." Dad laughs. He coughs again, raises the water to his lips and gulps some down. "I woke up with this annoying dry cough," he explains. "I hope I'm not coming down with something."

"Yeah, well, I better get to bed," I tell him. "I'll see you tomorrow."

"Night, Mason," he says to my back.

I head up to my room and collapse into bed with my musty sex clothes on. Some of the smell fades during the night, but when my alarm goes off in the morning the first thing I do is sprint for the shower. Brianna's the only one in the kitchen when I get there.

168

Lately we've been getting along okay, but now her face creases up like a seventy-nine-year-old woman's. *Shit. Do I still reek?*

"Morning," I say guardedly.

She nods and pushes another spoonful of cereal between her lips. She's wearing blue eye shadow all the way up to her brows and gloopy mascara. It's a terrible look, especially first thing Monday morning. I'm surprised Nina hasn't said something to her.

Then Burke stomps into the kitchen behind Nina, which makes four of us sitting around the table for breakfast. "Your dad's canceling his appointments and staying home today," Nina tells me as she shakes a serving of Lucky Charms out of the box for Burke. "He's not feeling very well."

The way Dad sounded last night I'm not surprised to hear he's taking a sick day. But that parallel universe where I can touch, taste and even be inside Colette makes this one—sitting around munching cereal with Nina and the two Bs—feel fuzzy and surreal, and it takes me a couple of seconds to muster a response. "I guess that cough medicine he was drinking down last night didn't do the trick, huh?"

Burke folds his ankles up under his legs and watches Nina pour milk into his bowl. "Didn't seem to," Nina says. "Poor guy. He was up most of the night."

I wonder if Nina knows about me coming home late. Next time I have to be more careful. *Next time.* I fixate on the details of my golden secret life all through breakfast and morning classes. Colette's mouth. Her skin. Her gorgeous legs. The incredible things we've done together, the things we'll do again. I'm on fire inside, tumbling over the memory of last night, hoarding the images.

I'm so gone that I don't realize how quiet I'm being until Jamie sidles up to me in the cafeteria lunch line later and asks where I've checked out to. I smile to acknowledge that I've been spacing.

Meanwhile Monica G and Hugo are play-fighting over possession of a blueberry muffin in front of me in line, arms swinging and bodies twisting.

Hugo slips his fingers into her armpit and tickles. Monica jumps back, accidentally elbowing me in the rib. "Sorry!" she exclaims, jaw dropping as she spins to look at me. "You okay, Mason?"

"Just a punctured lung," I joke.

She hugs my shoulder apologetically, Hugo frowning as he looks on. The last time I talked to Monica she was telling me the bad news about the lotto ad (she didn't get it). She said she'd learned her lesson and that if anything else came up she wouldn't breathe a word unless she'd locked down the role. There are benefits to keeping quiet if you can; I understand that.

I buy a Gardenburger, which is less grim than either the hamburger or cheeseburger, sit down with Jamie and try to stay in the moment. I could tell him where my mind's at—he already knows about Colette anyway—but for now I just want to keep the news to myself.

So I stay tuned in to the present for lunch and then switch my thoughts back to Colette and let the rest of the afternoon blur right by me. It's not until I'm home from school later that the feeling that I've swallowed a star begins to jog towards something else. Needing to talk to her. Needing to know when next time will be.

I check my cell for messages but won't let myself call. I fucked things up with Kat; I can't let that happen with Colette. It's more important than ever that I be cool.

Unfortunately Colette doesn't get in touch for three days, during which my brain runs wild imagining the worst—that she's busy with Ari, her palms on his chest, straddling him the way she straddled me. The worst thing about imagining the worst is that in this case it's probably true. But I don't call; I can't. And when *she* does I'm as cool as James Bond in a custom-made Italian suit.

Day four I'm back in her apartment, acting like Ari or whatever happened in the three days between doesn't matter. Colette whips up a seafood risotto while I stand in the kitchen dicing whatever she needs me to dice and measuring whatever she needs me to measure, but mainly leaning against the counter and comparing notes on Vancouver with her because I just found out she and Andrea were there visiting a mutual friend a couple of years ago.

We eat the risotto and pile the dishes into the sink. Then we're stripping down on her couch and I honestly forget about every single thing in the universe except what we're doing. There's the couch, Colette's legs folded tightly around my back, and then the floor beside the coffee table, where we both get carpet burn on our knees and laugh about it afterwards. "I hope you don't have gym class tomorrow," Colette jokes, tapping my chest with her foot as we lounge naked on the couch. "How would you explain your injuries?"

"You don't think they'd believe the truth?" I kid back.

"They probably would." Colette's foot pushes harder against my chest. "And then all the teenage girls at your school would hate me."

A goofy smile bursts onto my lips. I love when she says cheesy things like that. "No reason to hate you," I say, pinching her big toe. "There's plenty of me to go around."

Colette's sexy laugh makes me want to start over again and we do, a little, but then she tells me it's getting late and that "people will want to know where you are."

Generic people. Maybe that's easier for her to say than "your father and Nina." She's right, though, and I promised myself that I'd be careful this time, but careful in theory is easier than careful in practice. Once I step inside her apartment I never want to leave.

Colette slides closer to me on the couch and presses my hand to her lips like she knows I'm disappointed. "I'll drive," I say. We both know she lets me do it to make me feel better about not having a car and not being twenty-three. But if I actually was a twenty-three-year-old version of myself, with a career as a struggling actor and a secondhand Volkswagen Rabbit, maybe she wouldn't like me as much as she does right now. Maybe my potential is what she gets off on. My hot-young-thing status.

She's never really pretended otherwise so it shouldn't bother me. It doesn't really. I just . . .

I don't know.

This time I'm conscientious about washing the sex smell off before we leave. It's twenty to twelve when I walk through my front door and everyone's already in bed, which means I could've spent another few hours at Colette's after all.

There's always more to want. I'm already thinking about next time again. And the rug burns on my knees. The days in between. Ari Lightman. The way Colette's breasts fit in my hands. The things I know about her body now. The same things Ari knows.

Considering how great tonight and last time were, there shouldn't be any space for him in my mind. I need to keep my head on the pluses of this arrangement, not the minuses. What Colette and I have should feel like a thing of wonder, lighter than oxygen.

I remind myself that it does, mostly. It's the leftover bit I need to work on.

nineteen

BRIANNA'S SLATHERED ON the mascara and blue eye shadow again, making my head hurt as she glances up from her cereal bowl at me the next morning. "Hey," she mumbles as I pour myself a glass of orange juice.

Brianna's not a big morning talker so I don't take the minimalism personally. Like I said before, we've been getting along all right lately. Not well enough for me to advise her that she shouldn't wear blue eye shadow, but okay.

"Hey," she repeats with added volume as I raise the orange juice to my lips. "Was that Colette's car you got out of last night?"

"What?" I stop with my glass in midair.

"You know, my aunt's friend Colette. The one who was here for the engagement party." Brianna shovels a spoonful of cereal into her mouth and scrutinizes me.

"So now you're spying on me?" My skull throbs.

"Hardly," she says sarcastically. "Your dad keeps waking me up with all his coughing."

He's been coughing for days now, despite the medication his doctor put him on. *And Brianna's bedroom overlooks the street.* My eyeballs go dry in their sockets as I stare at her. "Who I was with is none of your business, you got it?" My voice is tinged with anger but I don't shout. I put my glass down on the counter and say, "You need to shut up about that fast."

Brianna stops chewing and glares at me. "You don't have to freak, you know." Her spoon scrapes against the bottom of the bowl. "I was just asking." Her superior tone reverberates in my ears and I grind my teeth together, panic mixing with anger in my gut.

"I really need you to do me a favor on this one," I plead, changing tactics. "Just don't say anything about what you saw, okay?" If Nina hears about this we're done. Colette won't let me within a hundred feet of her.

"Whatever." Brianna stares down at her bowl so that all I can see is BLUE.

"Thanks," I say.

"Uh-huh."

I leave for school with an empty stomach. I need to put some distance between me and the house. My stomach churns as I walk. Trusting Brianna's a gigantic leap of faith but I don't have a choice. I can't tell Colette about this either, not now that things are really happening between us. I mean, that stuff about Ari and the days in between could be purely my imagination. She might even be finished with him. That could be part of the reason the timing was right for us to finally do it.

I speed up, determined to track down Jamie or Miracle as soon as I get to GS. I need a damage control plan. Fast. Unfortunately Y's the first person I run into in the hall. "You look like hell," she observes.

"Thanks. You seen Jamie or Miracle around?"

"Nope." Her lips form a thin line. "You know, every time I see you lately you look like a version of this." She motions to my distressed form. "Is it Kat?"

"No." I slouch, my gaze still searching the area for any sign of Jamie or Miracle. "Everything's fine with Kat. I mean, the usual. Why? Have you heard something about Kat?"

Yolanda's eyes shrink as she processes my words. *There she goes monitoring me again. Exactly what I don't need right now.* "No," she says. "But she's not the one acting strange." She pats me on the back, opting to take pity on me. "If I see Jamie or Miracle I'll let them know you're looking for them."

"Great." I hurry off to find one of them before homeroom, desperate to spill my guts. I rush past their lockers and homerooms. *No luck.* I check the cafeteria and then the parking lot. *Nope. Nope. Nope.* I don't see either of them until lunch and then it's too late. I'm burnt out on anxiety. The tension's turned a corner and nothing anyone says will make a difference.

Of course I have the conversation anyway. I pull Jamie aside and tell him. Maybe I'll tell Miracle tomorrow and get her take on things too. I haven't decided. Anyway, a pensive look hangs over Jamie's eyes, like he's thinking all the info over. "You think Brianna will say anything?" he asks.

My stomach clenches again as I shrug. "I don't have a good feeling about this."

"Maybe you should give Colette the heads-up," Jamie says slowly. "And have some kind of backup story ready for your dad."

"A backup story that involves running into Colette and

somehow ending up in her car at eleven-thirty at night but which I failed to bring up earlier," I snap. "Like anything I could come up with would make for an even close to believable coincidence." I work my hands into my pockets and stand there exhaling jagged bursts of air. I should've parked farther down my street. This is my fault. Bumping into Miracle and Ian in Toronto should've been enough to let me know we needed to be profoundly careful.

"I know." Jamie shrugs too. "It's rough. I'm just saying you need to be prepared." He cocks his head and adds, "You had to know this was coming. It's one crazy situation."

I'm wasting my time. He thinks I have it coming because of Kat. I can't believe everything comes back to this. I turn to walk away, tension spiraling into anger and pounding in my chest. "Where do you think you're going?" Jamie shouts.

"You're still mad," I yell back. "I don't want to talk to you if you're still mad."

"I'm not mad," Jamie insists. "Fuck. Would you come back? You're acting like a total spaz."

"And you're not acting like a friend," I shout. Two freshman guys sharing a pair of earphones on the bleachers glance over at us with puzzled expressions. "Just admit you're still jealous. Kat and I are barely even speaking and you're still jealous."

"You're being a prick." Jamie scowls. "I thought this was about Colette—or is it just about being able to bone whoever you want without getting caught?"

"You're never going to let it go, are you?" I stop dead in my tracks and swing around to face him. His mouth's hanging open and he looks like he wants to rip my arms out of their sockets. If this wasn't about Kat, it is now.

Jamie jerks his head back and laughs hollowly. "Why don't you try that line on Kat and see how she takes it?"

"Fuck you," I mutter. "You don't know anything about that. You think that because the three of us were friends you're some kind of expert on the situ—"

"She's not talking to me because of something that you did," Jamie interrupts. "Don't give me that shit about it not having anything to do with me. It's like you don't even care about her—you're already in it up to your eyes with this"—he waves both hands frenetically in front of himself—"this twenty-three-year-old *woman*—and now you expect me to give you advice on your love life."

I watch his hands drift slowly back to his sides. My arms feel like lead. I don't know where to start with what he just said.

"Of course I care." I pull at my hair and scratch at my hand, right where the bandage used to be. "There's nothing I can do about Kat. There's nothing else I can say to her. It's all . . ." I shrug helplessly and the truth is I don't even know whether I'm angry with Jamie anymore. All I know is I'm losing it. The things he's talking about are done and over with, whether I want them to be or not, but this thing with Colette's still happening and it's about to explode in my face. If I were any more shaken up I'd be having a frigging seizure.

Jamie eyes me neutrally. He jerks his fingers inside his sleeve and listens to the silence.

"All what?" he asks finally. His gaze shoots skyward as his fingers slip back out of his sleeve. "Forget it," he mumbles. "That's none of my business."

His mouth makes a clicking noise when he opens it again. "This is about Colette," he says squarely. "So this is what you do—you talk to her. You go over there tonight and tell her about Brianna. You do it in person. In case she takes it really bad. It's harder for her to break it off if you're there in the flesh." He shrugs and buries his hands in his sweatshirt pockets. "Either that or you just hold your breath and wait for Brianna to crack, right?"

He's got my options covered and they suck. I bob my head up and down, approximating a nod. We walk back to the cafeteria together and I don't feel any better than I did ten minutes ago but I stay quiet. There's nothing else to say.

The house is empty when I walk through the front door later. Burke and Brianna both have dentist appointments straight after school and Nina won't have them home until after five-thirty. For a minute after I remember that, I feel like I can breathe again. I lie down on the basement couch with my shoes on and blast the TV volume up until the entire house pulses with sound. There are so many things that I don't want to think about lately, and before today they all went back to that Saturday-night party and this faceless guy named Ari Lightman.

The idea that my relationship with Colette hinges on Brianna's ability to keep a secret eclipses both of them but I can still feel Ari questions burning a hole in my brain. It sounds like Colette's friend Leslie knows him fairly well (enough to barrel downstairs to say hello when she thought I was him) and you don't leave a prescription in just anyone's bathroom. How long have they been hooking up and is it still happening?

I might be kidding myself if I think I can force myself to stop caring about what they are to each other. The further I get into this, the more it seems to matter. I cringe just thinking Ari's name. The situation with Colette is complicated enough without him and I have to wonder, why am I doing this to myself when there are countless other hot girls in Glenashton? I have at least three untried phone numbers crumpled up in various pockets.

Is it possible that I could be imagining the whole Colette Fournier addiction? That I just like the idea of being a junkie? It's a comforting thought, that I'm the root of all this drama. I don't have a problem with being the center of my own universe. The opposite is what scares me.

So I've got the TV booming and my mind racing and I'm doing what I can to convince myself that at the core I'm okay with everything but the noise is too much, even for me. I turn down the volume and then the phone rings, as if to make up for it. Chris Cipolla talks into my ear and his voice sounds like part of my past, in the best, most uncomplicated way.

"You still interested in working at JB?" Chris wants to know. "Letitia quit this morning. She's moving to Montreal with her boyfriend. Anyway, there's a spot open and Darlene wants to talk to you around five if you still want the job." Darlene is his manager. Chris says she's an okay boss, as long as you have a good attitude and no visible tattoos or piercings, which she apparently considers unhygienic.

"I still want the job," I confirm. "I'll be there at five." It looks like money's one issue I can strike from my list. Now if there was only a way I could keep Brianna quiet and get Colette to ditch Ari, I'd really be on to something. "Thanks."

Chris wishes me luck and hangs up and I turn off the TV and head upstairs to get ready for my interview with Darlene. This battle's still raging in my mind, asking me what I really want for myself, but in the meantime I'm changing my clothes and remembering that night I spent fondling Colette's Lunatic Fringe T-shirt. I can't stop thinking about her. Ari's invisible presence in her life and the headache our secret status has become almost make me wish I could, but it's impossible. I can conjure exactly how Colette tastes anytime I want. Or the way she coughs when she comes or her special sleepy smile in the middle of the night, one hand melting into my chest. How do you purge those details from your mind when they're swimming along with you every second of the day?

I don't have time to work it all out now. I down a glass of water fresh out of the kitchen tap, check the time and calculate how long it will take me to walk down to JB. The way I figure it I have another twenty minutes to spare. All of a sudden I glimpse a clump of black fur out of the corner of my eye. I spin around and stare at Billy curled up under the kitchen table. He looks peaceful but I don't need another claw tearing through my hand to convince me otherwise. I got the message last time. The thing is, he's not moving.

I don't mean that he's quiet or still. I mean he's completely motionless. He's fourteen years old, for God's sake; he could be dead. I step tentatively towards the table, expecting him to scurry away or screech out a sinister meow.

Billy stays coiled up, as passive as I've ever seen him. I get down on my knees and stretch out my arm but I know he's gone before I touch him. My fingers stroke his fur for the first time. I've never touched anything dead before but I don't feel sad. I don't feel anything much about it.

The big problem here is that I'm running out of time. I can't leave him as he is and let Nina and the kids discover him later but I don't have time to bury him in the backyard. What else do you do with dead animals?

I phone the local humane society and the answering machine picks up on the third ring. The message quotes an emergency number but Billy's emergency is over with. I just need to find out how to clean up the mess, hopefully in under ten minutes. My next call's to Jamie, because he used to have a dog, and he tells me that Nina's vet will dispose of the remains. Of course, I don't know who Nina's vet is and this isn't the kind of news I want to break over the phone.

In the end I pick up Billy, lay him in one of Nina's old moving boxes and carry his makeshift coffin into the garage. Then I call my dad at work and explain about my interview and finding Billy dead under the kitchen table. Dad's subdued over the phone. "Brianna loves that cat," he says. "She'll be so upset."

"I know." A brief spasm of sympathy grips me. "I have to go. I'll be late for my interview."

"You go," Dad tells me. "I'll get in touch with Nina and let her know what happened."

"Okay." *There goes my sympathy button again.* You'd think I slaughtered the damn cat. Haven't I done the best I can here? "I'll see you later."

"Good luck with the interview," Dad tells me.

"Thanks." Somehow, even though I know it's stupid, I can't shake the feeling that I don't deserve it.

twenty

BILLY'S CROSSED MY path enough times to give me permanent bad luck but the interview unfolds textbook perfect. After about two minutes I can tell Darlene likes me and after another twenty we're discussing a training schedule. Chris gives me a thumbs-up from the counter when I leave. I smile back and celebrate by buying homemade gelato from the ice cream place across the street.

Colette must be late leaving work because I bump into her out on the sidewalk, coffee in her right hand. Between Billy dying and my impromptu interview the possibility of running into her didn't occur to me. There's so much to talk about that I don't know what to say first.

"Mason," she says, her eyes scanning cautiously around before holding on mine. "How're you today?" It's a weird way to greet someone you slept with the night before. I want to fling my arms around her, bury my fingers in her hair and smell her skin.

"Not bad." I smile despite her lukewarm reaction to running into me in the street. I can't help but be happy to see her, especially after our last couple of nights together. "I just landed a job at The Java Bean. I'll be serving your coffee from now on."

It's meant to be good news but Colette shields her eyes from the sun and pulls her head abruptly back. "I didn't know you were looking for a job," she says sharply.

"It's almost summer," I remind her, smile dying on my lips. She has such a capacity to make me feel like shit and I don't even think she realizes it. I was going to call her later and ask about dropping by her place tomorrow night. I need to warn her about Brianna but before that I want to explain how amazing our last few nights together have been. It's nothing I haven't said before but the next time I say it needs to be different. I have to confess. I'm not just having a good time with her; it means more than that.

If I was smart I'd keep both of the above a secret. I guess I don't know how to feel the way I do about Colette and be smart about it. Something inside me's sure she deserves the truth, even if she doesn't want to hear it.

"We need to talk," I tell her. "Can I call you later?" I'm not about to suggest going back to her place now. She was unhappy enough with my job offer.

"Leslie's coming over tonight," she says. "We're planning a road trip to Florida next month and we're trying to work out the details." She never mentioned the trip before. Maybe that's something else Ari was first to hear. My confidence level's plummeted in the last sixty seconds. I'm right about those days in between. Just because Colette and I slept together doesn't mean Ari's out of the picture. "We can talk tomorrow." She ventures a restrained smile. "Call me around nine?"

"Sure." I comb my fingers swiftly through my hair. It's starting to get long at the back. Last night she couldn't stop playing with it. "You know this job doesn't have anything to do with you. It was the summer plan all along."

Colette clasps her hands in front of her and stands ballerina straight. Her legs are bare under a floral skirt that comes down well past her knees and she's wearing this purple beaded bracelet thing on her wrist. I picture the silky thong she's wearing under all those flowers. If we were down in her apartment I could hike up her skirt and slide my fingers inside the silk. We could do it against the wall, still wearing our clothes.

Colette blinks in slow motion as she stares at me. A hint of her perfume wafts through the air between us and it occurs to me that this is the closest I'm going to get to her today. "It's fine, Mason," she says. "Don't worry."

But she does worry me. All that stuff about the other phone numbers is bullshit. I don't want to call any other girls.

"I should go," she says hastily. "Congratulations on the new job."

"Yeah, thanks." Suddenly I don't give a shit about JB. "I'll call you tomorrow." It's official; I'm a hardcore junkie. I want to kiss her so much that every cell in my body is straining towards hers, singing like an army of crickets.

"Terrific," she says, charging off towards the parking lot.

I swallow a spoonful of melting gelato and watch her go. This could be the beginning of the end and I'm powerless to do anything about it. Maybe I should take my chances with Brianna after all. Just because she's bitchy doesn't mean she can't keep a secret. The two things are completely unrelated.

I consider that on the way home but when I walk through the

front door my thoughts skid back to Billy in the garage. Dad and Burke are in the kitchen toasting cheese sandwiches and I stand beside Burke and say, "I'm really sorry about your cat."

Burke stares silently up at me and Dad says, "Nina and Brianna took it to the vet."

"Him," I correct.

"Of course." Dad flips the sandwiches over with a spatula. "*Him.* Anyway, they're going to grab something on the way home, so we thought we'd have a boys' dinner tonight." He points at me with the spatula. "Which includes you, of course. Can I interest you in a cheese sandwich?"

"I'm more in a tuna melt mood," I say, pulling out a can. "Anyone else?"

"Sure," Dad says, trying to sound cheerful. "I can put away two sandwiches."

I glance automatically down at Burke, who is warily eyeing the tuna. "Do you like tuna fish, Burke?"

"Sometimes," he says cautiously. "Can I see it?" I open the can and hold it under his chin. He peeks inside and takes a huge sniff, like he's trying to clear his sinuses.

"What's the verdict?" I ask, relieved that he doesn't seem too bad off and that the hard job of telling him about Billy's been handled by someone else.

Burke shakes his head and pulls at his shorts. "It looks weird and lumpy," he announces.

I hold it under my own nose and inhale, trying to understand what he finds objectionable. This would've been Billy's favorite meal. It's funny to think we had anything in common, but honestly, I could eat tuna just about any minute of the day, even first thing in the morning.

"That's okay, Burke," Dad says, raising his fist to his mouth to cover his lingering cough. "You can just have the cheese."

So we fry up a bunch of sandwiches and eat them at the kitchen table with a side of sour-cream-and-onion potato chips. Burke finishes his sandwich first. He sits there swinging his legs under the chair and staring hungrily at my tuna melt. "Do you wanna try?" I ask. "You can have some of mine."

"Okay," Burke says.

I pass him my sandwich and he takes an ant-sized bite and chews thoughtfully. Then he tears off a second, humongous chunk with his front teeth and breaks into a grin. "I like it," he declares.

"Have it," I tell him. "I can make another one." The frying pan's still on the stove and I toss on another sandwich and tell the two of them about my new job at JB. Dad congratulates me and I say thanks and that if I seem jumpy from now on it's due to caffeine overconsumption.

In the middle of that Nina and Brianna come home. Brianna's in flip-flops and she shuffles into the kitchen with raccoon eyes, gaping at our sandwiches.

"I'm sorry about Billy," I say gently.

Nina drapes one arm around Brianna, squeezing her shoulder. "We had him a long time," she says. "We were lucky."

I stare at the new white skin on the back of my hand and silently disagree. A pit bull would've been friendlier.

"You put him in that box," Brianna says, looking over at me.

At first I don't know what she's getting at. "He was under the table," I explain. "He was already gone when I got here."

"You could've stayed with him," she argues. "He's not a piece of garbage to put in your garage." This morning's shock of blue eye shadow is gone and she rubs her messy black-lined eyes and talks into her fist. "Just because he's not yours doesn't mean he doesn't matter."

"I know that." I've never seen her like this. She's taking Billy's death even harder than I expected, but what surprises me most is that somehow she's turned this into my fault. "I had an interview. Otherwise I would've stayed. I don't know who your vet is. I didn't know what else to do."

"You did the right thing," Nina assures me. "She's just upset." Nina strokes Brianna's hair and kisses her head and for the briefest second there I actually miss my mother. Not even my mother but the idea of a mother.

"An interview with Colette," Brianna says mockingly. "That kind of interview?"

My shoulders twitch as I glare at her, hands shaking with anger. My secret didn't last a day. She shot me down the first chance she got.

Dad and Nina swap perplexed looks, but Brianna's eyes stay fixed on mine. "That's enough, Brianna," Nina commands. "This isn't Mason's fault. What happened to Billy is no excuse for you to act like this."

"I'm not acting like anything." Brianna's red-rimmed eyes glower at me. "Do you think he would've done that if it was his cat?"

"You just can't keep your mouth shut, can you?" I say bitterly, my mouth gritty.

"Keep my mouth shut about what exactly?" She pokes her bottom lip out at me and I can't believe how much I can hate someone I hardly know.

"Brianna, I could've wrapped your frigging cat in a burial shroud—it wouldn't make any difference to you." The cat's just an easy excuse. She never intended to keep her mouth shut. Taking a sledgehammer to my gut is all in a day's work. "You're just one fucked-up girl. I've tried to be nice to you, you know? Did you even notice that?" I don't give her a chance to answer. "Then the second I need you to do one thing for me you throw it back in my face like that." I snap my fingers and frown down at my sizzling tuna melt. I shove it with the spatula and snap, "And it's not going to bring your cat back either. You're doing it for nothing." Everyone's gawking at me, clueless and shocked, and I turn my back to them and study my sandwich, my jaw vibrating and my blood humming under my skin.

"This isn't one of your finer moments, Mason," Dad says from across the kitchen. *And here I was expecting thunderous applause.* Thank you, Dad. Thanks, audience. It's been a blast. "Would you just pick up that sandwich and go, please?"

"Where?" I say numbly.

"How about upstairs?" His face is white and his voice is coated in sarcasm. I've embarrassed him in front of his new family.

I leave the sandwich sizzling in the pan and brush by Brianna. She doesn't look at me. She doesn't need to. She's done enough damage for one day.

Dad comes up to talk to me thirty minutes later. He sits on the edge of my bed and says, "I don't ever want to hear you talk to Brianna like that again—no matter what comes out of her mouth. Do you understand?" I fold my arms silently in front of me, anger simmering just below the surface, and listen to him say, "I thought we cleared this up last time. What happened?"

"You saw what happened. She just blamed me for Billy dying. She twists everything around and treats people like shit. I'm not going to apologize for anything. If she can't act like a normal human being with me she can't expect me to act like one with her."

"I know she has issues," Dad concedes. "And Nina's talked to her about that—and will speak to her about it again—but I can't have you escalating the problems, Mason. You know how she feels about that cat. Have some empathy." I don't give a shit about his analysis. I'm waiting, I'm just waiting for him to say Colette's name. Brianna must've told him and Nina the rest of the story by now. I'm doomed. "I'd like you to come downstairs with me and talk to her."

"I'm not apologizing," I maintain. I'll spontaneously combust if we don't get to this in another two seconds; I've had enough. "Aren't you going to ask me about Colette?" Her name on my lips makes me shiver.

"I don't know who that is." Dad's eyes bear down on me. "Is it supposed to be a secret?"

"It was." He honestly doesn't know. I can tell by the way he's looking at me. "Andrea's friend from the shower, Colette Fournier."

"What about her?" he asks.

I crunch my fingers into fists. "Do you remember her?" I must be feeling destructive. There's no other explanation.

"Sure," Dad says, frowning. "I remember her."

"We've been seeing each other." I stare him in the face, waiting for a reaction.

Dad's head bobs uneasily on his shoulders. "How old is she? Andrea's age?"

This weird feeling of relief spreads through my shoulder blades. I straighten out my fingers and rest them flat against my stomach. "Twenty-three," I admit. "Almost twenty-four." In three weeks there'll be eight years between us. I'm always conscious of the number that separates us. Colette never forgets and I'm not sure I could either, even if given the chance.

Dad whistles through his teeth. "How long has this been going on?"

"About a month."

"And you're still seeing each other?" he asks.

"We won't be when she finds out you know." I've just nailed the coffin shut and I couldn't tell you why. I'm so broken up that I just stare at him for a few seconds. "She didn't want anyone to know about us." There's such a feeling of release in telling him that it's almost worth the ache. "I need to go talk to her."

"This discussion isn't finished, Mason. I expect some resolution to the antagonism between you and Brianna." Dad's eyes flicker and then he turns slowly away, like he needs time to process what I've just told him. "Go speak to this woman if that's what you need to do. We'll get to the bottom of all this tomorrow."

twenty-one

I FEEL LIKE somebody's pet hamster racing desperately to
nowhere on one of those stationary wheels. What's the point? Is
this supposed to feel like progress? The truth is I've never really
broken up with someone. Technically I won't be the one to do it
now either and I feel horrible. I feel like throwing up in Jamie's car
as he chauffeurs me over to Colette's place.

I didn't think it would be like this in the end. I thought we'd
fight or get sick of each other. No, I didn't even think that. I don't
know what I thought but it wasn't this. I'm torn straight down the
middle—half of me crushed to pieces and the other half staring
out the window, looking past this to the next time when it'll be less
messy, when I won't be sharing with some guy named Ari or looking over my shoulder, expecting to be caught at any minute.

Maybe I should thank Brianna. It's over with; it's done. Once
Colette hears we've been outed she won't be able to get rid of me

fast enough. I tear my eyes away from the window and glance tentatively at Jamie. "Do you want me to wait for you?" he asks.

"I don't know how long it's going to take." If I was in love with Colette would a sense of relief be knotted up with the pain like this? I try to hold on to that thought as we idle in front of her landlord's house. "Maybe you should just take off."

"You can phone me if you need me to come back," Jamie offers.

"Thanks." Remind me to take back every bad thing I ever said about Jamie. He's awesome. He can leap tall buildings in a single bound, snare bad guys in his mighty web and hurtle through the highways of Glenashton in his mom's metallic blue Honda Civic, searching for signals from people in desperate need of emergency transportation.

I thank him again as I get out of the car. My face is numb with nerves and sadness as I step away from him. I wish this didn't have to be so final, that Colette and I could just break up the normal way, leaving the possibilities open.

I trudge towards the door and it seems to me that it should be pouring rain or something dramatic like that but it's not. It's sticky-warm and Colette's neighbor is out watering his front garden in sunglasses and a baseball hat. I feel more like a paperboy than Colette's lover. I don't understand how all this happened in the first place.

I knock at the side door and this tall guy in his late twenties, skinny as me but not half as good-looking, opens it. He's wearing an orange T-shirt with the Orange Crush logo on it and black pants and he's got that stubble look going for him but that's about it. Ari Lightman in the flesh. I don't even have to ask. He looks like he belongs there. I mean, it would never occur to me to answer Colette's door.

"I'm looking for Colette," I tell him. "Is she here?"

"Col's here," he says in a vaguely Eastern European accent. "You want to come down?" He opens the door wider and gestures for me to follow him downstairs. It never would've occurred to me to call her Col either. This guy's miles ahead of me in the Colette Fournier department. I still don't even know whether she's French or what.

"Col," he calls at the bottom of the stairwell. "You have a visitor." I walk into the basement with him and spy two open beer bottles on the living room coffee table. It's a familiar scenario and my gaze shoots over to the kitchen where Colette's standing in the middle of the tile floor in a purple top and white jeans. So much for the floral skirt. So much for making plans with Leslie.

Colette peers back at me with parted lips but Ari speaks first. "I'll leave you two," he says with a backwards step.

"Ari," she protests.

"This is Mason, no?" He runs a hand over his wavy hair and stares casually in my general direction.

"Yes," I tell him. It's such a wicked joke, the three of us hanging out here in her apartment. I'm still waiting for the camera crew to give themselves away.

"It's okay." Ari nods at me. He plucks his car keys out of his pocket and heads for the stairs. I'm not even angry with him. The situation seems bizarrely civilized.

Colette watches him go, the tension in her limbs radiating out towards me. "I thought you were going to call me tomorrow," she says.

"Because you have plans with Leslie tonight." I look at the space where Ari stood seconds ago. "I know. I guess we both had a change in plans."

Colette's hands reach back for the counter. She leans against it and stares at the floor. "You didn't want me to talk about Ari anymore." Her gaze darts up to meet mine. "I told you about him. I wasn't hiding it. You knew."

"I know." I almost laugh, a weird mechanical sound like I'm on the verge of short-circuiting. "That's the really pathetic thing." I rest my hands on the opposite counter, the width of the kitchen separating us. "You must think I'm . . ." I tap my fingernails gingerly against the counter; it sounds like rain. "I guess it doesn't matter to him about us, huh?"

"Is that why you're here?" Colette asks. "To catch me at something you already knew about?"

"No." She's so far away that she might as well be in Florida. Last night feels more like last year. "My dad knows about us. Brianna saw you drop me off last night."

Colette stares past me, deep in thought. I know what she's worried about and it's not me. "Does Nina know?"

"She probably does by now. I don't think her and my dad keep secrets like that." Besides, I didn't ask him to.

"Shit," Colette says vehemently to herself. "Shit." She kneads her forehead with one hand. "This is a disaster." To me it's a much smaller disaster than facing Ari on her doorstep. Obviously we're not on the same wavelength here. I should've already realized that before. I guess maybe I did.

"Don't worry," I tell her. "It's not that bad. They won't do anything about it."

"Maybe it's not that bad for you. I don't think you have a concept of what this is like for me." Colette wraps her arms snugly around herself. Her chin is inches away from sinking into her chest.

She's so frazzled that I want to look after her. How screwed up is that?

"That's okay," I say wryly. "Worry about yourself first, I completely understand."

"Don't get annoying at a time like this," Colette warns. "This is serious, Mason."

"Oh, I know." I force myself to smile. "Before this happened I was going to tell you how much the last couple of nights have meant to me and all this completely sentimental bullshit. You would've hated it. I mean, I knew that. I don't know what I was thinking. You're the shameless, soulless good-time girl. I know that. So now you don't have to listen to my crap and tell me how wrong I am. We can skip straight to the end."

"Mason." Colette's eyes are sad. She feels sorry for me. I'm not the good-time boy she thought I was. "Last night was wonderful. *You're wonderful.* Maybe if I was sixteen it'd be different for us but you can see how things are." She shrugs her elbows helplessly. "You don't need me."

"I never said I needed you." My shoulders hunch forward. I lean on her counter and blink at her like a lost puppy. It feels pathetic but I need to say it anyway. "I just like you more than you like me. It happens."

"*I like you a lot,*" she says forcefully. "You know I do."

"Not enough, though. Not enough to do without Ari or whoever else there is."

"There isn't anyone else," she insists. "There's just Ari."

It should help that he doesn't look like much but it doesn't. There must be some other remarkable thing about him that I've missed.

"He's like an obsession," she confesses, her eyes apologetic. "It doesn't have anything to do with you. It's like quicksand. The harder I try to stay away from him, the worse it gets."

She motions helplessly to the last spot Ari occupied before leaving. "It never really works but it's never really over either." She shakes her head, pausing like she's torn between telling the truth and not wanting to hurt me, and then she says, "You have no idea how angry I make myself, falling into the same stupid pattern, wasting the past two and a half years on something that will probably never be anything more than it is right now. Whenever he asks if he should leave me alone for good, whether that would be better, I know I should say yes—and mean it—but I can't. I fuck it up every time. I call him . . . or he calls me and we're—"

"You don't have to explain," I break in. I've already heard too much. We never stood a chance. Her feelings for him run down to the roots. Sooner or later that would've ruined us, even if we managed to stay a secret.

"I've tried to stop," Colette says, her face earnest and her voice pleading. She wants me to understand. This is what she meant when she talked about *twisted romantic webs,* the secretly remarkable Ari Lightman.

I know exactly what she means. I'm trying to stop at this exact moment.

"Do they know you're here?" she continues. "Your father and Nina?" Her eyes fill with worry again.

"It's fine," I assure her. "I told my dad it was over between us."

"It is." She steps quickly towards me. Her hand reaches for mine on the counter. It's such a feeble gesture that I'm surprised I don't pull away. "I'm sorry."

I grip her fingers, angry with myself for going easy on her. The thing is, I can't make her like me any more than she does. It's exhausting caring about someone more than they care about you. I'll be almost glad to let it go.

I reach across the counter to curve my other hand around her neck. Colette's bottom lip droops in surprise. Her face springs towards me. She kisses me hard and then pulls back without warning. "You should go," she says.

So no last time. We're done. "Okay," I say quietly. "This is it then." My ribs throb with missing her. I squeeze her hand again over the counter and release it before she can squeeze back. I walk up her stairs for the final time, surprised all over again when I get to the top and find the sun still blazing through the laundry room window.

I breathe in sunshine as I open the side door and step onto the lawn. As terrible as this feels, it's over.

I don't know Colette Fournier anymore.

I'm free.

twenty-two

Jamie answers my call on the second ring. He picks me up at the 7-Eleven three blocks from Colette's apartment and talks nonstop to make up for my silence. It's cool; I haven't heard him talk so much since the night of the party almost two months ago. I'm not even paying attention to where we're going; I'm just listening and nodding at him.

He pulls into the North Star Chinese Buffet parking lot and tells me he's hungry and would I mind? Nope, I'm starving too. Burke finished my tuna melt and Brianna blindsided me before I had a chance to eat its replacement.

We grab two seats in the corner and down so much barbecued pork and Shanghai noodles that we make the guy in *Super Size Me* look like an anorexic. Jamie asks whatever happened to the dead psycho cat and I tell him about the box in the garage and Brianna going fierce diva on me.

"At least the cat's gone," Jamie offers. "One less enemy on the premises."

"The cat was easier to deal with," I say. Poor old Billy. I could've won him over with a palm full of tuna. Why didn't I think of that before?

We go back to Jamie's place and watch TV for a while. He drives me home after *The Daily Show* and I know I've been wrong about lots of things lately but this time the air between us feels clear.

The lights are off inside my house but I hear the TV on in the basement. I follow the noise and find Brianna stretched out on the couch in pink pajamas. Her eyes are closed and the *The O.C.*'s on behind her. I'm about to reach for the remote and switch it off when she opens her eyes.

"I thought you were asleep," I say. I'm too tired to fight with her and the anger's gone anyway.

"Sort of." Her voice is gravelly. "I think I'm going to stay down here tonight."

I guess she's pretty torn up about the cat but I don't want to talk about that either. "It's a comfortable couch," I tell her. "I've slept down here lots of times."

Brianna sucks in her cheeks as she sits up. "You know I wasn't actually going to tell them anything."

"They know now anyway."

Brianna's pupils bulge as she looks at me. "It was just seeing him in that box," she says haltingly. "You shouldn't have moved him."

"I had to go. I told you that. I had a job interview. He was already *gone*."

"I know." The accusatory tone's missing from her voice. "Your dad said you got the job."

"Yeah, that's right." I glance impatiently at Mischa Barton and Benjamin McKenzie on the screen. I got the job and lost the girl. Does that mean I balance?

"I really wasn't going to say anything," Brianna repeats.

"It doesn't make any difference anymore." After saying goodbye to Colette and gorging on Chinese food I can't get too excited about anything. My throat's burning. I can't tell if it's indigestion or misery. "Just remember that next time, okay?" Brianna's lips twitch like she's on the verge of anger and I add, "I don't want to fight with you anymore, Brianna. You'll win every time."

"You'll win," Brianna counters. "That's the way you are."

"Jesus, you can't even stop fighting with me now." I stare wearily at the ceiling. "Don't you recognize a white flag flying in your face? Look, I'm sorry about Billy. I'm sorry I said you were fucked up and bitchy." I fold my hands on top of my head and smooth down my hair. "If you want to keep this hostility up until we're seventy I guess I can't stop you. You'll do what you want. *That's the way you are.*"

"I don't want to fight with you." She snuggles back down into the couch. "I told you that before."

The potential for debate is endless and I sigh in defeat.

Brianna rubs her eyes and adds, "If you liked Billy maybe you'd understand."

"He didn't like *me*," I remind her. "I was ready to like him and he stabbed me in the hand."

A crooked smile forces its way onto Brianna's lips. I don't have photographic evidence; you'll just have to trust me on its existence because a moment later it's gone. "Why does everybody have to like you all the time, anyway?" she asks.

This is the second time she's said that and I chuckle miserably.

She has no idea what kind of night I've had. "Everybody doesn't like me—and I don't just mean you."

Brianna doesn't contradict me and tell me she likes me. She covers her lips with her hand and says, "I don't have to like you—I just have to live with you." She reaches for the remote and presses rewind, forcing the *O.C.* cast to zip through their story lines backwards in futility. "Why do you even care? Burke likes you. My mom likes you. My stupid friends like you."

I pop my shoulders up, suddenly feeling like we're trapped in a popularity contest. I don't know how much of this is about Brianna being thirteen, like Nina says, and how much is her making a choice to dislike me because it's one of the easiest things she can do right now. It could be something else entirely—I'm no TV psychologist—but I do feel bad about her losing Billy.

"You don't have to like me," I agree, taking a step away from the couch. "I'm really sorry about Billy. I know you guys had him a long time."

Brianna hides her mouth behind her hand again so I can't read her expression. "He really didn't like very many people, you know. It's not that he didn't like you specifically."

I bow my head at that and her eyes actually sparkle as she says, "I thought you knew karate. You should've been able to defend yourself against him."

I never said anything about karate; Dad must've told her. "This is what I'm saying. That's evidence that I'm a nice guy." A half smile bites into my mouth because, as unlikely as it seems, now I know she's capable of kidding around. "I never fought back."

"Okay," Brianna says resignedly. "Fine. You're nice. You're perfect. I'm the evil one."

"I'm gonna remind you that you said that."

"I know." Brianna rolls her eyes but I guess we're okay for the moment. It's not the big make-up scene that Dad wanted but I have the feeling we'll never get around to those.

"I'm going up," I announce. "I'll see you tomorrow."

"Good night," Brianna says. She's already closed her eyes.

The house is deserted again when I wake up on Saturday morning. Dad's left a note under my bedroom door explaining everything: Nina's gone to the hairdresser with Brianna and he's taken Burke to the doctor with hives. I don't know anything about the hives, but considering my luck lately Burke's probably allergic to tuna fish. Then Brianna can complain that I murdered her cat, attempted to poison her brother and, still more heinous, apologized to her afterwards, insisting that I was nice. *No wonder she doesn't like me.*

Seriously, though, I'm not in a great frame of mind today. That breakup with Colette yesterday really happened. She wasn't perfect but I'm already missing the flaws. Not that I want her back. Not really. Her Ari mania aches like a broken rib. I can't handle it. The fact that I knew all along just makes it hurt worse.

Now that we're over I don't know what to do. It feels like subtracting her from my life changed everything, even the parts she didn't touch. The reality of her absence mingles with a blistering awe at the fact that I was ever able to kiss her or sit next to her on her couch talking about everything from plot twists on *24* to reproductive rights. Every conversation and interaction between us is impossibly fresh in my mind and they shoot randomly out at me until my brain starts to hurt and I stumble out of my room and towards the bathroom. Then I shuffle around with a savage headache and do all the normal things that you usually don't give a second thought.

After a while Dad comes home with Burke asleep in his arms. "We stopped off for his prescription on the way home," he whispers, glancing at one of Burke's arms. "I guess it's working. You should've seen these babies first thing this morning."

I check out the miniature bumps on Burke's arms. "Do they know what it was?"

"No idea," Dad says. "They say it could've been anything. Nina says he's never had a reaction like this before." He balances Burke's weight as he steps towards the stairs. "He was scratching himself silly this morning. No other symptoms."

Dad carries Burke up to bed and then tries to talk to me about last night. It's exhausting enough having him in the house with me; I definitely don't want to talk. To speed things up I race to the part of the conversation where I agree to do my best to get along with Brianna. Then I point out that she needs to do some major work in the congeniality department herself. Dad agrees and makes a comment about adjusting to the nuances of the estrogen contingent. Then he goes serious on me again and asks about Colette. I confirm that it's over, expecting him to tell me that it's for the best because she was too old for me. I watch his hands, waiting for the words to come out of his mouth. "Nina and I talked about it," he says. "I expect that she'll tell Andrea."

I expect that too.

"I should check on Burke," he says slowly. "Are you doing all right?"

"Yeah, I'm okay." Better when I can keep my mouth shut. "It's just not how I wanted things to go."

Dad stares with uncertain eyes. "I know, Mason." He gives my arm a squeeze, making me feel simultaneously better and worse, before walking away.

I go down to the basement and hide out with the lights off,

playing video games. I can't remember the last time I did that. It must've been before Nina moved in.

After a bit I hear female voices upstairs but nobody disturbs me until hours later when Burke comes down with *Ice Age 3*. I tell him he can put on the DVD and he sticks both arms in my face, fascinated by his temporary affliction (although the only remaining trace of the hives is a couple of scratch marks). "The cream smells," he says, pressing his nostrils into one arm.

Twenty minutes after that I'm asleep. When I wake up Dad's yelling for me to get the phone. I mumble hello and Charlie Kady tells me his parents made a last-minute decision to go to some charity gala thing tonight and that his pool's ready for the season so he's inviting a bunch of people over to his place to swim or whatever (even Monica Gregory, who looks like a *Maxim* cover girl when she squeezes into a bikini). I can't think of a good way to tell him no, so I say yes and spend most of the night on this half-broken deck chair next to Dustin.

Monica G doesn't show, and Y and Z fight about something that I don't have the energy to understand, while Jamie hangs out with my old *Supernatural* buddy, the Whole Foods girl's best friend. Charlie barbecues regular hot dogs and these gourmet turkey burgers his girlfriend brought from work. The Black Eyed Peas blast out of speakers planted in the garden and everyone dances but I just want to escape. It's an okay party; I'm the problem. I slip away without telling anyone and Y phones my cell as I'm walking home.

"Where are you?" she says impatiently. "Do you realize you're MIA like last time? This is getting to be a habit with you."

It's nothing like last time. For one thing, I'm alone. "I'm walking home," I explain. "I just wasn't in the mood. I should've stayed home tonight."

"Ohhh." Y makes concerned noises into the phone. "I'm sorry I didn't come over to talk to you earlier—I've been immersed in the Zoe drama—but I thought something was the matter with you. You've been quiet all night."

"I'm okay," I say. "What about you and Zoe? Everything all right?"

"Sometimes I think we're too in tune with each other—if that makes any sense. The slightest ripple between us can set off a tidal wave . . . but this is about you. Do you want to come back? We can talk if you come back."

"I don't want to talk right now. But thanks. Honestly, I'm fine. The pool and all that was just a bit much." Being unhappy at a party, surrounded by friends, is worse than being unhappy alone in my bedroom—or with a medicinal-smelling Burke watching *Ice Age 3*. I need to be someplace quiet.

"Are you sure?" Yolanda says sympathetically. "If you tell me where you are, Zoe can come get you."

I'm glad she called but I don't want to talk anymore, much less be dragged back to the party. "I'll call you tomorrow, okay, Yolanda? Tell everyone I got sick or something."

I hang up and take my time walking home; the closer I get, the less I'm in the mood to be there either. Nina slings me a strained look as I pass the living room, like she's been giving my involvement with Colette too much thought. "Mason," she calls after me, "I left some paella in the fridge for you if you want it."

"Thanks." I skipped dinner in favor of more video games but the hot dog at Charlie's did the trick; I'm not hungry at all.

I go upstairs and lie on my bed and it feels as though I never left. The headache's back with a vengeance and hot dog–flavored puke scratches around indecisively at the bottom of my throat. It's a definite low point. There's no one I want to talk to, nowhere

I want to be and nothing I want to do. I don't even have the energy to throw up.

After a long while I fall asleep and I don't remember what I dream about, but when I wake up at twenty after three I realize I was wrong earlier. There's still one person I want to speak to tonight, the person who promised she'd absolutely be there for me if I needed her. She sounded sincere when she said it, but alone at twenty after three in the morning, with that partially digested hot dog burning a hole in my throat, I can't convince myself that she actually meant it.

Maybe some promises aren't meant to be cashed in. Anyway, I wouldn't know what to say if I got Kat on the phone.

twenty-three

ANDREA PHONES ON Sunday afternoon and I make the mistake of answering. Her tone's disapproving, making it obvious that Nina already told her about Colette and me. My voice bumps up an octave as I talk to her and I immediately feel like an even bigger ass. I'm not sure what Andrea and Nina think of me but I can imagine the options. Either I'm some kind of sex addict or an impressionable young victim caught in Colette's hedonistic web.

I don't know which is worse and I don't want to think about what it's like for Colette. There's no way she'll show up at the wedding now, regardless of whether Nina lets the invitation stand; I'm positive about that without anyone having to tell me. And no matter what she does from this moment on, Colette could already have lost her best friend. Of course, she'll still have Ari but I don't want to think about that either.

I'm relieved when I run out of weekend and find myself surrounded by all the people I wanted to avoid on Saturday night. At lunch Monica Gregory totters over to our table in zebra-print high heels and apologizes for not being able to make it on Saturday on account of being in the middle of breaking up with Hugo. "I was all ready to go," she says, pulling up a chair between Chris Cipolla and me. "I had my swimsuit picked out and everything." Tears form in Chris's eyes as she says that, and I crack a grin knowing that we're both picturing Monica G's perfect body poured into a microscopic bikini. "Then Hugo starts coming out with all this crap about how I shouldn't be going to a party he's not invited to."

She doesn't seem particularly upset about the split; she never does. We tell her that it's okay, she can make the next party, and after she teeters off Jamie tells me about that Jody girl he was talking to all Saturday night and how he's thinking about giving her a call. I tell him she seems cool and that he probably should and he smiles and says yeah.

Meanwhile Miracle's glowing with happiness and it's hard to look at her without thinking about my breakup with Colette, so mostly I don't. I tell her the news as we're leaving the cafeteria and she clenches my arm and whispers a heartfelt "I'm sorry."

Words like that are supposed to make you feel better but that's not how it works. Now I feel sorry for myself on the way to English. Twentieth-Century History last period wouldn't be much better, except that Kat's staring at me again. I'd love to rest my cheek in my palm and stare back until she turns away but I'm as scared of her as ever. It's insane; we're barely speaking and I'm still afraid to lose something. The only thing left is that promise I'll never hold her to anyway and I'm still scared.

I don't make a move towards her.

I don't say a word.

I barely even look in her direction.

The fear's worse now because I'm messed up and I think she can sense that, the way she always seems to sense things about me, because she's staring more than usual. Her eyes are so intent on me that my neck reddens as I peer at Mr. Echler sweeping his Jesus hair over his shoulders. I wonder if Kat notices the blushing too but I stay focused on Echler, trying to ignore his voice and find meaning in the words.

I try but it's impossible. A handful of Xanax would be more stimulating.

So history goes on forever and when the bell rings it feels like I've aged forty years. I've even stopped blushing. I plod into the hall, towards my locker and then home, feeling lonelier than when I left for school this morning because Kat Medina and I will probably never have a real conversation again.

Once classes are done with in a couple weeks I might not even lay eyes on her again until September. I won't tell her that I've missed her and that maybe certain things shouldn't have happened between us. I won't explain about crashing into Colette's life and trying to carve some space there for myself. It would just sound like bullshit anyway; Kat would never want to hear any of that.

When I get home Brianna's hanging out on the front step with Merilee and Jane, the three of them in identical yellow miniskirts and flip-flops. Brianna had her hair streaked blond when she was at the hairdresser the other day so now it actually looks pretty. Jane's limbs are covered in freckles and Merilee's staring at me like she'd devour me whole if given the chance. "Hi, Mason," Merilee calls, energetically batting her thickly mascaraed eyelashes at me. "Want to hang out with us?"

On my front step? Sounds exciting. "Nah," I say amicably. "I'm gonna catch a few hours' sleep."

"You going out later?" she asks. Brianna, hands on her hips, grimaces but Merilee's not easily discouraged. "Where do you usually hang out?"

"Friends' houses mostly. Nowhere special." My eyelids are as heavy as elephant feet. No wonder I'm having triple vision—except for Merilee's toe rings and anklet. She wiggles her toes as I glance down at them. "Is Burke around?"

"Downstairs watching *Yu-Gi-Oh!*" Brianna volunteers. "If you can watch him we can go to the mall or something." This is the first time anyone's asked me to babysit and Brianna hastily adds, "You barely have to do anything—you know what he's like. You can just snooze in the basement while he watches TV."

She shoots me a pleading look and after a couple seconds (during which I relish my sudden power), I say, "Sure. Go ahead."

Brianna's face lights up (as much as this is possible considering we're talking about Brianna) as she thanks me. Three sets of legs and yellow skirts saunter away in the direction of the bus stop and I descend into the basement to hang out with Burke. We eat potato chip, pickle and tomato sandwiches while watching *Yu-Gi-Oh!* Then we play the most kid-friendly video game I own until Nina comes home from work with unhappy eyes and wants to know where Brianna "disappeared to."

I don't know precisely where she is, just who she's with, but I assure Nina that I agreed to watch Burke and that there's no problem. Nina gives me this stone-faced look like I don't know what I'm talking about. I'm sure it's because of my history with Colette, which is unfair, but I don't argue. How can you argue with a look? Anyway, Nina, still semi-frowning, thanks me for babysitting and goes upstairs to make dinner. If anyone's figured out a way to make everyone happy at the same time, let me know. I think I'm flunking Stepfamily Integration 101.

Time speeds up as soon as I start work at The Java Bean. We don't do latte art like some places and we don't have near enough outlets for people who want to plug in their laptops and make use of the free Wi-Fi, but the morning shifts are hectic as hell and the first time I work with Chris Cipolla we decide to start the day off with quad espresso shots. Our hands shake for two hours afterwards but it definitely helps us pick up the pace.

Sometimes I even get through an entire shift without thinking about Colette for more than ten seconds at a time. Of course there are also times that I expect her to step through the door at any moment, but then something usually happens to distract me—Chris will knock over a pitcher in the refrigerator and it'll take an army of towels to clean it up or I'll burn my knuckles with hot tea (Darlene tells me you get used to it but I suspect that's called nerve damage) or this guy who everyone says used to be infatuated with Letitia will stand around at the counter talking to me about his blues CD being released next month.

Anyway, that's what it's like and that's what my summer will be like. Classes are finished and I'm on exams now, which means I don't see most of the people from school as much as before. Brianna still tries to argue with me sometimes but I tell her I'm going to walk away if she continues being a pain, and then I do. Usually everything's more or less fine the next time I see her and one morning Nina tells me she's noticed that we're getting along better lately and that she really appreciates me making the effort because she knows Brianna hasn't made it easy for me.

I'm glad to hear someone else noticed that and I quote what Kat said months ago about living in a house with the two other people that have always belonged there. It sounds both simple and true and it feels strange all over again to have lost that perspective.

Later that same night Dad forces me to go out and look for a new barbecue with him (even though there's nothing wrong with the old one). He gets all moody when I'm quiet in the car and then I know he wants to talk to me about something but the only thing he works up to saying is "Things seem to be working out well for you at the coffee shop. It must be nice to have some time to yourself now . . . no classes and so on."

And so on . . . Yeah.

Aside from Jamie, no one mentions Colette again and it's almost like our relationship never happened. It makes me miss her worse—mostly when I'm sitting around doing nothing and then I have to phone someone and convince them to pick me up.

It's a strange in-between time because logically I know it's finished but somehow I can't really believe it's over. There's all that waiting for her to walk into JB, the fact that she's so often only four doors away, that I still know her phone number by heart and keenly remember how every part of her body looks and tastes in the dark. I even found some Lunatic Fringe MP3s on the Net and she was right; they're incredible.

Given all this I'm not surprised when Colette actually does drift into The Java Bean during the middle of my third week. She's with a tiny blond woman with masses of curly hair and the two of them look stress-free and lightly bronzed. I'm on the cash register for the shift so I have no choice but to take their order.

My teeth taste bitter in my mouth. I feel my stomach gurgle in protest as Colette and the blonde approach the counter. I lean against it with studied casualness, faintly queasy. *Ian Chappell could pull this off pantless.* I'd settle for a tenth of his confidence.

"Hi, Mason," Colette says, her tone giving no clue of the drama we've been through together. She's wearing sunglasses, so I can't see her eyes, but she smiles and orders a mango smoothie. Except for the tan she looks exactly like the last time I saw her. That shouldn't be a shock but it is.

Her friend/coworker orders chai tea and continues chatting away to Colette about Pilates. It's surreal. I smile, punch in their orders and make polite change but it's all an act. I'm professional Barista Boy, not the sixteen-year-old guy who slept with Colette Fournier.

Colette and her friend leave as quickly as they arrived and I don't have time to mentally process the encounter but it aches like fuck. By the end of my shift I'm so desperate to be alone that I bump into two Japanese girls on my way out of the staff room and nearly topple one over. She reaches out and falls into my arms with a harried laugh. I apologize and help her regain her footing but beneath the surface I'm suffering something brutal. We sidestep each other as Christopher's voice sails over the Barenaked Ladies tune on the stereo: "Mason, if you forget your cell phone one more time I swear I'll donate it to charity or put it out with the napkins."

I glance back at him behind the counter and he adds, "Under the coatrack in the staff room."

So I double back to the staff room where my phone's lying face-down on the tile floor, underneath the coatrack, exactly like Chris said. I have two messages and I listen to the first one as I make my way out the front door. Jamie wants me to call him when I get home. Then Colette's voice comes to life, tender and deliberate. It stings so much to hear that at first I can hardly comprehend her syllables as words.

"Mason, that wasn't as easy as it looked for me just now," she says softly. "I hope you understand that we can't speak privately anymore and I really hope you're doing okay. You've probably noticed that I've been avoiding The Java Bean lately and I don't think I'll be in there very often this summer. That's probably better, isn't it? . . . I'm sorry, I don't know what to say. I just hope that you're not mad at me and I'm sorry if I did anything to cause you pain. That wasn't my intention. Don't be mad at me. Please. I'm sorry, Mason."

That's it. That's all she has to say to me after three weeks. I wrench the phone away from my ear, open my fist and let it drop onto the sidewalk. It makes a pathetically tiny ping as it connects with the cement in front of my feet. The blue screen stares reproachfully up at me, offering the time and declaring itself "Ready." If I wanted to smash the damn thing I could pick it up again and hurl it full force; it's not a black box, for God's sake, it's breakable. Instead I kick it a few paces ahead of me and watch it glide like a hockey puck on ice. When I catch up with it a couple seconds later I snatch it up and delete her message before I can change my mind.

For the first few steps afterwards I'm proud of myself for being ruthless. I don't need that kind of reminder weighing me down. How many times did she tell me she was sorry during that message—two or three? How many times did she say my name? I've already forgotten the exact details.

What a pointless thing to do. Why'd she even bother?

I'm furious with myself for being sad. If I hadn't deleted the message I'd be listening to it at this very moment, twenty short seconds after I killed it. I sacrificed the message and spared my phone. Does that mean something?

I'm so fed up with this shit I can't even tell you.

twenty-four

MY LAST EXAM is Twentieth-Century History and I'm the fourth person to finish. I know you're supposed to sit there and look over your paper for a while but I've already done that too. The school year's officially over. I'm done.

I hand in my exam and head over to my locker one final time, feeling nostalgic. I get like that every year, no matter what happened, but this one was really memorable in lots of ways. During the last week of class I stopped Mr. Fiore in the hall and thanked him for riding us so hard during *All My Sons* rehearsals. He focused his eyes on me in that intense, ultra-intelligent drama teacher way and asked how I felt about musicals. So it looks like we're doing a musical next year and that I should ask Miracle to be my vocal coach over the summer.

Lynn's already announced that next time she'll fly out for the show. I spend a couple of weeks with her every summer and this year's no exception. I'm flying over to Vancouver at the end of August and this time I plan to tell her we should try bungee jumping.

Anyway, I guess I don't need to explain about the memorable things. Sometimes it's hard to think about them but that doesn't mean I wish they didn't happen. I'm okay when it comes down to it. Or I will be. It's still early.

So I stand in the hall digging the remaining crap out of my locker. There's mostly trash left and I throw out everything but an old gray sweatshirt with a tomato sauce stain down one arm and a postcard Y bought me in Cuba on Christmas break but forgot to mail. I shove the sweatshirt and postcard into my knapsack, shut my empty locker and turn to go.

I do that all quickly, thinking I'm alone, but I'm wrong. My body crashes smack into Kat Medina's in the hall. "Jesus!" I exclaim, immediately recoiling. "Sorry, I didn't see you." I think I may have stepped on one of her feet too and I glance down, checking for crushed toes. "You okay?"

"I'm okay," Kat replies, openly staring at me. "Are you okay?"

"Clumsy." I motion with my hands and try to avoid staring back. But you know how that goes. The second you aim for casual there's nowhere else to put your eyes. Plus, her hair's falling softly over her shoulders and her skin's this beautiful cappuccino shade. Why wouldn't I want to stare at her? "Sorry about that."

"I guess I was too quiet," she murmurs, her head tilted to one side. "I just wanted to say hi before you took off." Kat scrapes anxiously at a cuticle as she looks at me, and of course I haven't forgotten her staring during the last few weeks of class, but with the Colette breakup still fresh I haven't had much time to dwell on it either. "It looks like you and Jamie have patched things up lately," she adds, going to work on a second cuticle.

"Yeah. We're okay." I'm overwhelmingly grateful for my

pessimism on the night of Charlie Kady's pool party. Who knows what crazy things I might've said to her over the phone. When it comes to Kat, it's better to be cautious. I don't want her to let me down again.

"That's good," she says. "I'm glad."

Silence crowds in on us in the empty hallway and I ease myself backwards a few inches so that we're not standing too close for Kat's comfort.

"I'm glad," she repeats, glancing down at my legs with an un-readable expression. Her gaze shoots back up to mine just as silence threatens to take over again.

"Yeah," I say loudly. I peer carefully into her brown eyes and re-alize that Kat wasn't one of the three people to finish the history exam before me. What're the odds she'd finish hot on my heels like that? "Me too. So what'd you think of the exam?"

"No big surprises. What about you?"

"Same." Strangely breathless, like I've been out scrambling up mountainsides. It's a familiar feeling and I don't fight it.

"You must've aced it," Kat notes. "You were one of the first peo-ple finished." She hugs her pencil case to her hip and studies the spot of floor between us like we've run out of conversation. "This is too weird. I'm sorry; I'll let you go." She bumps her arm against mine before she has time to think better of it.

"Wait." I twist around and watch her freeze in place. "It's not that I don't want to talk to you; I just don't know what it means anymore." Is that too much to confess? I have no idea where we stand. If we could sit around and have a conversation about us like we were two other people, we might be able to figure it out.

"I know." Kat raises a hand to her lips. It's like a veil between us. "I don't know what to say to you. Not speaking to you is weird and speaking to you is weird. *Everything's weird.* I thought being apart might be easier, especially when we had class together and it felt so awkward, but now I don't see you anymore and it still feels weird."

We stare uneasily at each other as she lowers her hand. The tension escalates until I can't stop myself; the words rush to my mouth. "I almost called you a few weeks ago. I didn't let myself."

She blinks rapidly, that cute pout plumping up her lips. "I don't know what I would've said if you did."

I nod pensively. "That's why I didn't do it."

Two ninth graders rush noisily by, laughing and banging their lockers open. The interruption makes our discussion less daunting but that won't last; in a couple minutes the hallway will be empty again.

"And anyway, you wouldn't have liked what I had to say," I add. Those months of not speaking are crushing in on me full force. I want to tell her everything.

Kat runs her fingers roughly through her hair. "It's about some girl, right? I know there's somebody. You don't have to be so careful breaking the news to me."

"That's not what I'm trying to do." For somebody who starred in the school play two months ago I feel unbelievably inarticulate. "Come out to the bleachers with me and I'll explain." She might hate me but I'm going to do it anyway. I'm tired of secrets, sick to death of omissions.

We go outside together, Kat shivering in her flimsy white summer top. This time last year I'd have flung an arm around her and rubbed her shoulders to warm her up. Now I don't do anything.

We sit at the top of the bleachers and squint at three guys playing Frisbee out by the track. One of them is the barefoot Jedi Master that calmed me down months ago and seeing him gives my life this strange feeling of continuity. "I was involved with someone for a while," I admit, shifting my gaze to Kat. "I figured that you knew."

As I watch her I begin to realize things have changed between us for the second time. I don't know when it happened but I'm seeing her differently. That Saturday night isn't front and center in my brain anymore; it's the entire Kat there beside me, in all her complexity. "But it's over now. Everything fell apart and it was one of those situations where I knew it would but . . ." I shrug, resting my arms on my knees.

"You're rebounding," she offers, casting me a sideways glance.

"That wasn't why I wanted to call," I protest. "I just wanted to be able to talk to you, like we used to talk all the time when we had things going on in our lives." Sunshine's grilling the back of my neck but she still looks cold. "Did you mean that about us still being friends?" I ask. "Was that just something to say?"

Kat folds her arms snugly in front of her. "You know I don't just say things like that, don't you?" She answers her own question: "I guess you don't."

"I don't think I can avoid talking to you and still consider us friends," I tell her, my eyes on the track. "If you want to cut me out of your life you should just do it." My tone's surprisingly harsh. "Make it official. Otherwise it just goes on like this forever—you staring at me in class next year and talking to me in the hall for two seconds like that proves something." I train my eyes on hers. "If that's the extent of our friendship it's not worth anything, is it?" I want to dangle my arm around her shoulders and find out what's been happening in her life these past couple months but instead I'm giving her an ultimatum. It feels like fate.

"Maybe it's not," she says in a low voice. "Maybe we trashed it."

I breathe in slowly, expecting the air to sear my lungs. We're finally going to have this conversation. I'm ultra-awake in my own skin, swaying slowly from side to side to calm myself.

"I wish you wouldn't think that. I wish things were different." I wrap my hands around the back of my neck, still hunched over. A couple more twists and I'd be a human pretzel. "That night was my first time."

Kat hunches over next to me, her breasts pushed together under the weight of her arms. We look like a couple of food-poisoning victims. I feel like one too. This conversation's exponentially tougher than it would've been two months ago.

"I didn't know that," she says finally. She flicks her hair out of her eyes and looks at me in a way that makes me hold my breath.

"We never had a chance to talk." I'm not being judgmental; these are the facts. "I wanted to tell you but you were so shaken about the whole thing . . . and then . . . later we couldn't talk at all."

Kat smiles a little and I lift my head and stare at her with clear eyes. "I know," she says quietly. She smooths her hands over her jeans and looks away. "You're making me nervous." She shifts her gaze swiftly back to mine. "I'm glad you told me. I wish I knew that at the time."

I never even thought to tell her at the time and my stomach dips and then free-falls, like I'm some bottomless pit of bittersweet emotion. Maybe we would've felt closer if I'd told her that night and I made us miss out on something good. Or maybe it would've stopped everything dead. I thought I was over that night but the regret's more acute now than it was months ago.

"I should've told you before," I say, my mouth bone dry.

Kat presses her lips together and sits up straight. "It wasn't how I expected it to be," she confesses, her voice tentative. "Was it for you?"

"It was great." The awe's there in my throat and I don't try to hide it. "I thought it was amazing."

"Yeah." Kat doesn't look at me as she speaks. "I didn't expect that either. I thought it would be scary and awkward." Her knees draw together. "I thought I would bleed."

In some ways talking about that night feels more real, more raw, than living it. My stomach takes another dive and I quip, "And that I'd be Hugo, right?" The joke's unexpected but we both smile.

"Nooooo," Kat says vehemently. "I never thought that—I just didn't think it'd be you."

"So why would you bother having a boyfriend you never intended to sleep with?" We never talked about sex much when we were friends, not with any seriousness. This is uncharted territory. I can hardly believe I'm saying these things out loud.

"I never intended to sleep with anyone anytime soon," she says forcefully. "Why do you think I was so freaked out? Anyway, it was your first time too—what were you waiting for?"

"I don't know." That's the truth. "Something special, I guess."

"Yeah." Kat's laugh is streaked with sarcasm. "Does drunken fumbling on your father's couch qualify?"

I frown as I tap the aluminum under my feet and Kat frowns too. "It was more than that," I tell her. "You know how much I like you." This is the hardest thing I've had to say yet. "I mean for years, ever since we first met." Kat's silent next to me but I won't let it go. "You knew that, right?"

"Yeah." She folds her hands into her lap and studies her fingers. "You and Jamie both. That's what I meant about this being incestuous. It makes me wonder whether the three of us were ever really friends or if it was always this sexual thing."

"I think it was both." I rub my forehead with one hand. "Maybe that's why it was easier for me to deal with what happened. I didn't see it as a bad thing."

"It's not that it was a bad thing," Kat says slowly. "It just changes things. Since that night my feelings for you are all screwed up. Half the time I don't know what I want. I told you to leave me alone and then that day when you said you were out late . . ." She exhales heavily and rolls her eyes. "And now here you are telling me that you and this girl broke up and maybe I should be relieved but I don't know . . ." Her front teeth scrape across her bottom lip as she stares out at the track. "Hugo was so much easier to deal with. Less complicated."

"I'm not complicated." Part of me is ecstatic that she has enough feelings for me to be confused but that's what made her give up our friendship in the first place. It's too risky to even hope for more. "You're the complicated one. Don't worry about all this other stuff—it'll work itself out. Just tell me that we can be friends and pick up the phone to call each other once in a while. Can we do that?" She's still thinking that over and I raise my head to the cloudless sky and sigh inwardly. This all feels so critical that it's almost like Colette never happened.

"Just that?" she asks, and I have to admit she looks so beautiful with those wide brown eyes and pouting lips that I'll probably have a crush on her for the next twenty years.

"Just that," I confirm. "If that's all there is." I'm tapping my feet like wild but I mean it. We've been friends for too long to let this get in the way. If I have to listen to her rave about how sexy and hilarious Sanjay is, I will. To a certain degree I'll even get used to it. I've been there before.

Kat locks her fingers together and watches me. "You think we can just keep going like this? As friends?"

"I know we can. We just have to give it a real chance."

"I missed talking to you, Mason." Her words sound heavy. "I want to be friends too but I don't know . . ." She chews her bottom lip. "What if it turns out that I want more?" I jolt backwards on the bleachers, beyond shocked. I know she said she was confused but I thought she was doing her best to smother that. "Sometime," she adds hastily. "Maybe. Can we give it some time and see how things go?"

"I can't believe you just said that." Surprise surges through my voice. "Of course we can. You have no idea how much I've missed just talking to you—about everything."

"Me too," Kat says haltingly. "We need to talk more from now on." Relief softens her eyes. "But about normal things too, okay? Not just about that night and this crazy conversation. I'm glad we're getting things out in the open but it's . . . not easy for me . . . especially when it involves you, so can we talk about something else for a while?" She shoots me a pleading look. "Anything."

"Sure, Kat. Anything." I can't think of a single normal thing to say. This is Kat Medina. She's like a goddess and my best friend wrapped into one. I'm shivering in the sun.

After about ten seconds Kat tucks one hand under her chin and helps me out. "You know, Eric's going to the Philippines for six weeks this summer," she says. "You should see the way my mom's acting, making all these preparations. You'd think he was royalty. And she thinks she has to send presents for all her family over there too. It's a bigger production than *All My Sons*. I think it'll be good for him, though. I hate the way he just lies around on the couch all summer."

My mind's racing with possibilities and I swear I'm getting this happy ice cream headache in the middle of my forehead as my arms tan, but I'm listening too. "So who's filling in for him with the catering?" I ask. Her brother has about two friends (who never go out either) and no hobbies, unless you include his laptop and Xbox. His life's evenly divided between his parents' basement and his aunt and uncle's catering business. "You?"

223

Kat laughs, her eyes gleaming in the sun. "With Tita Teresa? I don't think so." Her aunt Teresa is the bossy, competitive one in the family. Kat spends every family gathering actively avoiding her. Anyway, Kat explains that her fifteen-year-old cousin Cecilia (who's this teenage Einstein with a ninety-nine percent average) is going to do it. Then we talk about me for a while. I fill her in on my most recent clash with Brianna, talk about how Burke cracks me up and how relieved I am that Chris hooked me up with the JB job because the house feels cramped sometimes, even now that we're all more or less getting along.

Kat smiles and says she'll have to meet Burke and Brianna sometime because she has this detailed picture in her head and meanwhile the two of them probably don't look anything like that. The conversation runs on pretty smooth and I seriously almost believe this can work on some level, that there'll be some kind of us again. Maybe just as friends; I don't know.

When we finally decide to go Kat scoops up her pencil case and says, "Call me tomorrow, okay?"

"I'm working at The Java Bean till late," I tell her. "I'll call you the day after."

"Sure. Whenever." She sounds casual but her eyes give her away. We're both making a concentrated effort to act normal.

"Yeah, sure." I get up next to her, careful not to stand too close. "I can't believe this year's really over." I throw all my will into resisting the instinct to give her a hug. We're supposed to be doing *sometime, maybe* and anyway, I need more time to put Colette behind me. I don't want to use Kat as a shortcut to get over Colette. I've already tried that in reverse and it only makes things messier.

We smile self-consciously at each other as we head back to the school and it's weird to feel this lingering sadness in the pit of my stomach while I'm so happy. I'm grateful for the two Bs in the basement, distracting me when I get home afterwards, and that feels weird too. *Everything's weird,* just like Kat said. Colette's written me off like a bad check. Kat's offered me *sometime, maybe* and Brianna actually lets me watch *Relic Hunter* downstairs without complaining. For the second time this year, it's a whole new world.

twenty-five

I TELL JAMIE the very next day. Straight out without any intro or excuses. I explain that Kat and I are going to try to be friends again but that neither of us knows where that will go, maybe nowhere. I say that I really hope he won't be mad at me but that I realize he might be. Jamie's face crumples but he keeps his voice even. "From the moment I found out about you guys I knew you'd end up together," he says.

"You can't have known that," I insist. "*I didn't know.* I still don't."

"It's okay." Jamie's cheeks deflate. "I'm just saying that I saw it coming, Mason."

I don't want to go through this with Jamie again—the crack in our friendship's barely healed—but I can't choose between him and Kat; they're both too important for that. "I don't know what else to say to you," I tell him. "I don't want to be sorry about it; this is a good thing."

"I know it's a good thing." Jamie holds himself as still as a photograph. It feels like one of those decisive moments that shift your life into a whole new phase. I watch him blink, his lashes and lungs the only parts of him in motion. "And I'm sure I'm supposed to be able to be happy for you now that I'm hanging out with Jody, so let's just skip the rest of the conversation, okay?" He scratches his arms, suddenly back in real time. "Just be careful this time, all right?" He plunges his hands into his pockets and stares at me. "Do I sound crazy?"

He says that like he really wants to know, and I stare wistfully back at him, wondering if, for once, the three of us will be happy at the same time. "You don't sound crazy," I tell him. "I was jealous about Hugo even after they broke up. Fuck, I was jealous about Sanjay when I saw them walking through the hall together—and that was while I was with Colette."

"So you know how it is," Jamie says.

I definitely know how it is. "Are we good, though?" I gesture between us, and Jamie nods quickly like there's no question.

"Just don't ask me to hang out with you guys during the honeymoon phase," he adds, jaw clenching. "I don't want to hear about . . ." He stops midsentence to avoid saying it. "Keep me out of the loop, okay?"

"No problem." I think he already likes Jody more than he realizes—and I'm hoping he'll figure that out for himself soon. She's got him listening to lots of classical music lately and he's not the type that's normally influenced by other people's musical tastes. Plus, it looks like he's in the process of growing out his hair for the first time in about two years, which may not mean anything but I bet it does.

Supposedly the fastest way to get over someone is to distract yourself with somebody else, but I'm living proof that doesn't always work the way you want it to. Colette and I may have started out as simple distractions for each other, but something else happened along the way, at least for me.

The fact is, I still feel varying degrees of bad about Colette. I'm sure she still hooks up with Ari Lightman on a regular basis, but sometimes I wonder what she's doing about changing the world and if she called her new puppy Gracie in the end. And of course I wonder if she thinks about me and what she would say about Kat and me being friends again. For some reason I think she'd be happy about it.

Anyway, these thoughts whirl through my mind on a regular basis, and meanwhile Kat and I try really hard to be friends. Sometimes we talk on the phone until well after midnight and one time we go to the movies with Y and Z, almost like a double date except we're still just friends. You can actually be friends with someone and want to crush your mouth against theirs every minute of the time you're together. It's the weirdest thing but comfortingly familiar.

One night when Nina and Dad are out on a dinner date Kat comes over to meet Brianna and Burke. The four of us stand around the kitchen heating up pizza in the microwave (except Burke, who's already munching on one of his famous potato chip sandwiches). Kat's wearing a denim skirt, tan clogs and a bunch of bangles on both arms. She looks gorgeous, as usual, and Brianna, who just met her three minutes earlier, grabs her left arm and says, "Where did you get these?"

"Ella Bee's at the mall," Kat replies. "It's one of those stands right outside Club Monaco, next to the T-shirt place."

"I didn't know they had cool stuff like that." Brianna appraises Kat's arms and then shifts her stare to the clogs.

"I get a twenty-percent discount if you want to drop by and have a look sometime," Kat offers. She started there just three weeks ago and since then there's been all kinds of new jewelry showing up on her person. I take her in again as Brianna ogles her clogs. In fact, I've probably spent more time staring at Kat during the past few weeks than she ever spent staring at me in history.

"Cool," Brianna says. "Thanks."

After pizza the four of us watch a PG action movie in the basement. Brianna almost acts like a normal person, which makes it seem like I've been exaggerating her tendency to turn into a queen bitch at the slightest provocation, but that's okay. Then it's time for Burke to go to bed and for me to walk Kat home because she has to be up early to go to the airport with her family tomorrow.

It's almost dark, but since it's July it's still warm out on the sidewalk. Kat and I talk about the two Bs and how weird it'll be not having Eric around her house for the rest of the summer. "You should come over sometime," she suggests. "We'll have space for a change." Her eyes flicker with shyness as she realizes how that could be misinterpreted. "Well, you know what I mean."

"Judging by our history, that sounds like something we should avoid," I say lightly, and her body swings away from mine as her lips quiver. "I know what you mean, though," I add, serious this time. "It's like we've switched places this summer. Now I'm the one that doesn't have any space at home."

"Only for a year," Kat reminds me. "It'll go fast."

Now I completely understand why that upset her when I said it three months ago. We really have traded places. I'm having too good a time in the moment to think about next year.

"What is it?" Kat asks, staring hard. "Are you okay?"

I swing my arms at my sides as I look at her. "Yeah, I'm good." I give her a slow smile and I know I'm being weird but she's better off without an explanation. We're in balance right now; I don't want to upset that. "I'm perfect." Three months ago all my best moments were dramatic; today I'm happy enough just to walk her home.

"My feet are starting to hurt," Kat confesses. "I don't know what I was thinking wearing these shoes." She stops and tears off one clog at a time. "That's better." She walks along next to me in her bare feet. I scan the sidewalk for bits of glass and dog shit as we talk.

There's a slight breeze starting up and a Great Dane barks from its backyard as we pass. Kat's been quiet awhile and I glance into her eyes, catching a contemplative expression. She fastens her hand around a set of bangles and says, "I'm glad I came after you the day of the history exam. I couldn't imagine not seeing you the whole summer. It wouldn't feel right."

"I know. I thought the same thing but I never would've done anything about it—you had me too confused."

"I confused *you*?" I hear her tickle of an accent in her laugh. The sound makes me smile. "Mason, you have no idea." She shakes her head as her arm brushes against mine. "You should've seen me in the history exam. I was completely panicked when you got up and left so early." She slows down, her arms resting against her chest. "I was just starting the second-last short-essay question, you know. I never actually finished the exam."

I guessed that but hearing her admit it makes me insanely happy. "You're crazy." Now I'm all-out grinning, realizing that this time she doesn't sound miserable about coming clean. We're evolving on the spot, leaping over lines together. "You could've called me anytime. You didn't have to do that."

"I know." A sweet smile creeps onto Kat's lips. "But at the time it felt urgent. Like if I didn't do it then, I never would."

I know. I stop on the pavement, my heart hammering in my chest.

The breeze smooths her hair back as I reach out to stroke her cheek. Neither of us seems surprised. Kat stands there in her bare feet, a clog in each hand, and stares steadily back at me. We pull silently together. Slow. Like there's no rush this time. My fingertips graze her back. Then her breath's on my chin, her arms dangling over my shoulders as she tilts her head up. We're so soft together, so beautiful, that the moment hangs in the air, dreamlike.

There are certain things you know you'll always remember.

Our mouths slip together in a perfect fit.

C. K. KELLY MARTIN is the critically acclaimed author of *I Know It's Over* and *One Lonely Degree*. She began writing her first novel in Dublin and currently lives in greater Toronto with her husband. She's perpetually working on new novels and redesigning her Web site and blog. Visit them both at www.ckkellymartin.com.